The Writings of
Henry D. Thoreau

*Translations*

*Textual Center*
*The Writings of Henry D. Thoreau*
*University of California*
*Santa Barbara*

HENRY D. THOREAU

# Translations

EDITED BY K. P. VAN ANGLEN

PRINCETON, NEW JERSEY

PRINCETON UNIVERSITY PRESS

MCMLXXXVI

The Committee emblem means that one of a panel of textual experts serving the Committee has reviewed the text and textual apparatus of the original volume by thorough and scrupulous sampling, and has approved them for sound and consistent editorial principles employed and maximum accuracy attained. The accuracy of the text has been guarded by careful and repeated proofreading of printer's copy according to standards set by the Committee.

The editorial preparation of this volume, and costs associated with its publication, were supported by grants from the Editing and Publication Programs of the National Endowment for the Humanities, an independent federal agency. During the early stages of editing, support was provided through the Center for Editions of American Authors of the Modern Language Association.

# Editorial Board

# The Writings

*Walden*, J. Lyndon Shanley (1971)

*The Maine Woods*, Joseph J. Moldenhauer (1972)

*Reform Papers*, Wendell Glick (1973)

*Early Essays and Miscellanies*,
   Joseph J. Moldenhauer et al. (1975)

*A Week on the Concord and Merrimack Rivers*,
   Carl F. Hovde et al. (1980)

*Journal 1: 1837-1844*, Elizabeth Hall Witherell et al.
   (1981)

*Journal 2: 1842-1848*, Robert Sattelmeyer (1984)

*Translations*, K. P. Van Anglen (1986)

# Contents

# Translations

# The Prometheus Bound.

[We present our readers with a new and careful translation of the tragedy of Æschylus, in which fidelity to the text, and to the best text, is what is mainly attempted. We are the more readily drawn to this task, by the increasing value which this great old allegory is acquiring in universal literature, as a mystical picture of human life, and the most excellent work in that kind that exists in Greek poetry. Coleridge said of this play, that "it was more properly tragedy itself, in the plenitude of the idea, than a particular tragic poem."]

PERSONS OF THE DRAMA.

> KRATOS and BIA, (*Strength and Force.*)
> HEPHAISTUS, (*Vulcan.*)
> PROMETHEUS.
> CHORUS OF OCEAN NYMPHS.
> OCEANUS.
> IO, *Daughter of Inachus.*
> HERMES.

KRATOS *and* BIA, HEPHAISTUS, PROMETHEUS.

> KR.   WE are come to the far-bounding plain of earth,
>       To the Scythian way, to the unapproached solitude.
>       Hephaistus, orders must have thy attention,
>       Which the father has enjoined on thee, this bold one
>       To the high-hanging rocks to bind,
>       In indissoluble fetters of adamantine bonds.

For thy flower, the splendor of fire
 useful in all arts,
Stealing, he bestowed on mortals; and
 for such
A crime 't is fit he should give
 satisfaction to the gods;
That he may learn the tyranny of Zeus
To love, and cease from his man-loving
 ways.

HEPH. Kratos and Bia, your charge from Zeus
Already has its end, and nothing further
 in the way;
But I cannot endure to bind
A kindred god by force to a bleak
 precipice,–
Yet absolutely there's necessity that I
 have courage for these things;
For it is hard the father's words to
 banish.
High-plotting son of the right-
 counselling Themis,
Unwilling thee unwilling in brazen
 fetters hard to be loosed
I am about to nail to this inhuman hill,
Where neither voice [you'll hear,] nor
 form of any mortal
See, but scorched by the sun's clear
 flame,
Will change your color's bloom; and to
 you glad
The various-robed night will conceal
 the light,
And sun disperse the morning frost
 again;

And always the burden of the present ill
Will wear you; for he that will relieve
    you has not yet been born.
Such fruits you've reaped from your
    man-loving ways,
For a god, not shrinking from the wrath
    of gods,
You have bestowed honors on mortals
    more than just,
For which this pleasureless rock you'll
    sentinel,
Standing erect, sleepless, not bending a
    knee;
And many sighs and lamentations to no
    purpose
Will you utter; for the mind of Zeus is
    hard to be changed;
And he is wholly rugged who may
    newly rule.

KR.    Well, why dost thou delay and pity in
    vain?
Why not hate the god most hostile to
    gods,
Who has betrayed thy prize to mortals?

HEPH.    The affinity indeed is appalling and the
    familiarity.

KR.    I agree, but to disobey the Father's
    words
How is it possible? Fear you not this
    more?

HEPH.    Aye you are always without pity, and
    full of confidence.

KR.    For 't is no remedy to bewail this one;
Cherish not vainly troubles which avail
    nought.

HEPH.    O much hated handicraft!

KR.    Why hatest it? for in simple truth, for
    these misfortunes
Which are present now Art 's not to
    blame.

HEPH.    Yet I would't had fallen to another's lot.

KR.    All things were done but to rule the
    gods,
For none is free but Zeus.

HEPH.    I knew it, and have nought to say
    against these things.

KR.    Will you not haste then to put the
    bonds about him,
That the Father may not observe you
    loitering?

HEPH.    Already at hand the shackles you may
    see.

KR.    Taking them, about his hands with firm
    strength
Strike with the hammer, and nail him
    to the rocks.

HEPH.    'T is done, and not in vain this work.

KR.    Strike harder, tighten, no where relax,
For he is skilful to find out ways e'en
    from the impracticable.

HEPH.    Aye but this arm is fixed inextricably.

KR.    And this now clasp securely; that
       He may learn he is a duller schemer
           than is Zeus.

HEPH.  Except him would none justly blame
           me.

KR.    Now with an adamantine wedge's
           stubborn fang
       Through the breasts nail strongly.

HEPH.  Alas! alas! Prometheus, I groan for thy
           afflictions.

KR.    And do you hesitate, for Zeus' enemies
       Do you groan? Beware lest one day you
           yourself will pity.

HEPH.  You see a spectacle hard for eyes to
           behold.

KR.    I see him meeting his deserts;
       But round his sides put straps.

HEPH.  To do this is necessity, insist not much.

KR.    Surely I will insist and urge beside,
       Go downward, and the thighs surround
           with force.

HEPH.  Already it is done, the work, with no
           long labor.

KR.    Strongly now drive the fetters, through
           and through,
       For the critic of the works is difficult.

HEPH.  Like your form your tongue speaks.

KR.    Be thou softened, but for my
           stubbornness

Of temper and harshness reproach me
not.

HEPH.    Let us withdraw, for he has a net about
his limbs.

KR.    There now insult, and the shares of
gods
Plundering on ephemerals bestow;
what thee
Can mortals in these ills relieve?
Falsely thee the divinities Prometheus
Call; for you yourself need one
    *foreseeing*
In what manner you will escape this
fortune.

PROMETHEUS, *alone.*

O divine ether, and ye swift-winged
winds,
Fountains of rivers, and countless
smilings
Of the ocean waves, and earth, mother
of all,
And thou all-seeing orb of the sun I call.
Behold me what a god I suffer at the
hands of gods.
See by what outrages
Tormented the myriad-yeared
Time I shall endure; such the new
Ruler of the blessed has contrived for
me,
Unseemly bonds.
Alas! alas! the present and the coming
Woe I groan; where ever of these
sufferings
Must an end appear.

But what say I? I know beforehand all,
Exactly what will be, nor to me strange
Will any evil come. The destined fate
As easily as possible it behoves to bear,
    knowing
Necessity's is a resistless strength.
But neither to be silent, nor unsilent
    about this
Lot is possible for me; for a gift to
    mortals
Giving, I wretched have been yoked to
    these necessities;
Within a hollow reed by stealth I carry
    off fire's
Stolen source, which seemed the teacher
Of all art to mortals, and a great
    resource.
For such crimes penalty I pay,
Under the sky, riveted in chains.
Ah! ah! alas! alas!
What echo, what odor has flown to me
    obscure,
Of god, or mortal, or else mingled,–
Came it to this terminal hill
A witness of my sufferings, or wishing
    what?
Behold bound me an unhappy god,
The enemy of Zeus, fallen under
The ill will of all the gods, as many as
Enter into the hall of Zeus,
Through too great love of mortals.
Alas! alas! what fluttering do I hear
Of birds near? for the air rustles
With the soft rippling of wings.
Everything to me is fearful which
    creeps this way.

PROMETHEUS *and* CHORUS.

CH.    Fear nothing; for friendly this band
Of wings with swift contention
Drew to this hill, hardly
Persuading the paternal mind.
The swift-carrying breezes sent me;
For the echo of beaten steel pierced
    the recesses
Of the caves, and struck out from me
    reserved modesty;
And I rushed unsandalled in a
    winged chariot.

PR.    Alas! alas! alas! alas!
Offspring of the fruitful Tethys,
And of him rolling around all
The earth with sleepless stream
    children,
Of father Ocean; behold, look on me,
By what bonds embraced,
On this cliff's topmost rocks
I shall maintain unenvied watch.

CH.    I see, Prometheus; but to my eyes a
    fearful
Mist has come surcharged
With tears, looking upon thy body
Shrunk to the rocks
By these mischiefs of adamantine
    bonds;
Indeed new helmsmen rule Olympus;
And with new laws Zeus strengthens
    himself, annulling the old,
And the before great now makes
    unknown.

Pr.   Would that under earth, and below
         Hades
      Receptacle of dead, to impassible
      Tartarus, he had sent me, to bonds
         indissoluble
      Cruelly conducting, that neither god,
      Nor any other had rejoiced at this.
      But now the sport of winds, unhappy
         one,
      A source of pleasure to my foes I suffer.

Ch.   Who so hard-hearted
      Of the gods, to whom these things are
         pleasant?
      Who does not sympathize with thy
      Misfortunes, excepting Zeus? for he in
         wrath always
      Fixing his stubborn mind,
      Afflicts the heavenly race;
      Nor will he cease, until his heart is
         sated;
      Or with some palm some one may take
         the power hard to be taken.

Pr.   Surely yet, though in strong
      Fetters I am now maltreated,
      The ruler of the blessed will have need
         of me,
      To show the new conspiracy, by which
      He's robbed of sceptre and of honors,
      And not at all me with persuasion's
         honey-tongued
      Charms will he appease, nor ever
      Shrinking from his firm threats, will I
      Declare this, till from cruel

Bonds he may release, and to do justice
For this outrage be willing.

CH.  You are bold; and to bitter
Woes do nothing yield,
But too freely speak.
But my mind piercing fear disturbs;
For I'm concerned about thy fortunes,
Where at length arriving you may see
An end of these afflictions. For
     manners
Inaccessible, and a heart hard to be
     dissuaded has the son of Kronos.

PR.  I know, that Zeus is stern and having
Justice to himself. But after all
Gentle-minded
He will one day be, when thus he's
     crushed,
And his stubborn wrath allaying,
Into agreement with me and friendliness
Earnest to me earnest he at length will
     come.

CH.  The whole account disclose and tell us
     plainly,
In what crime taking you Zeus
Thus disgracefully and bitterly insults;
Inform us, if you are nowise hurt by
     the recital.

PR.  Painful indeed it is to me to tell these
     things,
And a pain to be silent, and every way
     unfortunate.
When first the divinities began their
     strife,

And discord 'mong themselves arose,
Some wishing to cast out Kronos from
   his seat,
That Zeus might reign, forsooth, others
   the contrary
Striving, that Zeus might never rule the
   gods;
Then I the best advising, to persuade
The Titans, sons of Uranus and
   Chthon,
Unable was; but crafty stratagems
Despising with rude minds,
They thought without trouble to rule
   by force;
But to me my mother not once only,
   Themis,
And Gæa, of many names one form,
How the future should be accomplished
   had foretold,
That not by power, nor by strength
Would it be necessary, but by craft the
   victors should prevail.
Such I in words expounding,
They deigned not to regard at all.
The best course therefore of those
   occurring then
Appeared to be, taking my mother to
   me,
Of my own accord to side with Zeus
   glad to receive me;
And by my counsels Tartarus'
   black-pitted
Depth conceals the ancient Kronos,
With his allies. In such things by me
The tyrant of the gods having been
   helped,

With base rewards like these repays
   me,
For there is somehow in kingship
This disease, not to trust its friends.
What then you ask, for what cause
He afflicts me, this will I now explain.
As soon as on his father's throne
He sat, he straightway to the gods
   distributes honors,
Some to one and to another some, and
   arranged
The government; but of unhappy
   mortals account
Had none; but blotting out the race
Entire, wished to create another new.
And these things none opposed but I,
But I adventured; I rescued mortals
From going destroyed to Hades.
Therefore indeed with such afflictions
   am I bent,
To suffer grievous, and piteous to
   behold,
And holding mortals up to pity, myself
   am not
Thought worthy to obtain it; but
   without pity
Am I thus corrected, a spectacle
   inglorious to Zeus.

CH.    Of iron heart and made of stone,
Whoe'er, Prometheus, with thy
   sufferings
Does not grieve; for I should not have
   wished to see
These things, and having seen them I
   am grieved at heart.

PR.     Indeed to friends I'm piteous to behold.

CH.     Did you in no respect go beyond this?

PR.     True, mortals I made cease foreseeing
          fate.

CH.     Having found what remedy for this ail?

PR.     Blind hopes in them I made to dwell.

CH.     A great advantage this you gave to men.

PR.     Beside these, too, I bestowed on them
          fire.

CH.     And have mortals flamy fire?

PR.     From which indeed they will learn
          many arts.

CH.     Upon such charges then does Zeus
          Maltreat you, and nowhere relax from
            ills?
          Is there no term of suffering lying
            before thee?

PR.     Nay, none at all, but when to him it
          may seem good.

CH.     And how will it seem good? What hope?
            See you not that
          You have erred? But how you've erred,
            for me to tell
          Not pleasant, and to you a pain. But
            these things
          Let us omit, and seek you some release
            from sufferings.

PR.     Easy, whoever out of trouble holds his
          Foot, to admonish and remind those
            faring

Ill. But all these things I knew,
Willing, willing I erred, I'll not deny;
Mortals assisting I myself found
    trouble.
Not indeed with penalties like these
    thought I
That I should pine on lofty rocks,
Gaining this drear unneighbored hill.
But bewail not my present woes,
But alighting, the fortunes creeping on
Hear ye, that ye may learn all to the
    end.
Obey me, obey, sympathize
With him now suffering. Thus indeed
    affliction
Wandering round, sits now by one, then
    by another.

CH.    Not to unwilling ears do you urge
This, Prometheus.
And now with light foot the swift-
    rushing
Seat leaving, and the pure ether,
Path of birds, to this peaked
Ground I come; for thy misfortunes
I wish fully to hear.

PROMETHEUS, CHORUS, *and* OCEANUS.

Oc.    I come to the end of a long way
Travelling to thee, Prometheus,
By my will without bits directing
This wing-swift bird;
For at thy fortunes know I grieve.
And, I think, affinity thus
Impels me, but apart from birth,

There's not to whom a higher rank
I would assign than thee.
And you will know these things as true,
    and not in vain
To flatter with the tongue is in me.
    Come, therefore,
Show how it is necessary to assist you;
For never will you say, than Ocean
There's a firmer friend to thee.

PR.    Alas! what now? And you then of my
       sufferings
Come spectator? How didst thou dare,
       leaving
The stream which bears thy name, and
       rock-roofed
Caves self-built, to the iron-mother
Earth to go? To behold my fate
Hast come, and to compassionate my
       ills?
Behold a spectacle, this, the friend
       of Zeus,
Having with him stablished his
       tyranny,
With what afflictions by himself I'm
       bent.

OC.    I see, Prometheus, and would admonish
Thee the best, although of varied craft.
Know thyself, and fit thy manners
New; for new also the king among the
       gods.
But if thus rude and whetted words
Thou wilt hurl out, quickly may Zeus,
       though sitting
Far above, hear thee, so that thy
       present wrath

Of troubles child's play will seem to be.
But, O wretched one, dismiss the
    indignation which thou hast,
And seek deliverance from these woes.
Like an old man, perhaps, I seem to
    thee to say these things;
Such, however, are the wages
Of the too lofty speaking tongue,
        Prometheus,
But thou art not yet humble, nor dost
    yield to ills,
And beside the present wish to receive
    others still.
But thou wouldst not, with my counsel,
Against the pricks extend your limbs,
    seeing that
A stern monarch, irresponsible reigns.
And now I go, and will endeavor,
If I can, to release thee from these
    sufferings.
But be thou quiet, nor too rudely speak.
Know'st thou not well, with thy superior
    wisdom, that
On a vain tongue punishment is
    inflicted?

Pr.     I congratulate thee that thou art
            without blame,
        Having shared and dared all with me,
        And now leave off, and let it not
            concern thee.
        For altogether thou wilt not persuade
            him, for he's not easily persuaded,
        But take heed yourself lest you be
            injured by the way.

Oc.   Far better thou art to advise those near
      Than thyself; by deed and not by word
          I judge.
      But me hastening by no means mayest
          thou detain,
      For I boast, I boast, this favor will Zeus
      Grant me, from these sufferings to
          release thee.

Pr.   So far I praise thee, and will never
          cease;
      For zeal you nothing lack. But
      Strive not; for in vain, nought helping
      Me, thou'lt strive, if aught to strive
          you wish.
      But be thou quiet, holding thyself aloof,
      For I would not, though I'm unfortunate,
          that on this account
      Evils should come to many.

Oc.   Surely not, for me too the fortunes of
          thy brother
      Atlas grieve, who towards the evening-
          places
      Stands, the pillar of heaven and earth
      Upon his shoulders bearing, a load not
          easy to be borne.
      And the earth-born inhabitant of the
          Cilician
      Caves, seeing, I pitied, the savage
          monster
      With a hundred heads, by force
          o'ercome,
      Typhon impetuous, who stood 'gainst
          all the gods,
      With frightful jaws hissing out
          slaughter;

And from his eyes flashed a gorgonian
    light,
Utterly to destroy by force the
    sovereignty of Zeus;
But there came to him Zeus' sleepless
    bolt,
Descending thunder, breathing flame,
Which struck him out from lofty
Boastings. For struck to his very heart,
His strength was scorched and
    thundered out.
And now a useless and extended
    carcass
Lies he near a narrow passage of the
    sea,
Pressed down under the roots of Ætna.
And on the topmost summit seated,
    Hephaistus
Hammers the ignited mass, whence will
    burst out at length
Rivers of fire, devouring with wild jaws
Fair-fruited Sicily's smooth fields;
Such rage will Typhon make boil over
With hot discharges of insatiable fire-
    breathing tempest,
Though by the bolt of Zeus burnt to a
    coal.

Pr.   Thou art not inexperienced, nor dost
    want
My counsel; secure thyself as thou
    know'st how;
And I against the present fortune will
    bear up,
Until the thought of Zeus may cease
    from wrath.

Oc. Know'st thou not this, Prometheus, that
Words are healers of distempered
wrath?

Pr. If any seasonably soothe the heart,
And swelling passion check not rudely.

Oc. In the consulting and the daring
What harm seest thou existing?
Teach me.

Pr. Trouble superfluous, and light-minded
folly.

Oc. Be this my ail then, since it is
Most profitable being wise not to
seem wise.

Pr. This will seem to be my error.

Oc. Plainly homeward thy words remand
me.

Pr. Aye, let not grief for me into hostility
cast thee.

Oc. To the new occupant of the all-
powerful seats?

Pr. Beware lest ever his heart be angered.

Oc. Thy fate, Prometheus, is my teacher.

Pr. Go thou, depart, preserve the present
mind.

Oc. To me rushing this word you utter.
For the smooth path of the air sweeps
with his wings
The four-legged bird; and gladly would
In the stalls at home bend a knee.

PROMETHEUS *and* CHORUS.

CH.    I mourn for thee thy ruinous
       Fate, Prometheus,
       And tear-distilling from my tender
       Eyes a stream has wet
       My cheeks with flowing springs;
       For these, unenvied, Zeus
       By his own laws enforcing,
       Haughty above the gods
       That were displays his sceptre.
       And every region now
       With groans resounds,
       Mourning the illustrious
       And ancient honor
       Of thee and of thy kindred;
       As many mortals as the habitable seat
       Of sacred Asia pasture,
       With thy lamentable
       Woes have sympathy.
       And of the Colchian land, virgin
       Inhabitants, in fight undaunted,
       And Scythia's multitude, who the last
       Place of earth, about
       Mæotis lake possess,
       And Arabia's martial flower,
       And who the high-hung citadels
       Of Caucasus inhabit near,
       A hostile army, raging
       With sharp-prowed spears.
       Only one other god before, in sufferings
       Subdued by injuries
       Of adamantine bonds, I've seen,
          Titanian
       Atlas, who always with superior
          strength

The huge and heavenly globe
On his back bears;
And with a roar the sea waves
Dashing, groans the deep,
And the dark depth of Hades murmurs
    underneath
The earth, and fountains of pure-
    running rivers
Heave a pitying sigh.

Pr.   Think not indeed through weakness or
    through pride
That I am silent; for with the
    consciousness I gnaw my heart,
Seeing myself thus basely used.
And yet to these new gods their shares
Who else than I wholly distributed?
But of these things I am silent; for I
    should tell you
What you know; the sufferings of
    mortals too
You've heard, how I made intelligent
And possessed of sense them ignorant
    before.
But I will speak, not bearing any
    grudge to men,
But showing in what I gave the good
    intention;
At first, indeed, seeing they saw in vain,
And hearing heard not; but like the
    forms
Of dreams, for that long time, rashly
    confounded
All, nor brick-woven dwellings
Knew they, placed in the sun, nor
    wood-work;

But digging down they dwelt, like puny
Ants, in sunless nooks of caves.
And there was nought to them, neither
    of winter sign,
Nor of flower-giving spring, nor fruitful
Summer, that was sure; but without
    knowledge
Did they all, till I taught them the
    risings
Of the stars, and goings down, hard to
    determine.
And numbers, chief of inventions,
I found out for them, and the
    assemblages of letters,
And memory, Muse-mother, doer of
    all things,
And first I joined in pairs wild animals
Obedient to the yoke; and that they
    might be
Alternate workers with the bodies of
    men
In the severest toils, harnessed the
    rein-loving horses
To the car, the ornament of over-
    wealthy luxury.
And none else than I invented the
    sea-wandering
Flaxen-winged vehicles of sailors.
Such inventions I wretched having
    found out
For men, myself have not the ingenuity
    by which
From the now present ill I may escape.

CH.     You suffer unseemly ill, deranged in
       mind

You err; and as some bad physician,
    falling
Sick you are dejected, and cannot find
By what remedies you may be healed.

PR.     Hearing the rest from me more will
        you wonder,
What arts and what expedients I
    planned.
That which was greates., if any might
    fall sick,
There was alleviation none, neither
    to eat,
Nor to anoint, nor drink, but for the
    want
Of medicines they were reduced to
    skeletons, till to them
I showed the mingling of mild remedies,
By which all ails they drive away.
And many modes of prophecy I settled,
And distinguished first of dreams what
    a real
Vision is required to be, and omens
    hard to be determined
I made known to them; and tokens by
    the way,
And flight of crooked-taloned birds I
    accurately
Defined, which lucky are,
And unlucky, and what mode of life
Have each, and to one another what
Hostilities, attachments, and
    assemblings;
The entrails' smoothness, and what
    color having

They would be to the divinities
   acceptable,
Of the gall and liver the various
   symmetry,
And the limbs concealed in fat; and
   the long
Flank burning, to an art hard to be
   guessed
I showed the way to mortals; and
   flammeous signs
Explained, before obscure.
Such indeed these; and under ground
Concealed the helps to men,
Brass, iron, silver, gold, who
Would affirm that he discovered
   before me?
None, I well know, not wishing in vain
   to boast.
But learn all in one word,
*All arts to mortals from Prometheus.*

CH.   Assist not mortals now unseasonably,
   And neglect yourself unfortunate; for I
   Am of good hope, that from these bonds
   Released, you will yet have no less
      power than Zeus.

PR.   Never thus has Fate the Accomplisher
   Decreed to fulfil these things, but by
      a myriad ills
   And woes subdued, thus bonds I flee;
   For art's far weaker than necessity.

CH.   Who then is helmsman of necessity?

PR.   The Fates three-formed, and the
      remembering Furies.

CH.    Than these then is Zeus weaker?

PR.    Aye, he could not escape what has
        been fated.

CH.    But what to Zeus is fated, except
        always to rule?

PR.    This thou wilt not learn; seek not
        to know.

CH.    Surely some awful thing it is which
        you withhold.

PR.    Remember other words, for this by
        no means
    Is it time to tell, but to be concealed
    As much as possible; for keeping this
        do I
    Escape unseemly bonds and woes.

CH.    Never may the all-ruling
    Zeus put into my mind
    Force antagonist to him.
    Nor let me cease drawing near
    The gods with holy sacrifices
    Of slain oxen, by Father Ocean's
    Ceaseless passage,
    Nor offend with words,
    But in me this remain,
    And ne'er be melted out.
    'T is something sweet with bold
    Hopes the long life to
    Extend, in bright
    Cheerfulness cherishing the spirit.
    But I shudder, thee beholding
    By a myriad sufferings
        tormented. * * *

For not fearing Zeus,
In thy private mind thou dost regard
Mortals too much, Prometheus.
Come, though a thankless
Favor, friend, say where is any
     strength,
From ephemerals any help? Saw you
     not
The powerless inefficiency,
Dream-like, in which the blind * * *
Race of mortals are entangled?
Never counsels of mortals
May transgress the harmony of Zeus.
I learned these things looking on
Thy destructive fate, Prometheus.
For different to me did this strain come,
And that which round thy baths
And couch I hymned,
With the design of marriage, when
     my father's child
With bridal gifts persuading, thou
     didst lead
Hesione the partner of thy bed.


PROMETHEUS, CHORUS, *and* Io.

Io.     What earth, what race, what being
             shall I say is this
         I see in bridles of rock
         Exposed? By what crime's
         Penalty dost thou perish? Show, to
             what part
         Of earth I miserable have wandered.
         Ah! ah! alas! alas!
         Again some fly doth sting me wretched,

Image of earth-born Argus, cover it
    earth;
I fear the myriad-eyed herdsman
    beholding;
For he goes having a treacherous eye,
Whom not e'en dead the earth conceals.
But me, wretched from the Infernals
    passing,
He pursues, and drives fasting along
    the sea-side
Sand, while low resounds a wax-
    compacted reed,
Uttering sleep-giving law; alas! alas!
    O gods!
Where, gods! where lead me far-
    wandering courses?
In what sin, O son of Kronos,
In what sin ever having taken,
To these afflictions hast thou yoked me?
    alas! alas!
With fly-driven fear a wretched
Phrenzied one dost thus afflict?
With fire burn, or with earth cover, or
To sea monsters give for food, nor
Envy me my prayers, king.
Enough much-wandered wanderings
Have exercised me, nor can I learn
    where
I shall escape from sufferings.

CH.    Hear'st thou the address of the
        cow-horned virgin?

PR.    And how not hear the fly-whirled
        virgin,

Daughter of Inachus, who Zeus' heart
    warmed
With love, and now the courses over
    long,
By Here hated, forcedly performs?

Io.    Whence utterest thou my father's
    name,
Tell me, miserable, who thou art,
That to me, O suffering one, me born
    to suffer,
Thus true things dost address?
The god-sent ail thou'st named,
Which wastes me stinging
With maddening goads, alas! alas!
With foodless and unseemly leaps
Rushing headlong, I came,
By wrathful plots subdued.
Who of the wretched, who, alas! alas!
    suffers like me?
But to me clearly show
What me awaits to suffer,
What not necessary; what remedy
    of ill,
Teach, if indeed thou know'st,
    speak out,
Tell the ill-wandering virgin.

Pr.    I'll clearly tell thee all you wish
    to learn.
Not weaving in enigmas, but in simple
    speech,
As it is just to open the mouth to
    friends.
Thou seest the giver of fire to men,
    Prometheus.

Io.    O thou who didst appear a common
              help to mortals,
         Wretched Prometheus, to atone for
              what do you endure this?

Pr.    I have scarce ceased my sufferings
              lamenting.

Io. .  Would you not grant this favor to me?

Pr.    Say what you ask; for you'd learn all
              from me.

Io.    Say who has bound thee to the cliff.

Pr.    The will indeed of Zeus, Hephaistus'
              the hand.

Io.    And penalty for what crimes dost thou
              pay?

Pr.    Thus much only can I show thee.

Io.    But beside this, declare what time
              will be
         To me unfortunate the limit of my
              wandering.

Pr.    Not to learn is better for thee than
              to learn these things.

Io.    Conceal not from me what I am to
              suffer.

Pr.    Indeed, I grudge thee not this favor.

Io.    Why then dost thou delay to tell the
              whole?

Pr.    There's no unwillingness, but I hesitate
              to vex thy mind.

Io.    Care not for me more than is pleasant
           to me.

Pr.    Since you are earnest, it behoves to
           speak; hear then.

Ch.    Not yet indeed; but a share of pleasure
           also give to me.
       First we'll learn the malady of
           this one,
       Herself relating her destructive
           fortunes,
       And the remainder of her trials let her
           learn from thee.

Pr.    'T is thy part, Io, to do these a favor,
       As well for every other reason, and as
           they are sisters of thy father.
       Since to weep and to lament
           misfortunes,
       There where one will get a tear
       From those attending, is worth the
           delay.

Io.    I know not that I need distrust you,
       But in plain speech you shall learn
       All that you ask for; and yet e'en
           telling I lament
       The god-sent tempest, and dissolution
       Of my form—whence to me miserable
           it came.
       For always visions in the night moving
           about
       My virgin chambers, enticed me
       With smooth words; "O greatly
           happy virgin,
       Why be a virgin long? it is permitted
           to obtain

The greatest marriage. For Zeus with
  love's dart
Has been warmed by thee, and wishes
  to unite
In love; but do thou, O child, spurn
  not the couch
Of Zeus, but go out to Lerna's deep
Morass, and stables of thy father's
  herds,
That the divine eye may cease from
  desire."
With such dreams every night
Was I unfortunate distressed, till I
  dared tell
My father of the night-wandering
  visions.
And he to Pytho and Dodona frequent
Prophets sent, that he might learn what
  it was necessary
He should say or do, to do agreeably to
  the gods.
And they came bringing ambiguous
Oracles, darkly and indistinctly uttered.
But finally a plain report came to
  Inachus,
Clearly enjoining him and telling,
Out of my home and country to
  expel me,
Discharged to wander to the earth's
  last bounds,
And if he was not willing, from Zeus
  would come
A fiery thunderbolt, which would
  annihilate all his race.
Induced by such predictions of the
  Loxian,

Against his will he drove me out
　　unwilling,
And shut me from the houses; but
　　Zeus' rein
Compelled him by force to do these
　　things.
Immediately my form and mind were
Changed, and horned, as you behold,
　　stung
By a sharp-mouthed fly, with frantic
　　leaping
Rushed I to Cenchrea's palatable
　　stream,
And Lerna's source; but a herdsman
　　born-of-earth
Of violent temper, Argus, accompanied,
　　with numerous
Eyes my steps observing.
But unexpectedly a sudden fate
Robbed him of life; and I, fly-stung,
By lash divine am driven from land
　　to land.
You hear what has been done; and if
　　you have to say,
What's left of labors, speak; nor
　　pitying me
Comfort with false words; for an ill
The worst of all, I say, are made-up
　　words.

CH.　Ah! ah! enough, alas!
　　　Ne'er, ne'er did I presume such cruel
　　　　words
　　　Would reach my ears, nor thus
　　　　unsightly,

And intolerable hurts, sufferings, fears
   with a two-edged
Goad would chill my soul;
Alas! alas! fate! fate!
I shudder, seeing the state of Io.

PR.   Before hand sigh'st thou, and art full
   of fears,
Hold till the rest also thou learn'st.

CH.   Tell, teach; for to the sick 't is sweet
To know the remaining pain beforehand
   clearly.

PR.   Your former wish ye got from me
With ease; for first ye asked to learn
   from her
Relating her own trials;
The rest now hear, what sufferings 't
   is necessary
This young woman should endure from
   Here.
But do thou, offspring of Inachus,
   my words
Cast in thy mind, that thou may'st
   learn the boundaries of the way.
First, indeed, hence toward the rising of
   the sun
Turning thyself, travel uncultivated
   lands,
And to the Scythian nomads thou wilt
   come, who woven roofs
On high inhabit, on well-wheeled carts.
With far-casting bows equipped;
Whom go not near, but to the sea-
   resounding cliffs

Bending thy feet, pass from the region.
On the left hand the iron-working
Chalybes inhabit, whom thou must
    needs beware,
For they are rude and inaccessible to
    strangers.
And thou wilt come to the Hybristes
    river, not ill named,
Which pass not, for not easy is't to pass,
Before you get to Caucasus itself,
    highest
Of mountains, where the stream spurts
    out its tide
From the very temples; and passing
    over
The star-neighbored summits, 't is
    necessary to go,
The southern way where thou wilt
    come to the man-hating
Army of the Amazons, who Themiscyra
    one day
Will inhabit, by the Thermodon,
    where's
Salmydessia, rough jaw of the sea,
Inhospitable to sailors, step-mother
    of ships;
They will conduct thee on thy way, and
    very cheerfully.
And to the Cimmerian isthmus thou
    wilt come,
Just on the narrow portals of a lake,
    which leaving
It behoves thee with stout heart to pass
    the Mæotic straits;
And there will be to mortals ever a
    great fame

Of thy passage, and Bosphorus from
    thy name
'T will be called. And leaving
    Europe's plain
The continent of Asia thou wilt
    reach.—Seemeth to thee, forsooth,
The tyrant of the gods in everything
    to be
Thus violent? For he a god with this
    mortal
Wishing to unite, drove her to these
    wanderings.
A bitter wooer didst thou find, O virgin,
For thy marriage. For the words you
    now have heard
Think not yet to be the prelude.

Io.    Ah! me! me! alas! alas!

Pr.    Again dost shriek and heave a sigh?
       What
Wilt thou do when the remaining ills
    thou learn'st?

Ch.    And hast thou any further suffering
    to tell her?

Pr.    Aye, a tempestuous sea of baleful woe.

Io.    What profit then for me to live, and
    not in haste
To cast myself from this rough rock,
That rushing down upon the plain I
    may be released
From every trouble? For better once
    for all to die,
Than all my days to suffer evilly.

Pr.  Unhappily my trials would'st thou bear,
To whom to die has not been fated;
For this would be release from
    sufferings;
But now there is no end of ills lying
Before me, until Zeus falls from
    sovereignty.

Io.  And is Zeus ever to fall from power?

Pr.  Thou would'st be pleased, I think, to see
this accident.

Io.  How should I not, who suffer ill
from Zeus?

Pr.  That these things then are so, be thou
assured.

Io.  By what one will the tyrant's power be
robbed?

Pr.  Himself, by his own senseless counsels.

Io.  In what way show, if there's no harm.

Pr.  He will make such a marriage as one
day he'll repent.

Io.  Of god or mortal? If to be spoken, tell.

Pr.  What matter which? For these things
are not to be told.

Io.  By a wife will he be driven from the
throne?

Pr.  Aye, she will bring forth a son superior
to his father.

Io.  Is there no refuge for him from this
fate?

PR.   None, surely, till I may be released from
      bonds.

Io.   Who then is to release thee, Zeus
      unwilling?

PR.   He must be some one of thy
      descendants.

Io.   How sayest thou—that my child will
      deliver thee from ills?

PR.   Third of thy race after ten other births.

Io.   This oracle is not yet easy to be
      guessed.

PR.   But do not seek to understand thy
      sufferings.

Io.   First proffering gain to me, do not
      then withhold it.

PR.   I'll grant thee one of two relations.

Io.   What two propose, and give to me my
      choice.

PR.   I give; choose whether thy remaining
      troubles
      I shall tell thee clearly, or him that
      will release me.

CH.   Consent to do her the one favor,
      Me the other, nor deem us undeserving
      of thy words;
      To her indeed tell what remains of
      wandering,
      And to me, who will release; for I
      desire this.

Pr.   Since ye are earnest, I will not resist
To tell the whole, as much as ye ask for.
To thee first, Io, vexatious wandering I
    will tell,
Which engrave on the remembering
    tablets of the mind.
When thou hast passed the flood,
    boundary of continents,
Towards the flaming orient sun-
    travelled * * *
Passing through the tumult of the sea,
    until you reach
The gorgonean plains of Cisthene,
    where
The Phorcides dwell, old virgins,
Three, swan-shaped, having a common
    eye,
One-toothed, whom neither the sun
    looks on
With his beams, nor nightly moon ever.
And near, their winged sisters three,
Dragon-scaled Gorgons, odious to men,
Whom no mortal beholding, will have
    breath;
Such danger do I tell thee,
But hear another odious sight;
Beware the gryphons, sharp-mouthed
Dogs of Zeus, which bark not, and the
    one-eyed Arimaspian
Host, going on horse-back, who dwell
    about
The golden-flowing flood of Pluto's
    channel;
These go not near. But to a distant land
Thou'lt come, a dusky race, who near
    the fountains

Of the sun inhabit, where is the
&AElig;thiopian river.
Creep down the banks of this, until
thou com'st
To a descent, where from Byblinian
mounts
The Nile sends down its sacred
palatable stream.
This will conduct thee to the
triangled land
Nilean, where, Io, 't is decreed
Thou and thy progeny shall form the
distant colony.
If aught of this is unintelligible to
thee, and hard to be found out,
Repeat thy questions, and learn clearly;
For more leisure than I want is
granted me.

CH. If to her aught remaining or omitted
Thou hast to tell of her pernicious
wandering,
Speak; but if thou hast said all, give us
The favor which we ask, for surely thou
remember'st.

PR. The whole term of her travelling has
she heard.
But that she may know that not in vain
she hears me,
I'll tell what before coming hither she
endured,
Giving this as proof of my relations.
The great multitude of words I will
omit,
And proceed unto the very limit of thy
wanderings.

When then you came to the
    Molossian ground,
And near the high-ridged Dodona,
    where
Oracle and seat is of Thesprotian Zeus,
And prodigy incredible, the speaking
    oaks,
By whom thou clearly, and nought
    enigmatically,
Wert called the illustrious wife of Zeus
About to be, if aught of these things
    soothes thee;
Thence, driven by the fly, you came
The seaside way to the great gulf
    of Rhea,
From which by courses retrograde you
    are now tempest-tossed.
But for time to come the sea gulf,
Clearly know, will be called Ionian,
Memorial of thy passage to all mortals.
Proofs to thee are these of my
    intelligence,
That it sees somewhat more than the
    apparent.
But the rest to you and her in common
    I will tell,
Having come upon the very track of
    former words.
There is a city Canopus, last of the
    land,
By Nile's very mouth and bank;
There at length Zeus makes thee sane,
Stroking with gentle hand, and
    touching only.
And, named from Zeus' begetting,

Thou wilt bear dark Epaphus, who
    will reap
As much land as broad-flowing Nile
    doth water;
And fifth from him, a band of fifty
    children
Again to Argos shall unwilling come,
Of female sex, avoiding kindred
    marriage
Of their cousins; but they, with minds
    inflamed,
Hawks by doves not far left behind,
Will come pursuing marriages
Not to be pursued, but heaven will
    take vengeance on their bodies;
For them Pelasgia shall receive by Mars
Subdued with woman's hand with
    night-watching boldness.
For each wife shall take her husband's
    life,
Staining a two-edged dagger in his
    throat.
Such 'gainst my foes may Cypris
    come.–
But one of the daughters shall love
    soften
Not to slay her bed-fellow, but she
    will waver
In her mind; and one of two things
    will prefer,
To hear herself called timid, rather
    than stained with blood;
She shall in Argos bear a royal race.––
Of a long speech is need this clearly
    to discuss.

From this seed, however, shall be born
   a brave,
Famed for his bow, who will release me
From these sufferings. Such oracle
   my ancient
Mother told me, Titanian Themis;
But how and by what means, this needs
   long speech
To tell, and nothing, learning, wilt
   thou gain.

Io.   Ah me! ah wretched me!
Spasms again and brain-struck
Madness burn me within, and a fly's
   dart
Stings me—not wrought by fire.
My heart with fear knocks at my breast,
And my eyes whirl round and round,
And from my course I'm borne by
   madness'
Furious breath, unable to control my
   tongue;
While confused words dash idly
'Gainst the waves of horrid woe.

CH.   Wise, wise indeed was he,
Who first in mind
This weighed, and with the tongue
   expressed,
To marry according to one's degree is
   best by far;
Nor being a laborer with the hands,
To woo those who are by wealth
   corrupted,
Nor those by birth made great.
Never, never me
Fates * * *

May you behold the sharer of Zeus'
  couch.
Nor may I be brought near to any
  husband among those from heaven,
For I fear, seeing the virginhood of Io,
Not content with man, through
  marriage vexed
With these distressful wanderings by
  Here.
But for myself, since an equal marriage
  is without fear,
I am not concerned lest the love of the
  almighty
Gods cast its inevitable eye on me.
Without war indeed the war, producing
Troubles; nor do I know what would
  become of me;
For I see not how I should escape the
  subtlety of Zeus.

PR.    Surely shall Zeus, though haughty now,
Yet be humble, such marriage
He prepares to make, which from
  sovereignty
And the throne will cast him down
  obscure; and father Kronos'
Curse will then be all fulfilled,
Which falling from the ancient seats he
  imprecated.
And refuge from such ills none of the
  gods
But I can show him clearly.
I know these things, and in what
  manner. Now therefore
Being bold, let him sit trusting to lofty
Sounds, and brandishing with both
  hands his fire-breathing weapon,

For nought will these avail him, not
To fall disgracefully intolerable falls;
Such wrestler does he now prepare,
Himself against himself, a prodigy
    most hard to be withstood;
Who, indeed, will invent a better flame
    than lightning,
And a loud sound surpassing thunder;
And shiver the trident, Neptune's
    weapon,
The marine earth-shaking ail.
Stumbling upon this ill he'll learn
How different to govern and to serve.

CH.    Aye, as you hope you vent this against
        Zeus.

PR.    What will be done, and also what I
        hope, I say.

CH.    And are we to expect that any will
        rule Zeus?

PR.    Even than these more grievous ills
        he'll have.

CH.    How fear'st thou not, hurling such
        words?

PR.    What should I fear, to whom to die has
        not been fated?

CH.    But suffering more grievous still than
        this he may inflict.

PR.    Then let him do it; all is expected by
        me.

CH.    Those reverencing Adrastia are wise.

PR.    Revere, pray, flatter each successive
        ruler.
    Me less than nothing Zeus concerns.
    Let him do, let him prevail this short
        time
    As he will, for long he will not rule the
        gods—
    But I see here, indeed, Zeus' runner,
    The new tyrant's drudge;
    Doubtless he brings us some new
        message.

PROMETHEUS, CHORUS, *and* HERMES.

HER.    To thee, the sophist, the bitterly bitter,
    The sinner against gods, the giver of
        honors
    To ephemerals, the thief of fire, I speak;
    The father commands thee to tell the
        marriage
    Which you boast, by which he falls
        from power;
    And that too not enigmatically,
    But each particular declare; nor cause
        me
    Double journeys, Prometheus; for thou
        see'st that
    Zeus is not appeased by such.

PR.    Solemn-mouthed and full of wisdom
    Is thy speech, as of the servant of the
        gods.
    Ye newly rule, and think forsooth
    To dwell in griefless citadels; have I
        not seen
    Two tyrants fallen from these?

And third I shall behold him ruling
    now,
Basest and speediest. Do I seem to thee
To fear and shrink from the new gods?
Nay, much and wholly I fall short of
    this.
The way thou cam'st go through the
    dust again;
For thou wilt learn nought which thou
    ask'st of me.

HER.    Aye, by such insolence before
    You brought yourself into these woes.

PR.    Plainly know, I would not change
    My ill fortune for thy servitude,
    For better, I think, to serve this rock
    Than be the faithful messenger of
        Father Zeus.
    Thus to insult the insulting it is fit.

HER.    Thou seem'st to enjoy thy present state.

PR.    I enjoy? Enjoying thus my enemies
    Would I see; and thee 'mong them I
        count.

HER.    Dost thou blame me for aught of thy
        misfortunes?

PR.    In plain words, all gods I hate,
    As many as well treated wrong me
        unjustly.

HER.    I hear thee raving, no slight ail.

PR.    Aye, I should ail, if ail one's foes to
        hate.

HER.    If prosperous, thou couldst not be
        borne.

Pr.    Ah me!

Her.   This word Zeus does not know.

Pr.    But time growing old teaches all things.

Her.   And still thou know'st not yet how to be
       prudent.

Pr.    For I should not converse with thee a
       servant.

Her.   Thou seem'st to say nought which the
       father wishes.

Pr.    And yet his debtor I'd requite the favor.

Her.   Thou mock'st me verily as if I were a
       child.

Pr.    And art thou not a child, and simpler
       still than this,
       If thou expectest to learn aught from
       me?
       There is not outrage nor expedient, by
       which
       Zeus will induce me to declare these
       things,
       Before he loose these grievous bonds.
       Let there be hurled then flaming fire,
       And with white-winged snows, and
       thunders
       Of the earth, let him confound and
       mingle all.
       For none of these will bend me till I tell
       By whom 't is necessary he should fall
       from sovereignty.

Her.   Consider now if these things seem
       helpful.

PR.    Long since these were considered and
       resolved.

HER.    Venture, O vain one, venture, at length,
       In view of present sufferings to be wise.

PR.    In vain you vex me, as a wave,
       exhorting.
       Ne'er let it come into thy mind, that,
       I, fearing
       Zeus' anger, shall become woman-
       minded,
       And beg him, greatly hated,
       With womanish upturnings of the
       hands,
       To loose me from these bonds. I am
       far from it.

HER.    Though saying much I seem in vain to
       speak;
       For thou art nothing softened nor
       appeased
       By prayers; but champing at the bit
       like a new-yoked
       Colt, thou strugglest and contend'st
       against the reins.
       But thou art violent with feeble wisdom.
       For stubbornness to him who is not
       wise,
       Itself alone, is less than nothing strong.
       But consider, if thou art not persuaded
       by my words,
       What storm and triple surge of ills
       Will come upon thee not to be avoided;
       for first this rugged
       Cliff with thunder and lightning flame
       The Father 'll rend, and hide

Thy body, and a strong arm will bury
    thee.
When thou hast spent a long length
    of time,
Thou wilt come back to light; and Zeus'
Winged dog, a blood-thirsty eagle,
    ravenously
Shall tear the great rag of thy body,
Creeping an uninvited guest all day,
And banquet on thy liver black by
    eating.
Of such suffering expect not any end,
Before some god appear
Succeeding to thy labors, and wish to
    go to rayless
Hades, and the dark depths of Tartarus.
Therefore deliberate; since this is not
    made
Boasting, but in earnest spoken;
For to speak falsely does not know
    the mouth
Of Zeus, but every word he does. So
Look about thee, and consider, nor ever
    think
Obstinacy better than prudence.

CH.   To us indeed Hermes appears to say
       not unseasonable things,
    For he directs thee, leaving off
    Self-will, to seek prudent counsel.
    Obey; for, it is base for a wise man
       to err.

PR.   To me foreknowing these messages
    He has uttered, but for a foe to suffer ill
    From foes, is nought unseemly.

Therefore 'gainst me let there be
    hurled
Fire's double-pointed curl, and air
Be provoked with thunder, and a
    tumult
Of wild winds; and earth from its
    foundations
Let a wind rock, and its very roots,
And with a rough surge mingle
The sea waves with the passages
Of the heavenly stars, and to black
Tartarus let him quite cast down my
Body, by necessity's strong eddies;
Yet after all he will not kill me.

HER.    Such words and counsels you may hear
From the brain-struck.
For what lacks he of being mad?
And if prosperous, what does he cease
    from madness?
Do you, therefore, who sympathize
With this one's suffering,
From these places quick withdraw
    somewhere,
Lest the harsh bellowing of thunder
Stupify your minds.

CH.    Say something else, and exhort me
To some purpose; for surely
Thou hast intolerably abused this word.
How direct me to perform a baseness?
I wish to suffer with him whate'er is
    necessary,
For I have learned to hate betrayers;
Nor is there pest
Which I abominate more than this.

HER.    Remember then what I fore-tell;
Nor by calamity pursued
Blame fortune, nor e'er say
That Zeus into unforeseen
Ill has cast you; surely not, but
    yourselves
You yourselves; for knowing,
And not suddenly nor clandestinely,
You'll be entangled through your folly
In an impassible net of woe.

PR.    Surely indeed, and no more in word,
Earth is shaken;
And a hoarse sound of thunder
Bellows near; and wreaths of lightning
Flash out fiercely blazing, and
    whirlwinds dust
Whirl up; and leap the blasts
Of all winds, 'gainst one another
Blowing in opposite array;
And air with sea is mingled;
Such impulse against me from Zeus
Producing fear, doth plainly come.
O revered Mother, O Ether
Revolving common light to all,
You see me, how unjust things I
    endure!

# Anacreon.

WE lately met with an old volume from a
London bookshop, containing the Greek Minor Poets,
and it was a pleasure to read once more only the
words,–Orpheus,–Linus,–Musæus–those faint poetic
sounds and echoes of a name, dying away on the
ears of us modern men; and those hardly more substantial sounds, Mimnermus–Ibycus–Alcæus–Stesichorus–Menander. They lived not in vain. We can
converse with these bodiless fames, without reserve
or personality.

We know of no studies so composing as those of
the classical scholar. When we have sat down to
them, life seems as still and serene as if it were very
far off, and we believe it is not habitually seen from
any common platform so truly and unexaggerated as
in the light of literature. In serene hours we contem-
plate the tour of the Greek and Latin authors with
more pleasure than the traveller does the fairest
scenery of Greece or Italy. Where shall we find a
more refined society? That highway down from
Homer and Hesiod to Horace and Juvenal is more
attractive than the Appian. Reading the classics, or
conversing with those old Greeks and Latins in their
surviving works, is like walking amid the stars and
constellations, a high and by-way serene to travel.
Indeed, the true scholar will be not a little of an
astronomer in his habits. Distracting cares will not
be allowed to obstruct the field of his vision, for the

higher regions of literature, like astronomy, are above
storm and darkness.

But passing by these rumors of bards, we have
chosen to pause for a moment at Anacreon, the
Teian poet, and present some specimens of him to
our readers.*

There is something strangely modern about him.
He is very easily turned into English. Is it that our
lyric poets have resounded only that lyre, which
would sound only light subjects, and which Simonides tells us does not sleep in Hades? His odes are
like gems of pure ivory. They possess an etherial and
evanescent beauty like summer evenings, ὃ χρή σε
νοεῖν νόου ἄνθει, *which you must perceive with the
flower of the mind,*—and show how slight a beauty
could be expressed. You have to consider them, as
the stars of lesser magnitude, with the side of the
eye, and look aside from them to behold them. They
charm us by their serenity and freedom from exaggeration and passion, and by a certain flower-like
beauty, which does not propose itself, but must be
approached and studied like a natural object. But,
perhaps, their chief merit consists in the lightness
and yet security of their tread;

> "The young and tender stalk
> Ne'er bends when *they* do walk."

True, our nerves are never strung by them;—it is
too constantly the sound of the lyre, and never the
note of the trumpet; but they are not gross, as has
been presumed, but always elevated above the sen-
sual.

* The following, with the odes to the Cicada and to Spring,
in the ninth number of the Dial, pp. 23, 24, are, in the opinion of the translator, the best that have come down to us.

## On His Lyre.

I wish to sing the Atridæ
And Cadmus I wish to sing;
But my lyre sounds
Only love with its chords.
Lately I changed the strings
And all the lyre;
And I began to sing the labors
Of Hercules; but my lyre
Resounded loves.
Farewell, henceforth, for me,
Heroes! for my lyre
Sings only loves.

—

## To a Swallow.

Thou indeed, dear swallow,
Yearly going and coming,
In summer weavest thy nest,
And in winter go'st disappearing
Either to Nile or to Memphis.
But Love always weaveth
His nest in my heart. * * *

—

## On a Silver Cup.

Turning the silver,
Vulcan, make for me,
Not indeed a panoply,
For what are battles to me?
But a hollow cup,
As deep as thou canst.
And make for me in it
Neither stars, nor wagons,

Nor sad Orion;
What are the Pleiades to me?
What the shining Bootes?
Make vines for me,
And clusters of grapes in it,
And of gold Love and Bathyllus
Treading the grapes
With the fair Lyæus.

---

### ON HIMSELF.

THOU sing'st the affairs of Thebes,
And he the battles of Troy,
But I of my own defeats.
No horse have wasted me,
Nor foot, nor ships;
But a new and different host,
From eyes smiting me.

---

### TO A DOVE.

LOVELY Dove,
Whence, whence dost thou fly?
Whence, running on air,
Dost thou waft and diffuse
So many sweet ointments?
Who art? What thy errand?–
Anacreon sent me
To a boy, to Bathyllus,
Who lately is ruler and tyrant of all.
Cythere has sold me
For one little song,
And I'm doing this service
For Anacreon.
And now, as you see,

I bear letters from him.
And he says that directly
He'll make me free,
But though he release me,
His slave I will tarry with him.
For why should I fly
Over mountains and fields,
And perch upon trees,
Eating some wild thing?
Now indeed I eat bread,
Plucking it from the hands
Of Anacreon himself;
And he gives me to drink
The wine which he tastes,
And drinking, I dance,
And shadow my master's
Face with my wings;
And, going to rest,
On the lyre itself do I sleep.
That is all; get thee gone.
Thou hast made me more talkative,
Man, than a crow.

—

## ON LOVE.

LOVE walking swiftly
With hyacinthine staff,
Bade me to take a run with him;
And hastening through swift torrents,
And woody places, and over precipices,
A water-snake stung me.
And my heart leaped up to
My mouth, and I should have fainted;
But Love fanning my brows
With his soft wings, said,
Surely, thou art not able to love.

## ON WOMEN.

NATURE has given horns
To bulls, and hoofs to horses,
Swiftness to hares,
To lions yawning teeth,
To fishes swimming,
To birds flight,
To men wisdom.
For woman she had nothing beside;
What then does she give? Beauty,–
Instead of all shields,
Instead of all spears;
And she conquers even iron
And fire, who is beautiful.

—

## ON LOVERS.

HORSES have the mark
Of fire on their sides,
And some have distinguished
The Parthian men by their crests;
So I, seeing lovers,
Know them at once,
For they have a certain slight
Brand on their hearts.

—

## TO A SWALLOW.

WHAT dost thou wish me to do to thee–
What, thou loquacious swallow?
Dost thou wish me taking thee
Thy light pinions to clip?
Or rather to pluck out

Thy tongue from within,
As that Tereus did?
Why with thy notes in the dawn
Hast thou plundered Bathyllus
From my beautiful dreams?

—

## TO A COLT.

THRACIAN colt, why at me
Looking aslant with thy eyes,
Dost thou cruelly flee,
And think that I know nothing wise?
Know I could well
Put the bridle on thee,
And holding the reins, turn
Round the bounds of the course.
But now thou browsest the meads,
And gambolling lightly dost play,
For thou hast no skilful horseman
Mounted upon thy back.

—

## CUPID WOUNDED.

LOVE once among roses
Saw not
A sleeping bee, but was stung;
And being wounded in the finger
Of his hand cried for pain.
Running as well as flying
To the beautiful Venus,
I am killed, mother, said he,
I am killed, and I die.
A little serpent has stung me,

Winged, which they call
A bee—the husbandmen.
And she said, If the sting
Of a bee afflicts you,
How, think you, are they afflicted,
Love, whom you smite?

# The Seven Against Thebes.

Persons of the Drama
Eteocles
Scout.
Chorus of Virgins
Ismene
Antigone
Herald

Et.   Citizens of Cadmus, it behoves that he
      should speak that which the times
      require
Whoever has in charge the common-
      wealth, managing the helm
In the city's stern, not closing his
      (eye)lids in sleep.
For if we should do well, the gods are
      thanked for it;
But if, on the other hand, which be not
      so, misfortune happen,
Then may be Eteocles would be blamed
      throughout the city
By the citizens, with lengthy preludes
And lamentations—from which May
      Zeus called the Defender
indeed defend the city of the Cadmeans
But it behoves you now, both him who
      wants as yet
The perfect bloom of youth, and who
      exceeds in time,
Increasing much the vigor (firmness)
      of his body
And of whatever age, so as is fit,
To aid the city, and the altars of his
      country's

Gods, so that their honors may ne'er be
    effaced;
And His children, and mother Earth,
    his dearest nurse,
Who indeed your creeping youth with
    friendly plain,
Supporting all the miseries of your
    childhood,
Has nourished up shieldbearing
    colonists,—
And faithful, that you might be against
    this need.
And even to this day is Heaven well
    inclined;
For to us now this long while besieged
war for the most part has succeeded
    well by favor of the gods.
But now, as the soothsayer says,
    herdsman of birds,
Considering in his ears and under-
    standing, apart from fire,
Oracular omens with unfailing art;—
This one, master of such oracles—
Says (that) Achaia leads on by night
    and intends
Against the city the greatest assault
    of all.
now to the ramparts and the bulwark
    gates
Hasten ye all, hurry with all your armor
Crowd to the breast works, and on the
    platforms
Of the towers stand, and at the
    passages of the gates
Abiding, be of good courage, nor fear
    much

The crowd of the besiegers; Heaven
    does well for us.
And I have sent out spys and watches
    to observe
The army, who will not loiter by the
    way I trust;
And hearing from these, by no means
    can I be taken by treachery.

———

Sc    Eteocles, most excellent king of the
    Cadmeans,
I come bearing sure tidings from the
    hosts.
For I myself am observer of the affairs.
Seven men forsooth impetuous
    captains,
Slaughtering a bull in to a black-bound
    shield,
And touching with their hands the
    bullock's blood,
By Ares Enyo, and blood-loving
    Phoebus,
Have taken oath, either destroying the
    town
To lay waste the city of the Cadmeans,
Or dying moisten this land with their
    blood.
And memorials of themselves for their
    parents at home
With  their hands they piled upon the
    chariot of Adrastes, shedding
A tear;—But there was no sigh escaped
    their lips.
For an iron spirit burning with bravery
Breathed in them, as lions beholding
    battle

And these things I inform you are not
    delayed by sloth
But I left them drawing lots, how each
    of them by lot
Should lead a band against the gates.
Therefore the best men chosen of the
    city
arrange quickly at the passages of the
    gates;
For now at hand completely Armed the
    Host of Argives
Approaches, raises the dust, and the
    plains the white foam
stains, in drops from the horses' breasts.
But do you like a skilful helmsman of a
    ship
Fortify the city, before the blasts of war
    burst on it.
For roars the savage wave of an army;
And seize the season of these things as
    quick as possible;
And I for the rest a faithful
    daywatching
Eye will have and with clearness of
    words
Knowing the things without the gates,
    thou wilt be uninjured.

Et   O Zeus and Gaea and gods who have
    the city in your charge,
And powerful curse, my father's fury,
Do not eradicate my city from the
    stern—
Utterly destroyed captured by the
    enemy, spending
The tongue of Hellas, and domestic
    houses

But may the free land and the city of
    Cadmus
Never support the yoke of slavery;
Be ye an aid; for I trust I express a
    common interest;
For a city faring well honors the
    divinities.

Ch.   I lament fearful great woes,
The army has been let loose leaving
    the camp,
Flows numerous this host, forerunning
    on horse back;
In air a dust persuades me appearing,
Without speech, a clear true messenger;
And a sound rousing from my couch,
    caused by the trampling of horses
Approaches, flies,
And roars like
An irresistible water resounding among
    the mountains.
Alas Alas alas alas. Gods and goddesses
Avert the rushing evil.
Resounds above the walls
The white-shielded army rushes
Ready, hastening against the city.
Who then will deliver,
Who then will succour
Of Gods or goddesses?
Shall I then fall down
Before the images of the divinities?
O blessed well-seated,
It is high time to draw near the images.
Why do we delay deeply mourning?
Hear ye or hear ye not the clashing of
    shields?
Shall we have robes and garlands

Ever, if not now, for prayer?
I perceived a clash; a rattling not of
     one spear.
What wilt thou do? Wilt thou betray,
Aboriginal Ares,
Thy own land?
O golden-helmed divinity—regard regard
     the city,
If ever you esteemed it dear;
Gods protectors of this region
Come come all,
Behold of virgins
A suppliant band
On account of bondage.
For a wave of men
With bended crests
Excited by the blasts
Of war roars.
But o Zeus father entirely
Ward off capture by our foes.
For the Argives surround
The city of Cadmus; and fear of hostile
     arms;
And the bridles fastened to the horses'
     jaws
Rattle slaughter.
And Seven brave and distinguished
     men of their host
With spear-shaking shields, stand
     'gainst
The Seven gates, having by lot drawn
     them.
And thou o Zeus-born
War-loving head,
Be a defender of the city
Pallas, and thou horseman

Sea-ruling king
Neptune with thy fish-striking
Weapon give release
From fears a release.
And thou Ares, alas! alas!
Guard the city of Cadmus
Bearing his name,
And visibly take care of it.
And Cypris, who art original mother
Of our race, defend; from thy blood
We sprang; With prayers
Addressed to the gods entreating
We draw near to thee. And thou
Lycian king, be wolf-like
To the hostile army,
Like a battle cry of groans; and thou
O virgin descended from Latona
Prepare well thy bow
Dear Artemis. alas alas. alas. alas.
I hear a din of chariots round the city,
O reverend Juno;
The boxes of the heavily laden axles
    resound
Dear Artemis, alas. alas. alas. alas.
The spear-vexed atmosphere is mad.
What does my city suffer, what will
    become of it?
To what end does heaven lead us?
    alas. alas. alas. alas.
And stones come to the pointed
    battlements.
O dear Apollo,
A clashing in the gates of brass-bound
    shields,
And from Zeus
A war finishing holy end in fight;

And thou blessed queen
Ongca before the city
Defend the seven-gated seat.
O ye all mighty gods
And goddesses of perfect power
Guardians of this land
Betray not the city exposed to the
    spear–
To a host speaking a strange tongue
Hear us Virgins,
Hear our wholly-just
And suppliant prayers.
O Dear divinities
With power to deliver surrounding
    the city,
Show yourselves friendly to the city
Care for the sacred gifts of the people,
And caring help;
And be mindful to me
Of the sacrifice-loving orgies
Of the city

Et.    I ask you, race not to be borne,
Are these things best and bringing
    safety to the city,
And courage to this besieged army,
Falling down before the images of the
    city-guarding gods,
To sigh, and shriek, objects of hatred to
    the wise?
Neither in ills nor in sweet prosperity–
Would I be a dweller with the race of
    woman.
For prevailing her insolence is not to
    be borne;
And fearing, to house and city the
    more evil.

And now producing in the citizens
    these flights
Running hither and thither, ye spread
    spiritless fear;
And the affairs of those without the
    gates as well as ye can assist;
And we by ourselves within are
    worsted.
Such things dwelling with a woman
    thou wouldst have.
And if any one shall not obey my
    authority,
Man or woman, or whatever is between
    them,
A ruinous decree shall be pronounced
    against them,
And by no means may he escape death
    by being stoned by the people.
For it concerns a man, let not a woman
    consider
Things without; but being within, do
    no harm.
Dost thou hear—or dost thou not hear,
    or do I speak to a deaf person?

Ch.    O dear offspring of OEdipus, I feared
        hearing
    The tumult of rattling chariots
    And when the hollow naves resounded,
        and
    The sleepless rudders in the mouths
        of the horses,
    The bridles wrought by fire.

Et.    What then; does the sailor forsooth
        flying to the prow
    From the stern find means of safety,

His vessel laboring with a wave of
   the sea?

Ch.   But to the ancient statues of the gods
       Hastening I came, trusting to the gods,
          when
       There was the roaring at the gates of a
          destructive snow storm falling,
       Then indeed through fear I offered
          up prayers to the gods,
       That they might hold their strength
          over the city.

Et.   Pray that our towers ward off the
          hostile spear.

Ch   Will not this be by favor of the gods.

Et                   But then as for the gods
       There is a saying that they desert a
          captured city.

Ch.   Never in my life may this general
          assembly of the gods
       Desert us, nor may I see
       This city taken by storm, and an army
       Setting to it hostile fire.

Et   Do not calling on the gods, consult ill.
       For obedience is the mother of success,
       The wife of the savior; such is the
          saying.

Ch.   There is to the gods a power superior;
       And often in evils, the remediless cloud
       Of severe woe hung o'er
       Our eyes, it may clear away

Et   These things are the duty of men, the
          slaughter and the sacrifice

To perform to the gods, the enemy
    endeavoring;
But thine on the other hand to be silent;
    and remain within the house.

Ch.   Through the gods we possess our city
    unsubdued
And our tower keeps off the host of
    enemies.
What wrath hates these things?

Et.   By no means am I unwilling that you
    should honor the race of the gods;
But that you may not make the citizens
    faint hearted,
Be composed, nor (greatly) fear
    (excessively).

Ch.   Hearing a strange noise, with
Trembling fear to this acropolis,
Honorable seat, I came.

Et.   Do not now, if ye hear of dead or
Wounded burst straightway into
    lamentations.
For Ares feeds upon this blood of men.

Ch.   Surely I hear the snorting of horses.

Et.   Hearing, hear not now too plainly.

Ch.   The city resounds from the ground, as
    if surrounded.

Et.   But it is enough that I consult for
    these things.

Ch.   I fear—for the clashing in the gates
    increases.

Et   Will you not be silent? Say none of
these things in the city.

Ch   O assembly, do not betray our towers.

Et   Destruction! will you not bear these
things in silence

Ch.   Citizen gods—let me not obtain slavery.

Et.   Thyself wouldst enslave both me—and
thee and the city.

Ch.   O all-powerfull Zeus, turn thy weapon
'gainst the enemy.

Et.   O Zeus of women what a race you have
bestowed.

Ch.   Wretched, as men, when their city is
taken.

Et.   Dost thou lament again, touching again
the statues?

Ch.   For want of energy fear possesses my
tongue.

Et   Me asking wouldst thou grant a slight
thing.

Ch.   Say it at once and quickly I shall
know it.

Et.   Be silent, o wretched one, frighten not
thy friends.

Ch.   I will be silent; with the rest I'll suffer
what is fated.

Et   This word instead of those I will prefer
of yours.

And beside these, being far from the
   statues,
Pray the gods to be our allies unto
   better things;
Hearing my wishes, then do thou
For thy lament sing the sacred and
   enlivening paean,
The Hellenic custom of the Priestess'
   shout.
Courage to thy friends, banishing the
   fear of the enemy
And I to the guardian deities of this
   region,
Guarding the plain and overseeing the
   market place,
At Dirce's fountains, nor do I refuse
   Ismenus,
Succeeding well, and the city having
   been saved,
Staining with blood of sheep the
   hearths of the gods,
And slaying bullocks to the gods, I
   here vow
To place trophies, the garments of the
   enemy
Spoils taken by the spear from our foes,
   in their sacred houses.
Such things vow not with lamentations
   to the gods,
Nor in vain and rude sighs.
For not at all the more mayst thou
   escape what's fated.
But I going will arrange six men,
Myself the seventh, Answering to the
   enemy in dreadful wise,

At the entrances of the seven gates,
Before fleet messages and, and
   swift-running
Words, arrive, and I am set on fire
   by necessity.

[EXIT ETEOCLES]

Ch.   It concerns, my mind will not rest;
     But near my heart cares
     Kindle fear,
     Of the host around the walls;
     As some all trembling dove,
     Sleepless upon her nest,
     Fears for her young
     The serpent.
     For some against the towers
     With all their host, with all their crowd,
     March. What may become of us?
     Others against the uncertain
     Citizens hurl
     The rough stone.
     By every means, O Zeus-born
     Gods, city and army
     Of Kadmus' race, protect.
     What plain of earth will ye receive
        in exchange
     More excellent than this, yielding to
        the enemy
     The deep-soiled ground,
     And the water of Dirce
     Fattest of drinks,
     As many as earth-shaking
     Neptune emits,
     And the children of Tethys?
     Therefore, O city-guarding
     Gods, Sending among

Those without the towers, Man-
Destroying Calamity, causing to cast
   away
The arms, take
Glory; And to the loud-wailing
Supplications of the citizens
May ye stand defenders of the city—
And well seated.
For pitiable this Ogygian city
To send before its time to Hades, prey
   of the spear—
The slave of filthy ashes,
Being laid waste disgracefully
By an Achaean man, with the help of
   heaven.
And the captured females lead,
Alas! alas! alas!, both young and old,
Like horses by halters,
Their garments rent.
And echoes the emptied city,
The confusedly murmuring herd
   being destroyed;
Indeed I fear heavy calamities.
And it is to be wept for those who have
   hardly passed the age of childhood
That they must go the hateful way
   from their homes
With the prospect of being violated
   before ripe.
What? For I declare that he dead
Does better than these.
For when a city is subdued,
Alas! alas! alas! many unfortunate
   things are done.
One attacks another,
Murders, and sets fire to things;

With smoke all the city is blackened
And furious Ares inspires,
Destroying the people, defiling piety.
And tumults through the city,
and Against the city a hedge of turrets.
And man by man is killed with the
    spear;
And the bloody bleatings
Of those at the breast—
new-born resound.
And kindred plunder of those running
    hither & thither
He carrying fights with him carrying,
And the empty calls to him empty,
Wishing to have a companion
Nor left with less, nor equal.
What can words compare to these
    things?
And fruit from various soils
Falling on the ground, makes it groan
    lighting upon it.
And sad the eye of the bridegrooms;
And many a gift of earth
Indiscriminately mingled, with trifling
Impetuosity is borne along
And the young members of the
    commonwealth newly afflicted,
Wretched, a man obtaining
Their captured bed, as
A superior enemy.
Hope is that a nightly end may come,
Defender from very grievous sufferings.

Semich.    The watch, as it seems to me, brings
    Some new account to us my friends, of
        the host,

With zeal impelling the carrying
   axletrees of his feet

Semich.   Indeed the king himself offspring of
      OEdipus
   Comes to learn the messengers report
      of new arrangements
   But his zeal does not equal the foot
      of this one.

Scout   I would tell, well knowing, the affairs
      of our opponents,
   How in the gates each one drew his lot
   Tydeus forsooth now thunders at the
      Proetian
   Gate, for the sooth sayer does not
      permit to pass
   The ford of Ismenus; for these victims
      are not good.
   But Tydeus furious and earnestly
      desiring battle,
   As a dragon raging with noonday
      hissings, shouts,
   And assaults with reproach the prophet,
      wise OEclides
   That he shakes through want of spirit
      at fate and battle;
   Shouting such things he shakes his
      three shady
   Crests, the hair of his helm, and under
      his shield
   The brazen driven bosses resound fear;
   And he has this proud design upon
      his shield,
   A heaven burning with stars wrought;
   And a bright full moon in the midst of
      the shield,

Oldest of stars, eye of night, excels.

Such furious with his overboasting
   shields,

He shouts along the river's banks,
   desirous of battle,

As a horse waits panting upon the bits,

Who waiting the sound of the trumpet,
   rushes in anticipation.

Whom will you range gainst him? Who
   at the gate of Proetus

The bars being loosed, to stand before
   them a sufficient surety?

E   I should not tremble at any ornament
   of a man,

Nor are symbols wounding;

And crest and boss do not wound
   without spear.

And this night which you describe to be

Upon a shield glittering with the stars
   of heaven

Perhaps, may be prophet the thought to
   some one.

For if night should fall over the eyes
   of him dying—

Him bearing this overboastful symbol,

It would be rightly and justly
   described,

And himself against himself will
   insolently foretel injury.

But to Tydeus, the prudent son of
   Astacus

Him will I oppose to stand before
   the gates,

Both well-born, and honoring the
   throne

Of modesty, and hating haughty words.
For he is not a doer of base deeds, and
    does not love to be a coward.
From Spartan men whom Ares spared
His root proceeded, and he is wholly
    of this region,
Melanippus; His work in dice Ares
    decides;
And kindred justice surely sends him
    to the field
To ward off from the mother who bore
    him the spear of the enemy.

Ch.   Him who now contends for me may the
       gods
    Give to succeed, since justly he rushes
    To fight before the city: but I tremble
    The blood-bringing fates to behold
    On account of my friends destroyed.

Sc.   To him indeed thus to succeed may
       the gods give
    But Kapaneus has drawn the Electraean
       gate;
    A giant he another than the before
       named
    Greater; And his boast not according
       to man is conceived;
    And he threatens terrible things to the
       towers, which may not fate perform;
    For Heaven willing he will utterly lay
       waste the city
    And not willing he says, nor the wrath
       of Zeus
    Rushing upon the plain shall hold him
       off.
    Lightnings and thunderbolts

He likens to noon-day heats;
And he has a device, a naked man
　　bearing fire,
And there burns a torch in his hands
　　furnished;
And in golden letters he says, I will
　　burn the city.
To such a man send, who will
　　withstand him,
Who a boasting man not trembling
　　will await.

Et　　And by this advantage another
　　　advantage is produced.
Of vain resolves indeed the true tongue
Is accuser to men.
But Capaneus threatens, prepared to
　　execute,
Dishonoring the gods, and exercising
　　his mouth,
With vain joy being mortal against
　　heaven
He sends joyful out-waving words to
　　Zeus.
But I trust the fire-bearing bolt will
　　come to him
With justice, made nothing like
The midday heats of the sun.
But a man against him, even if he is
　　prompt with his tongue very,
A burning resolution has been
　　stationed, Polyphontes' force,
A sufficient protection, by the good
　　will of Artemis
His protectress, and by the other gods.
Mention another having obtained
　　another gate.

Ch.    May he perish, who boasts great things
           against the city,
       And may a thunder-bolt restrain him,
       Before he leaps against my house,
           and utterly
       Lays waste the virgin apartments
       Ever with keen-cutting spear.

Sc.    And him next having obtained by lot
           (to stand) against the gates
       I will tell; for to Eteocles third the
           third lot
       Leaped from the high helm of fair
           brass,
       Against the gate of Neis to strike his
           band.
       And he whirls his horses in bridles
           raging against
       Wishing to fall against the gate–
       And their bridles rattle in a
           barbarous manner,
       With snorting breath filled
       And his shield has been fashioned not
           in a trivial manner;
       But an armed man marches to the
           ascents of the ladder
       Against an enemys tower, wishing to
           destroy it utterly.
       And this one shouts in syllables of
           letters,
       That not even would Ares thrust him
           out from the towers;
       And gainst this man send the
           sufficient surety;
       To keep off from this city the yoke of
           slavery.

Et   Such an one would I now send and with
fortune against him;

And indeed he has been sent having
his boast in his hands,

Megareus of the seed of Kreon, of the
race of the Spartans,

Who not at all fearing the loud sound
of the greedy snorting

Of the horses will go from the gate;

But either dying he will fully pay to
the earth the cost of his support,

Or having taken the two men, and the
city

On the shield, with the spoils will deck
his father's house.

Boast against another, nor envy me
words.

Ch.   I pray indeed that it may fare well with
this one,

O champion of my house, and ill with
them.

And as they go boastfully against the
city

With furious mind, thus Zeus the
dispenser of justice,

May behold them, angry.

Sc.   Fourth another, having the
neighboring gate

Of Onca Athene, with a shout stands
by,

The form of Hippomedon, and great
figure;

And the large halo, I mean the circle of
his shield,

I shuddered as he whirled it; not
  otherwise will I say.
He who wrought the device was not
  indeed any mean person,
Who bestowed this work upon the
  shield,
Typhon casting out through (his)
  fire-breathing mouth
Dark smoke, whirling brother of fire;
And the surrounding space of the
  hollow-bellied circle
With folds of serpents touches the
  ground.
And he raises the cry of battle, and
  inspired by Ares
Raves violently, as Thyas, looking fear.
Such a mans endeavor is well to be
  guarded against.
For fear already swaggers at the gates.

Et.  First Onca Pallas, who is near the city,
  Near to the gates hating the insolence
    of the man,
  Will restrain him from her young as a
    furious dragon;
  And Hyperbius, illustrious offspring
    of OEnops
  A man against this man has been
    chosen, wishing
  To seek out fate, in practice of fortune;
  Nor in form nor spirit nor the holding
    of his arms,
  To be blamed, but Hermes fitly
    conferred on him.
  For hostile thus man shall withstand
    man.

And it is to be contended by hostile
   gods upon
Their shields; for the one has fire-
   breathing Typhon
But to Hyperbius Zeus the father upon
   his shield
Sits firm, in his hand burning his bolt;
And not yet any one saw Zeus ever
   conquered.
Such then the friendship of the
   divinities;
We are under the protection of the
   victors, they of the defeated,
If Zeus indeed is stronger than Typhon
   in battle;
And it is probable that thus the
   contending men will do;
To Hyperbius, on account of his device,
Zeus may be savior happening to be on
   his shield.

Ch.   I trust that the antagonist of Zeus
     having
On his shield the unfriendly body of
   the earthly
Demon, an odious image to mortals and
To the long-lived gods, before
The gates will lay his head.

Sc.   So may it be! but the fifth again I tell,
Stationed at the fifth Borraean gate,
By the tomb itself of Zeus-born
     Amphion;
And he swears by the spear, which he
   holds, trusting

To reverence it more than a god, above
    his eyes,
That he will lay waste the city of the
    Cadmeans in spite
Of Zeus; this says the fair-browed
    offspring
Of a mountain-dwelling mother, a man-
    child man.
And the down lately goes through his
    cheeks,
His season producing it, thick hair
    rising.
He having a fierce thought that could
    by no means be attributed
To woman, and a terrible eye, stands
    against.
Not indeed without boast does he take
    his stand against the gate;
For the reproach of the city on a
    brazen-nailed
Shield, on the rounded prominence of
    its body,
A sphinx eating raw flesh with her
    jaws, fixed on,
He brandished, a bright raised body,
And she bears under her a man one of
    the Cadmeans,
As many weapons as possible against
    this man must be hurled.
For he seems to have come not to retail
    a trade of battle
And not to disgrace the delay of a
    long way,
Parthenopaeus of Arcadia, he such a
    man,

Who resided with us, repaying Argos for
    his fair nourishment,
He threatens the towers with such
    things, which may not heaven
    perform.

Et.    Aye may they obtain what they
    meditate, by the gods,
With those same unholy boasts;
Aye may he perish with all ruin and
    disgrace.
But there is to this one, whom you
    name the Arcadian,
A man without boast, and his hand sees
    what's to be done;
Actor brother of the before named,
Who will not permit the tongue,
    without deeds,
Rushing within the gate, to increase
    evils;
Nor him to enter into the city bearing
    the image of that
Most odious ravenous beast upon his
    hostile shield;
She shall blame him carrying her from
    without within,
Obtaining frequent blows under the
    city.
The gods willing I should speak truth.

Ch.    Comes the word through my breasts,
And the curls of my hair stand upright,
    hearing greatly boasting impious
Men. O that the gods would destroy
    them in the earth.

Sc.    Sixth I would mention a man wisest
    of all

And in strength best a prophet force of
    Amphiareaus;
And at the Omolaean gate stationed.
With evil words he utters many things
    against the force of Tydeus,
The man-slayer, the disturber of the
    city,
The greatest teacher of evils to Argos,
Caller of Erinnys, servant of murder,
Council chamber of these evils to
    Adrastus;
And thy brother too worthy of death
Inspecting his name—the force of
    Polynices,
And in two at last distributing the
    name,
He calls. And he says this word with
    his mouth;
Surely such a deed is both agreeable to
    the gods,
And fair to hear, and tell to those
    coming after,
Thy native city and thy country's gods,
To lay waste, leading against them a
    foreign host.
But what justice will extinguish the
    tears of thy mother?
And thy father land by thy zeal by the
    spear
Taken, how will it be to thee and ally?
I myself indeed shall make fat this
    ground,
A prophet buried under a hostile soil.
Let us fight, I hope no dishonorable
    fate.

Such things the prophet, brandishing a
  well rounded shield
All of brass, said. But there was no
  device upon its circle.
For not to seem best but to be so he
  wishes,
Bearing fruit in a deep furrow in his
  mind,
From which spring glorious counsels.
Gainst him both wise and good
  opponents
I exhort to send. Terrible he who
  reverences the gods.

Et   Alas the omen mingling a just man
With the more impious mortals.
In every deed there is than evil
  fellowship
Nothing worse, fruit is not to be
  derived;
(Ate's field bears death for fruit.)
Forsooth a pious man having embarked
  in a vessel
With sailors desperate and any craft,
perishes with the god-abhorred race
  of men;
He being just, with fellow citizen men,
Inhospitable and forgetful of the gods,
Falling unjustly into the same snare,
Struck by the all-common lash of
  heaven is subdued.
And this one the prophet, I mean the
  son of OEcleus,
Prudent, just, good, reverent man,
Great prophet, mingled with unholy
Bold-mouthed men in spite of sense

Aiming the long pomp again to go,
Zeus willing, shall be drawn down
   together with them.
I think therefore that he shall not
   smite the gate,
Not as wanting spirit, nor by cowardice
   of resolution;
But he knows, that it is necessary he
   should die in battle,
If there shall be fruit to the prophecies
   of the Loxian.
But he loves to be silent or to speak
   what is reasonable.
But however, against him a man force
   of Lasthenes,
An inhospitable doorkeeper I will
   oppose.
Old the mind, but a body blooming he
   bears,
A foot-swift eye, and he does not
   slowly move his hand
To grasp from the shield a naked spear,
But it is the gift of heaven for mortals
   to be fortunate.

Ch.   Gods hearing our just
     Prayers accomplish that the city may
        be prosperous,
     Turning aside from the land evils
        wrought by the spear against
     The invaders; And casting without the
        towers
     May Zeus kill them with his
        thunderbolt.

Sc.   The seventh indeed this one against the
     7$^{th}$ gate

I will mention, the brother of thyself,
What fates he imprecates and prays
    against the city;
Assaulting the towers, and menacing
    the land,
The captive paean vociferating against
    it,
With thee to encounter, and killing to
    die near,
Or living the thus dishonorer banishing,
    man
To requite with banishment in the
    same manner.
Such things says, and the native gods
Calls of his father land, to be wholly
    observers
of his prayers force of Polynices
And he has a new-put together and well
    made shield,
And a double device fixed to it.
For wrought of gold a soldier to see
Some woman leads modestly leading.
And (she) justice to be he says, as
    the letters
Say. I will restore this man and he
    shall have
His native city, and the return to
    his home.
Such of them are the inventions.
But do you yourself now know whom
    you think to send;
As never this man for his heraldings
Will you blame, but know yourself to
    steer the city.

Et.    O god-mad and great hatred of the gods,
       O all-wept my race of OEdipus;

Alas. Surely now the curses of my
    father are brought to an end.
But neither to weep nor to lament is
    becoming,
Lest then may be produced a more
    intolerable grief
And to Polynices surely named after
    (the fact) I say
Quickly we shall know where the
    devices end;
If gold-wrought letters shall restore
    him,
Boiling out upon his shield with rage
    of mind.
But if the virgin child of Zeus Dice
    were present
To his deeds and mind, perhaps would
    this be.
But neither him fleeing the darkness of
    his mother,
Nor in his education, Nor arriving at
    the age of puberty ever
Nor in the gathering of down upon
    his cheek,
Did Dice look upon and think him
    worthy (her attention);
Nor yet in this ill treatment of his
    father land
Do I think that she now stands by him.
Surely she would be quite falsely
    named
Dice, associating with a man daring
    all in his mind.
To these trusting I go, and will
    withstand him
Myself, what other more justly?

To ruler ruler, and to brother brother,
Foe with foe I will stand. Bring quick
   as possible
Greaves, spear, and shield of stones.

Ch.   Dearest of men, offspring of OEdipus,
     be
Not in wrath like him speaking the
   worst things.
But there are enough Cadmean men to
   go to blows
With the Argives; for their blood may
   be expiated.
But of men of the same blood the death
   thus self-slaying,
There is not old age of this pollution.

Et   If indeed anyone may bear evil, without
   disgrace,
Be it so; for alone is there gain to the
   dead;
But of evil and base things you will not
   say there is any glory.

Ch.   And dost thou remain a child? Let not
Calamity filled with rage spear-mad
   carry thee; Cast out
Beginning of evil desire.

Et   When the deed surely heaven urges on,
Let all the race of Laius hateful to
   Phoebus
Go with a favorable wind obtaining the
   wave of Cocytus.

Ch.   Very biting desire excites thee
Bitter-fruited manslaying to perform
Of unlawful blood.

Et  For my dear father's base-performing
curse
With dry unwept eyes sits near,
Saying gain before the after fate.

Ch.  But be thou not incited. Coward thou
wilt not
Be called, leading thy life well;
blackrushing Erinnys
Does not enter the houses, when from
the hands
The gods receive sacrifice.

Et.  By the gods now somehow we have
been neglected,
And favor ceases to respect us
destroyed;
Why then yet should we cringe to
destructive fate?

Ch  Now it stands near thee; since the
divinity
Changed by a timely change of
resolution
Would perhaps come with a more
genial
Breath; but now yet it rages.

Et.  Aye, the imprecations of OEdipus boil
over,
And very true visions of phantasms
in sleep
Distributing my father's possessions.

Ch.  Obey a woman, although not of like
breast.

Et.  What accomplishment of what (would
be said); nor is it necessary to be
long.

Ch.   Nay you may not go this way to the
        7<sup>th</sup> gate.

Et    Me whetted thou wilt not take off the
        edge with your words.

Ch.   Victory however if it is bad heaven
        punishes.

Et.   It does not behove an armed man to
        love this word.

Ch.   But dost thou wish to shed the blood
        of thy own brother?

Et.   The gods giving, he would not escape
        evils.

Ch.   I shudder at the house-destroying
        Goddess, not like the gods,
        All true, prophetess of ill
        O my father, Erinnys desired
        To perform the violent
        Curses of OEdipus deranged in mind.
        And this child-destroying strife excites
            her.
        But a foreign colonist from the mines
        Of the Scythians distributes the lots,
        A stern distributor
        Of possessions, cruel minded iron,
        shaking asunder ground to inhabit,
        Whatever they may slain occupy,
        Without any share in the great plains.
        When suicidally
        Slain by each others hands they may
            die,
        And dust of the earth may drink
        Their black-clotted bloody blood,
        Who would extend purifications,

Who would wash them? O
New afflictions of the houses
Mingled with former evils.
I mean forsooth the ancient
Transgression bringing swift
   vengeance;
And it remains to the third age.
When Laius, in spite
Of Apollo, thrice saying
In Pythian oracles
In the middle of the earth, that dying
Without progeny, he would save the
   city,
Overcome by the evil counsels of
   friends
He begat indeed death to himself,
Father-slaying OEdipus,
Who not in a holy
Field sowing, where he was nourished,
A bloody root
Suffered.  folly brought together
insane bride & bridegroom;
And a wave of ills like the sea strikes;
One fallen another rises
Threefold, which round the stern
Of the city roars.
but between a strength for a short time
Extends a tower in breadth.
But I fear with kings
Lest the city be subdued.
For to be performed are the old-spoken
   curses,
Severe the changes,
And the ruinous things omitted.
And wealth grown very fat
Of inventive men,

Brings a casting-overboard to the
  very stern.
For what man so much did the gods
Admire who dwelt with him
In the city, and the life of mortals
  nourishing many,
As then they honored OEdipus,
Having removed from the region
A man-seizing fate?
And when he became
Sensible of the oracle of wretched
Marriage, at grief of his misfortunes
With maddened heart
He did double evils;
With parricidal hand he wandered
From the eyes of those who had better
  children.
And to the children of accursed
Cherishing he furious discharged
Alas! alas! bitter-tongued curses,
And them with iron-lawed
Hand ever to obtain
Possessions; and now I tremble
Lest the crooked footed Erinnys
  perform. (them)

Sc.   Be of good courage children, cherished
        of your mothers.
      This city has escaped the yoke of
        slavery;
      The boasts of violent men have fallen;
      And the city in fair weather and in
        the many blows
      Of the billows did not receive (water
        into the hold)
      But the tower protects, And we fortified

The gates with sufficient single
  fighting champions;
Well are most things in six gates;
But the awful king Apollo has taken
The seven the chiefs
Performing the old ill counsels of Laius.

Ch.   What is the matter new raging present
      to the city?

Sc.   (The city has been saved, but the kings
      of one seed)
    Men have died, by their own-slaying
      hands * * *

Ch.   Who? What did you say? I am beside
      myself with fear of your word.

Sc.   Thoughtful now hear,–the race of
      OEdipus.

Ch.   O I wretched, prophetess I of evils.

Sc.   Nor doubtfully indeed–(that) they have
      been cut down.

Ch.   Did they come to that? Indeed it is
      heavy, but tell.

Sc.   Thus by fraternal hands they were
      destroyed with violence.

Ch   Thus the Fate was common to both
      together

Sc.   The same surely may destroy the
      illstarred race.
    Such things to rejoice and to bemoan it
      is allowed;
    The city on the one hand doing well,
      but the rulers

2 commanders, have shared by the
    hammer-wrought
Scythian iron the whole abundance of
    their possessions.
And they will have of land what they
    may take in burial,
According to the unhappy prayers of
    their father (taken away)
The city has been saved; and earth has
    drank the blood
Of kings of the same seed by one
    another's murder.

Ch.   O great Zeus and City-holding
Gods, who indeed these towers
Of Cadmus defend;
Whether shall I rejoice, and cry aloud
To the unhurt savior of the city,
Or weep the miserable & unfortunate
Childless polemarchs?
Who surely rightly according to the
    name
And much-striving
Were destroyed by impious thought.
O black and perfect
Curse of the race of OEdipus,
Some evil chill falls around my heart;
I composed a song for the tombs
As Priestess of Bacchus, blood-dropping
Dead weeping unfortunate
Having died; Surely illomened this
Concert of the spear.
The desired saying of the father
Accomplished, nor refused;
And the incredible counsels of Laius
    prevailed.

And miseries about the city,
And oracles of the gods are not blunted.
O causing many groans you have done
This incredible thing; And came
The bewailed sufferings not in word.
These of themselves—plain—before our
    eyes the messengers word.
Double sorrows, evils of two
Men slain by themselves, double
Perfect these sufferings. What may I
    say?
Some others labor surely may labor
Sitting on the hearths of the houses.
But, friends, with a fair wind of
    lamentations
Row around the head a conveying
    motion
Of the hands, which ever conveys
    through Acheron
The groanless, black-sailed
Navigated bark,
To the untracked by Apollo, the sunless,
All-receiving, invisible waste.
But these come to a sad affair
Antigone and Ismene,
The Mourning of their brothers, not
    dubiously
I think that they from their loving
    deep-bosomed
Breasts will send forth worthy grief.
But it is just that we howl before
Relating, the sad sounding hymn of
Erinnys, and to Hades
Chant the hostile paean.

Semich.     O most ill brothered of all, as many as
            Cast a girdle twisted round their
                clothing,
            I weep, I groan, and no deception
            That I do not in my mind rightly
                delight with sounds of joy.

Semich.     Oh oh. unfortunate,
            Not trusting your friends, and
                unexhausted of evils,
            Your fathers house taking
            Unfortunate with force.

Semich.     Unfortunate surely, who unfortunate
                deaths
            Found in the ruin of your house.

Semich      Oh Oh destroying the walls
            Of the houses, and the odious
                monarchies
            Looking after, now ye have obtained
            The lot of the sword,
            (Not by friendship
            But by murder ye determined;)
            And surely the awful Erinnys of father
            OEdipus has performed true things.

Semich      by well named struck.

Semich.     Struck indeed, of
            Kindred sides.

Semich      Alas! alas! unhappy
            Alas! Alas! curses
            Of deaths to be atoned for by deaths.

Semich.     You tell a piercing wound.

Semich      In houses and in bodies
            Struck I reproach.

Semich.   It remains to chide the untold
          & Accursed double
          Fate from the father.

Semich.   And A groan has gone through
          The city, the towers groan,
          Groans the man-loving plain;
          And possessions remain for the
              descendants,
          On account of which to them
              unfortunate
          On account of which strife arose,
          And the end of death;
          And they irascible obtained
          Possessions, such as it was just they
              should obtain;
          Reconciler not without blame to friends,
          Nor is Ares Agreeable.

Semich.   Struck with steel thus they fare.

Semich    And struck with steel await them
          Perhaps some one may say, Who?
          The lots (fates) of their paternal
              graves.

Semich.   Surely an echo of the houses against
              them
          Sends forth piercing lamentation,
          Groaning for itself, suffering–for itself,
          Hostile, not fond of mirth, truly
          Pouring out from the heart, which,
          I weeping, diminishes,
          For these two beings.
          And it is permitted to say to the
          Wretched, that they did
          Many things indeed to the citizens
          And the destructive ranks
          Of all foreigners in war.

Semich.    Unhappy she who bore them
           Of all women, as many as
           Have been called child-bearing.
           Making the child of herself husband
               to herself,
           She bore these; who thus have died by
           Oneanother's murderous kindred
               hands.

Ismene     Of one seed surely and wholly ruined,
           Not by friendly divisions
           By mad strife

Semich.    Stern deliverer from contentions, the
               marine
           Foreigner from fire shaken
           Whetted iron; Severe
           And evil distributer of property
                    Mars making
           True the curse of the father.

Antigone   They have their lot having obtained,
               o unfortunate,
           Zeus-given misfortunes;
           And under the body of the earth
           A very deep wealth shall be.

Is.        O houses blooming
           With many afflictions;
           And finally these curses
           Have screeched the stern law,
           The race being turned
           In all-turning flight.
           And the Demon has placed
           A trophy of Ate
           In the gates, in which they died,
           And conquering the two, has ceased.

Antigone.  Struck thou struck'st.

Is.                    And thou died'st
           killing

An.  By the spear thou didst kill.

Is.                    And with the
           spear thou didst die.

An.  Unfortunate–laborer

Is.                    Unfortunate
           sufferer.

An.  Flow tears

Is.           Flow lamentation.

An.  He that slew shall be exposed.
     Alas! Alas! my mind is mad with
        lamentations.

Is.  and within my heart groans.

An.  Alas alas much-wept thou.

Is.  and thou too all all-wretched.

An.  By a friend thou wast destroyed.

Is   And a friend thou slew'est

An.  Double to tell

Is                    And double to see.

An.  Such griefs are these things near

Is.  Near these sisters to their brothers.

An.  O Fate afflicting, unfortunate,
     And awful shade of OEdipus,
     Black Erinnys, surely of great strength
        some one thou art.

Is. Alas! alas! hurts not to be witnessed
   He showed from flight to me.

An. Nor did he come when he had slain.

Is. For being saved he lost his breath.

An. He lost it surely.

Is       And that of this one
   took away.

An. Wretched race.

Is       Wretched too they
   suffered
   Grievous woes of the same-name.

An. Twice wet with triple woes.

Is Sad to tell.

An.      And sad to see
   O Fate afflicting, intolerable,
   And awful shade of OEdipus,
   Black Erinnys, surely of great strength
     some one thou art.
   Thou then knowst entirely

Is. And thou nothing afterwards learning.

An. When you came to the city.

Is Antagonist with spear to him

An. Sad to tell.

Is     And sad to see.

An. Oh affliction.

Is      Oh oh. evils to the houses
   And the land, and before all to me.

An. Alas! Alas! and besides indeed to me.

Is    Alas alas of grievous ills
      King Eteocles author.

An    Oh most lamentable of all

Is.   Oh furious in woe.

An.   Oh oh. where shall we bury them in
          the land?
      Oh where (it is) most honorable.

Is.   Oh oh. the misery lying by the father.

Herald.   What seems good and has seemed good
              to the counsellors of the people
          It behoves me to announce–of this
              Cadmean city;
          This Eteocles for his good will to the
              land
          To bury has seemed good with friendly
              burial;
          For keeping off the enemy he received
              death in the city;
          And holy with respect to his country's
              rights, being without blame
          He died when it is beautiful for the
              young to die.
          So indeed about this one it has been
              ordered to say.
          But this one's brother this corse of
              Polynices–
          To cast out unburied, a prey to dogs,
          As being a destroyer of the Cadmean
              land,
          Unless some one of the gods had stood
              in the way of
          His spear. But a chief even dead he
              shall obtain

His countrys gods, whom he
   dishonoring,
A foreign army leading was taking the
   city.
So by winged birds it seems good that
   this one
Disgracefully buried, receive this
   reward;
And neither burial rights accompany,
Nor show respect by shrill-sounding
   lamentations,
And to be without the honor of burial
   by friends;
Such seemed good to this authority of
   the Cadmeans.

An.   But I say to the rulers of the Cadmean
If not any other wishes to bury him
   with me,
I will bury him, and renounce danger,
Burying my brother, nor am I
   ashamed
Having this disobedient anarchy to the
   city.
Terrible the common womb, from
   which we were born,
Of a wretched mother, and from an
   unfortunate father.
Therefore my soul willing shares the ill
   he suffered
Unwilling, alive him dead with kindred
   mind.
And his flesh hollow-bellied wolves
Shall not devour; Let it not seem good
   to any.
For sepulchre myself and burial I

Though I am a woman, for him I will
  contrive
Bearing in the bosom of my linen robe.
And myself will bury; Nor to any let it
  seem good otherwise;
To courage efficient invention is
  present.

Herald    I tell thee not to do violence to the city
  in this.

An.    I tell thee not to proclaim superfluous
  things to me.

H.    Stern however a people having escaped
  ills.

An.    Make them stern, unburied this one
  shall not be.

H.    But whom the city hates, wilt thou
  honor with burial?

An.    Already the affairs of this one have
  not been celebrated with honor to the
  gods.

H.    Not indeed before this region he
  invaded with danger.

An.    Suffering ill, with evils he repaid.

H.    But against all instead of one this
  work was.

An.    Eris accomplishes her word, lowest of
  gods.
  And I will bury him; do not long-
  harangue.

H    Then self-willed be, but I declare it.

Semich.  Alas! alas! o great-boasting and race-
                destroying
            Fates Erinnyes, who the race
            Of OEdipus thus utterly have
                destroyed.

An.      What may I suffer? and what may I
                do? and what shall I resolve?
            How shall I endure not to weep thee,
            Nor accompany to the tomb?
            But I fear, and I am turned aside
            By fear of the citizens.

Semich   Thou indeed wilt obtain many
                mourners;
            But he the wretched unmourned.
            Having one-wept lamentation of a
                sister
            Goes. Who would these obey?

Semich.  Let the city do and let it not do
            To those who weep Polynices.
            We indeed go and will bury with thou
            Accompanying. For by birth
            Common this grief, and the city
            At other times in other cases praises
                justice.

Semich   But we with this one, as the city—
            And justice approves.
            For after the blessed and the force
                of Zeus,
            This one defended the city of the
                Cadmeans—
            Not to be destroyed, nor by a wave
                of foreign men
            Inundated for the most part.

                        (END)

# Pindar.

PINDAR is an empty name to all but Greek scholars. We have no reputation in literature comparable to his, which is so ill supported in English translation. The most diligent and believing student will not find one glance of the Theban eagle in West and his colleagues, who have attempted to clothe the bird with English plumage. Perhaps he is the most untranslatable of poets, and though he was capable of a grand national music, yet did not write sentences, which alone are conveyed without loss into another tongue. Some of our correspondents, who found aid and comfort in Mr. Thoreau's literal prose translations of Anacreon and of Æschylus, have requested him to give versions of the Olympic and Nemæan Odes; and we extract from his manuscripts a series of such passages as contain somewhat detachable and presentable in an English dress.

### SECOND OLYMPIC ODE.—109.

*Elysium.*

Equally by night always,
And by day, having the sun, the good
Lead a life without labor, not disturbing the
    earth
With violent hands, nor the sea water,
For a scanty living; but honored
By the gods, who take pleasure in fidelity
    to oaths,
They spend a tearless existence;
While the others suffer unsightly pain.
But as many as endured threefold
Probation, keeping the mind from all

Injustice, go the way of Zeus to Kronos' tower,
Where the ocean breezes blow around
The island of the Blessed; and flowers of
    gold shine,
Some on the land from dazzling trees,
And the water nourishes others;
With garlands of these they crown their hands
    and hair;
According to the just decrees of Rhadamanthus;
Whom Father Kronos, the husband of Rhea
Having the highest throne of all, has ready
    by himself as his assistant judge.
Peleus and Kadmus are regarded among these;
And his mother brought Achilles, when she had
Persuaded the heart of Zeus with prayers;
Who overthrew Hector, Troy's
Unconquered, unshaken column, and gave
    Cycnus
To death, and Morning's Æthiop son.

—

### OLYMPIC V.–34.

Always around virtues labor and expense
    strive toward a work
Covered with danger; but those succeeding
    seem to be wise even to the citizens.

—

### OLYMPIC VI.–14.

                Dangerless virtues,
Neither among men, nor in hollow ships,
Are honorable; but many remember if a fair
    deed is done.

## OLYMPIC VII.–100.

### *Origin of Rhodes.*

Ancient sayings of men relate,
That when Zeus and the Immortals divided
    earth,
Rhodes was not yet apparent in the deep sea;
But in salt depths the island was hid.
But Helius* being absent no one claimed for
    him his lot;
So they left him without any region for his
    share,
The pure god. And Zeus was about to make a
    second drawing of lots
For him warned. But he did not permit him;
For he said that within the white sea he had
    seen a certain land springing up from the
    bottom,
Capable of feeding many men, and suitable
    for flocks.
And straightway He commanded golden-
    filletted Lachesis
To stretch forth her hands, and not contradict
The great oath of the gods, but with the son
    of Kronos
Assent, that to the bright air being sent by
    his nod,
It should hereafter be his prize. And his words
    were fully performed,
Meeting with truth. The island sprang from
    the watery
Sea; and the genial Father of penetrating
    beams,
Ruler of fire-breathing horses, has it.

* The Sun.

### Olympic VIII.–95.

A man doing fit things
Forgets Hades.

—

### Olympic X.–59.

*Hercules names the Hill of Kronos.*

He named the Hill of Kronos, for before
    nameless,
While Œnomaus ruled, it was moistened with
    much snow,
And at this first rite the Fates stood by,
And Time, who alone proves
Unchanging truth.

—

### Olympic X.–85.

*Olympia at Evening.*

With the javelin Phrastor struck the mark;
And Eniceus cast the stone afar,
Whirling his hand, above them all,
And with applause it rushed
Through a great tumult;
And the lovely evening light
Of the fair-faced moon shone on the scene.

—

### Olympic X.–109.

*Fame.*

When, having done fair things, O Agesidamus,
Without the reward of song, a man may come
To Hades' rest, vainly aspiring
He obtains with toil some short delight.

But the sweet-voiced lyre,
And the sweet flute, bestow some favor;
For Zeus' Pierian daughters
Have wide fame.

———

### THE FOURTEENTH OLYMPIC ODE.

*To Asopichus, of Orchomenos, on his Victory
in the Stadic Course.*

O ye, who inhabit for your lot the seat of
    the Cephisian
Streams, yielding fair steeds, renowned Graces,
Ruling bright Orchomenos,
Protectors of the ancient race of Minyæ,
Hear, when I pray.
For with you are all pleasant
And sweet things to mortals;
If wise, if fair, if noble,
Any man. For neither do the gods,
Without the august Graces,
Rule the dance,
Nor feasts; but stewards
Of all works in heaven,
Having placed their seats
By golden-bowed Pythian Apollo,
They reverence the eternal power
Of the Olympian Father;
August Aglaia, and song-loving
Euphrosyne, children of the mightiest god,
Hear now, and Thalia loving-song,
Beholding this band, in favorable fortune
Lightly dancing; for in Lydian
Manner meditating,
I come celebrating Asopichus,

Since Minya by thy means is victor at the
    Olympic games.
Now to Persephone's*
Black-walled house go Echo,
Bearing to his father the famous news;
That seeing Cleodamus thou mayest say,
That in renowned Pisa's vale
His son crowned his young hair
With plumes of illustrious contests.

* Cleodamus, the father of the hero, was dead.

—

### FIRST PYTHIAN ODE.—8.

*To the Lyre.*

Thou extinguishest even the spear-like bolt
Of everlasting fire. And the eagle sleeps on the
    sceptre of Zeus,
Drooping his swift wings on either side,
The king of birds.

—25.

Whatever things Zeus has not loved
Are terrified, hearing
The voice of the Pierians,
On earth and the immeasurable sea.

—

### PYTH. II.—159.

A plain-spoken man brings advantage to
    every government,
To a monarchy, and when the
Impetuous crowd, and when the wise rule a
    city.

—

As a whole, the third Pythian Ode, to Hiero, on his
victory in the single-horse race, is one of the most memo-
rable. We extract first the account of

*Æsculapius.*

As many therefore as came suffering
From spontaneous ulcers, or wounded
In their limbs with glittering steel,
Or with the far-cast stone,
Or by the summer's heat o'ercome in body,
Or by winter, relieving he saved from
Various ills; some cherishing
With soothing strains,
Others having drunk refreshing draughts, or
    applying
Remedies to the limbs, others by cutting off
    he made erect.
But even wisdom is bound by gain,
And gold appearing in the hand persuaded
    even him with its bright reward,
To bring a man from death
Already overtaken. But the Kronian, smiting
With both hands, quickly took away
The breath from his breasts;
And the rushing thunderbolt hurled him to
    death.
It is necessary for mortal minds
To seek what is reasonable from the
    divinities,
Knowing what is before the feet, of what
    destiny we are.
Do not, my soul, aspire to the life
Of the Immortals, but exhaust the practicable
    means.

In the conclusion of the ode the poet reminds the
victor, Hiero, that adversity alternates with prosperity in
the life of man, as in the instance of

*Peleus and Cadmus.*

The Immortals distribute to men
With one good two

Evils. The foolish therefore
Are not able to bear these with grace,
But the wise, turning the fair outside.

But thee the lot of good fortune follows,
For surely great Destiny
Looks down upon a king ruling the people,
If on any man. But a secure life
Was not to Peleus, son of Æacus,
Nor to godlike Kadmus,
Who yet are said to have had
The greatest happiness
Of mortals, and who heard
The song of the golden-filletted Muses,
On the mountain, and in seven-gated Thebes,
When the one married fair-eyed Harmonia,
And the other Thetis, the illustrious daughter
    of wise-counselling Nereus.
And the gods feasted with both;
And they saw the royal children of Kronos
On golden seats, and received
Marriage gifts; and having exchanged
Former toils for the favor of Zeus,
They made erect the heart.
But in course of time
His three daughters robbed the one
Of some of his serenity by acute
Sufferings; when Father Zeus, forsooth, came
To the lovely couch of white-armed Thyone.
And the other's child, whom only the immortal
Thetis bore in Phthia, losing
His life in war by arrows,
Being consumed by fire excited
The lamentation of the Danaans.
But if any mortal has in his
Mind the way of truth,

It is necessary to make the best
Of what befalls from the blessed.
For various are the blasts
Of high-flying winds.
The happiness of men stays not a long time,
Though fast it follows rushing on.

Humble in humble estate, lofty in lofty,
I will be; and the attending dæmon
I will always reverence in my mind,
Serving according to my means.
But if Heaven extend to me kind wealth,
I have hope to find lofty fame hereafter.
Nestor and Lycian Sarpedon–
They are the fame of men–
From resounding words which skilful artists
Sung, we know.
For virtue through renowned
Song is lasting.
But for few is it easy to obtain.

—

## PYTH. IV.–59.

### *Origin of Thera*,

Whence, in after times, Libyan Cyrene was settled by
Battus. Triton, in the form of Eurypylus, presents a clod
to Euphemus, one of the Argonauts, as they are about
to return home.

He knew of our haste,
And immediately seizing a clod
With his right hand, strove to give it
As a chance stranger's gift.
Nor did the hero disregard him, but leaping
    on the shore,
Stretching hand to hand,
Received the mystic clod.

But I hear it sinking from the deck,
Go with the sea brine
At evening, accompanying the watery sea.
Often indeed I urged the careless
Menials to guard it, but their minds forgot.
And now in this island the imperishable seed of
    spacious Libya
Is spilled before its hour.

—

### PYTH. V.–87.

*Apollo.*

He bestowed the lyre,
And he gives the muse to whom he wishes,
Bringing peaceful serenity to the breast.

—

### PYTH. VIII.–136.

*Man.*

(Σκιᾶς ὄναρ ἄνθρωποι.) The phantom of a shadow
are men.

—

### PYTH. IX.–31.

*Hypseus' Daughter Cyrene.*

He reared the white-armed child Cyrene,
Who loved neither the alternating motion of
    the loom,
Nor the superintendence of feasts,
With the pleasures of companions;
But with javelins of steel,
And the sword, contending,
To slay wild beasts;

Affording surely much
And tranquil peace to her father's herds;
Spending little sleep
Upon her eye-lids,
As her sweet bed-fellow, creeping on at dawn.

———

PYTH. X.–33.

*The Height of Glory.*

Fortunate and celebrated
By the wise is that man,
Who conquering by his hands, or virtue
Of his feet, takes the highest prizes
Through daring and strength,
And, living still, sees his youthful son
Deservedly obtaining Pythian crowns.
The brazen heaven is not yet accessible to him.
But whatever glory we
Of mortal race may reach,
He goes beyond, even to the boundaries
Of navigation. But neither in ships, nor going
    on foot,
Couldst thou find the wonderful way to the
    contests of the Hyperboreans.

———

THIRD NEMEAN ODE.–32.

*To Aristoclides, Victor at the Nemean Games.*

If, being beautiful,
And doing things like to his form,
The child of Aristophanes
Went to the height of manliness; no further
Is it easy to go over the untravelled sea,
Beyond the pillars of Hercules.

## NEM. III.–69.

### *The Youth of Achilles.*

One with native virtues
Greatly prevails; but he who
Possesses acquired talents, an obscure man,
Aspiring to various things, never with fearless
Foot advances, but tries
A myriad virtues with inefficient mind.

Yellow-haired Achilles, meanwhile, remaining
   in the house of Philyra,
Being a boy played
Great deeds; often brandishing
Iron-pointed javelins in his hands,
Swift as the winds, in fight he wrought death
   to savage lions;
And he slew boars, and brought their bodies
Palpitating to Kronian Centaurus,
As soon as six years old. And all the while
Artemis and bold Athene admired him,
Slaying stags without dogs or treacherous nets;
For he conquered them on foot.

—

## NEM. IV.–66.

Whatever virtues sovereign destiny has given
   me,
I well know that time creeping on
Will fulfil what was fated.

—

## NEM. V.–1.

The kindred of Pytheas, a victor in the Nemean games, had wished to procure an ode from Pindar for less than three drachmæ, asserting that they could purchase a statue for that sum. In the following lines he nobly re-

proves their meanness, and asserts the value of his
labors, which, unlike those of the statuary, will bear the
fame of the hero to the ends of the earth.

No image-maker am I, who being still make
    statues
Standing on the same base. But on every
Merchant-ship, and in every boat, sweet song,
Go from Ægina to announce that Lampo's son,
Mighty Pytheas,
Has conquered the pancratian crown at the
    Nemean games.

—

## NEM. VI.–1.

*The Divine in Man.*

One the race of men and of gods;
And from one mother
We all breathe.
But quite different power
Divides us, so that the one is nothing,
But the brazen heaven remains always
A secure abode. Yet in some respect we are
    related,
Either in mighty mind or form, to the
    Immortals;
Although not knowing
To what resting place
By day or night, Fate has written that we
    shall run.

—

## NEM. VIII.–44.

*The Treatment of Ajax.*

In secret votes the Danaans aided Ulysses;
And Ajax, deprived of golden arms, struggled
    with death.

Surely, wounds of another kind they wrought
In the warm flesh of their foes, waging war
With the man-defending spear.

—

## Nem. VIII.–68.

### The Value of Friends.

Virtue increases, being sustained by wise men
    and just,
As when a tree shoots up with gentle dews into
    the liquid air.
There are various uses of friendly men;
But chiefest in labors; and even pleasure
Requires to place some pledge before the eyes.

—

## Nem. IX.–41.

### Death of Amphiaraus.

Once they led to seven-gated Thebes an army
    of men, not according
To the lucky flight of birds. Nor did the
    Kronian,
Brandishing his lightning, impel to march
From home insane, but to abstain from the
    way.
But to apparent destruction
The host made haste to go, with brazen arms
And horse equipments, and on the banks
Of Ismenus, defending sweet return,
Their white-flowered bodies fattened fire.
For seven pyres devoured young-limbed
Men. But to Amphiaraus
Zeus rent the deep-bosomed earth
With his mighty thunder-bolt,
And buried him with his horses,

Ere being struck in the back
By the spear of Periclymenus, his warlike
Spirit was disgraced.
For in dæmonic fears
Flee even the sons of gods.

———

### Nem. X.–153.

#### *Castor and Pollux.*

Pollux, son of Zeus, shared his immortality with his
brother Castor, son of Tyndarus, and while one was in
heaven, the other remained in the infernal regions, and
they alternately lived and died every day, or, as some
say, every six months. While Castor lies mortally wounded by Idas, Pollux prays to Zeus, either to restore his
brother to life, or permit him to die with him, to which
the god answers,

Nevertheless, I give thee
Thy choice of these; if indeed fleeing
Death and odious age,
Thou wilt dwell on Olympus,
With Athene and black-speared Mars;
Thou hast this lot.
But if thou thinkest to fight
For thy brother, and share
All things with him,
Half the time thou mayest breathe, being
    beneath the earth,
And half in the golden halls of heaven.
The god thus having spoken, he did not
Entertain a double wish in his mind.
And he released first the eye, and then the
    voice,
Of brazen-mitred Castor.

### First Isthmian Ode.—65.

#### *Toil.*

One reward of labors is sweet to one man, one
    to another,
To the shepherd, and the plougher, and the
    bird-catcher,
And whom the sea nourishes.
But every one is tasked to ward off
Grievous famine from the stomach.

—

### Isth. II.—9.

#### *The Venality of the Muse.*

Then the Muse was not
Fond of gain, nor a laboring woman;
Nor were the sweet-sounding
Soothing strains
Of Terpsichore, sold,
With silvered front.
But now she directs to observe the saying
Of the Argive, coming very near the truth,
Who cried, "Money, money, man,"
Being bereft of property and friends.

—

### Isth. VI.—62.

#### *Hercules' Prayer concerning Ajax,*
#### *son of Telamon.*

If ever, O father Zeus, thou hast heard
My supplication with willing mind,
Now I beseech thee with prophetic
Prayer, grant a bold son from Eribœa
To this man my fated guest;

Rugged in body
As the hide of this wild beast
Which now surrounds me, which, first of all
My contests, I slew once in Nemea, and let
    his mind agree.
To him thus having spoken, Heaven sent
A great eagle, king of birds,
And sweet joy thrilled him inwardly.

# Fragments of Pindar.

[The following fragments of Pindar, found in ancient authors, should have been inserted at the end of the translations contained in our last number.]

## THE FREEDOM OF GREECE.

                    First at Artemisium
The children of the Athenians laid the shining
Foundation of freedom,
And at Salamis and Mycale,
And in Platæa, making it firm
As adamant.

———

## FROM STRABO.

*Apollo.*

                    Having risen he went
Over land and sea,
And stood over the vast summits of mountains,
And threaded the recesses, penetrating to the
    foundations of the groves.

———

## FROM PLUTARCH.

Heaven being willing, even on an osier thou
    mayest sail.
Thus rhymed by the old translator of Plutarch;
    "Were it the will of heaven, an osier bough
    Were vessel safe enough the seas to plough."

———

## FROM SEXTUS EMPIRICUS.

Honors and crowns of the tempest-footed
Horses delight one;

Others life in golden chambers;
And some even are pleased traversing securely
The swelling of the sea in a swift ship.

---

### From Stobaeus.

This I will say to thee,–
The lot of fair and pleasant things
It behoves to show in public to all the people;
But if any adverse calamity sent from heaven
    befall
Men, this it becomes to bury in darkness.

---

### From Clemens of Alexandria.

To Heaven it is possible from black
Night to make arise unspotted light,
And with cloud-blackening darkness to obscure
The pure splendor of day.

---

### From the Same.

First, indeed, the Fates brought the wise-
    counselling
Uranian Themis, with golden horses,
By the fountains of Ocean to the awful ascent
Of Olympus, along the shining way,
To be the first spouse of Zeus the Deliverer.
And she bore the golden-filletted, fair-wristed
Hours, preservers of good things.

---

Equally tremble before God
And a man dear to God.

### From Ælius Aristides.

Pindar used such exaggeration [in praise of poetry] as to say that even the gods themselves, when at his marriage Zeus asked if they wanted any thing, "asked him to make certain gods for them who should celebrate these great works and all his creation with speech and song."

——

### From Stobaeus.

Pindar said of the physiologists, that they "plucked the unripe fruit of wisdom."

——

### From the Same.

Pindar said that "hopes were the dreams of those awake."

# Pindaric Odes
# From HM 13204

But days that come after
Are the wisest witnesses.          I Olympic


That which is by nature, is best of all.
But many men
Labor to get renown
By acquired talents.
But without God, let it not be spoken.
Surely there is no lamer thing
Than this. For there are other
Ways beside ways.
And one care will not nourish
Us All. But wisdom is steep.          Olymp. IX


Of wisdom, yoked with the streams of
    words                              VII Isthmian


But my fear having departed
Has put an end to severe sadness.
And that which is before the foot is
    better always
Whatever it is. For treacherous time
Hangs over men
Revolving the course of life.
But are curable to mortals
With freedom
Even these.          VIII Isthmian

# The Transmigrations
of the Seven Brahmans.

The world is founded upon the *sraddha*[1]

The divine eye, which Sanatcoumara had given me, made me perceive the Seven Brahmans, of whom he had spoken, unfaithful to their sacred rules, but yet attached to the worship of the Pitris. They bore names answering to their works: they were called *Vagdouchta, Crodhana, Hinsa, Pisouna, Cavi, Swasrima* and *Pitrivarttin*: they were sons of Cosica, and disciples of Gargya. Their father dying they commenced the prescribed ceremonies under the direction of their master. By his order they took care of his foster cow, named Capila, who was accompanied by her calf already as large as herself. On the way, the sight of this magnificent cow, who supplied all the wants of Gargya, tempted them: hunger impelled them, their reason was blinded; they conceived the cruel and mad project of slaying her. Cavi and Swasrima endeavored to prevent them from it. What could they do against the others? But Pitrivarttin, that one among them who was always occupied with the *sraddha*,[2] having his mind then on the duty the thought of which possessed him, said to his missing or wandering brothers with anger: "Since we have a sacrifice to make to the Pitris, let this cow be sacrificed by us with devotion, and her death will profit us. Let us honor the Pitris, and no reproach can be made to us." "Well", cried they all, and the cow was sacrificed in honor of the Pitris. They told their master afterwards: "Your cow has been slain by a tiger,

---

[1] rites in honor of Ancestors
[2] Worship offered to the Pitris or fathers.

but here is her calf." The Brahman, without suspecting evil, took the calf which they delivered to him.

But they had failed in (the regard and) the respect which they owed to their master; and when Time came to take them all together from this world, for having been cruel and wicked, for having rendered themselves guilty of impiety toward their spiritual preceptor, they all seven reappeared in life in the family of a hunter, of the country of Dasarna. However, as in sacrificing the cow of their master, they had rendered homage to the Pitris, these brothers, filled with force and intelligence, preserved in this existence the remembrance of the past: they showed themselves attached to their duties, performing their functions with zeal, and abstaining from every act of cupidity and injustice: now holding in their breath as long a time as endured the recitation of a *mantra*,[3] now plunging themselves into profound meditations on their destiny. These were the names of these pious hunters: *Nirvera, Nirvriti*, Kchanta, *Nirmanyou, Criti, Veghasa* and *Matrivarttin*. Thus these same men who had formerly loved evil and injustice, were now so changed that they honored their mother bent (down) under the weight of age and rejoiced the heart of their father. When death had taken away their parents, then leaving their bow, they fixed themselves in the forest, where soon after they themselves also surrendered their souls.

As a recompense for their good conduct, they retained still in their following life the remembrance of the past: they were born upon the agreeable mountain Calandjara, under the form of stags with high branching horns, by turns experiencing and inspiring

[3] An act of piety in which the penitent collects himself, and holds his breath, until the prayer which he repeats mentally is ended.

fear. Their names were then *Ounmoukha, Nityavi-trasta, Stabdacarna, Vilotchana, Pandita, Ghasmara,* and *Nadin*. Thus going over in (their) memory their ancient actions, they wandered in the woods, detached from every sentiment, from every affection, submitting with resignation to the duties which they had to fulfil, and in their solitude delivering themselves to the exercises of the *Yoga*.[4] Extenuated by fasting and penitence, they died in the course of pious practices, by which the earth was worn bare and one sees yet, O son of Bharata, upon the mountain Calandjara the mark of their feet.

Their piety caused then that they passed into a class of beings more elevated; transported into the beautiful country of Sarodwipa, they had the form of those geese which inhabit the abode of the lakes: entirely isolated from all society, true Mounis occupied only with divine things, they were named then *Nihspriha, Nirmama, Kchanta, Nirdwandwa, Nichparigraha, Nirvriti* and *Nirbhrita*. In the midst of their austerities and their fastings, they died, and returned to life under the form of swans, frequenting the waves of Manasa. The names of these seven brothers were *Padmagarbha, Ravindakcha, Kchirag-arbha, Soulotchana, Ourouvindou, Souvindou* and *Himagarbha*. In the remembrance of their past life, they pursued their holy exercises; the fault committed toward their master, when they were Brahmans, had caused them to retrograde in the scale of beings; but the worship which they had then, in the midst even of their crime, rendered to the Pitris, had procured for them the faculty of adding to their knowledge at each new birth. Finally they returned to the world under the appearance of wild ducks, with

---

[4] An exercise of penance or extreme devotion

the names of *Soumanas, Swani, Souvak, Souddha, Tchitradarsana, Sounetra* and *Soutantra*. By the effect of the acts of penitence which they had performed in their various states, their exercises of devotion and their good works, the divine science which they had formerly learned in the lessons of their different masters, formed a treasure which went on always accumulating in their transmigrations. In their new condition of inhabitants of the air, they continued their holy practices; in their language they spoke only of sacred things, and the *yoga* was the only object of their meditations.

Such was their existence, when Vibhradja, descendant of Pourou and prince of the family of the Nipas, brilliant with beauty, glorious or illustrious with power, stately, and surrounded by all his house, entered into the forest where these birds lived. Soutantra saw him, and suddenly dazzled by so much riches, (he) formed this desire: "Might I become like this king, if I have acquired any merit by my austerities and my penitence! I am unhappy to have fasted and mortified myself without any fruit."

Then two of the wild ducks his companions said to him: "We wish to follow you, and share the destiny of our friend." "So be it" replied Soutantra, till then only animated by religious thoughts, and they associated themselves all three in this resolution. Souvak said to him: "Since consulting only your passion, you reject our pious exercises, in order to form earthly desires, hear my words. Be cursed by us: You shall be king at Campilya, and these two friends shall follow you thither". Thus the four birds, faithful to their vocation, addressed imprecations and reproaches to their old companions, whom the desire of a throne had turned aside from the good way. Cursed, fallen from their devotion, all lost, these three unhappy ones asked pardon of their comrades. Their despair was touching, and Soumanas spoke to them in the name of the others: "Our curse shall have its effect. You shall become men, but you shall return one day to the holy practices of devotion. Soutantra shall know the languages of all animals. It is to him we owe the favors with which the Pitris have loaded us. When we slew the cow of our master, it was he who counselled us to offer her as a sacrifice to the manes: it is therefore to him that we are to attribute the science which we possess, and the devotion which we have practised. Yes, one day, (in) hearing some words which will recall to you in a concise manner, a past, the knowledge of which shall have been concealed at the bottom of your souls, (then) you shall abandon all to return to devotion."

As I was saying, (that) while these seven birds, on the waves of Manassa, nourishing themselves only on air & water, suffered their bodies to waste away, the king Vibhradja betook himself to these woods, surrounded by all his court, and shining like Indra in the midst of his celestial garden of Nandana.[5] He saw there these seven birds occupied with their pious practices: humbled by the comparison which he made of them and himself, he came back all pensive into his city. He had a son extremely religious, who was named *Anouha*, because forgetting this body composed of material atoms, he elevated himself even to the contemplation of the soul. Souca gave him for wife his daughter, the illustrious Critwi, no less estimable for her good qualities than for her devotion. + + +

Vibhradja, having yielded the throne to his son Anouha, gave his last advice to his subjects, made his adieus to the Brahmans, and betook himself to the

[5] the Elysium of Indra

borders of the lake where he had seen the seven friends in order to do penance there. There, fasting, contenting himself with air for all nourishment, renouncing every kind of desire, he thought only of mortifying his body. His object, however, was to obtain by force of his austerities the privilege of becoming the son of one of these beings whom he admired. The ardor of his penitence soon gave to Vibhradja a luminous appearance. He was like a sun which enlightened all the forest. O son of Courou, this wood was from his name called *Vebhradja*, as well as the lake, where the four birds, constant in devotion, and the three others, who had strayed from the good road, abandoned their mortal coil.

Then all together & in harmony they betook themselves to Campilya; and there these seven noble and holy souls, purified by science, meditation, (&) penitence, (and) instructed in the Vedas and the Vedangas underwent a new birth. But there were only four who preserved the memory of the past; the three others found themselves in the shades of their folly.

Soutantra became the son of Anouha, and was the glorious Brahmadatta; the desire which he had formed, when he was a bird, was thus accomplished. As for Tchitradarsana and Sounetra, they were born into a family of Brahmans: they were sons of Babhravya and of Vatsa, able in the science of the Vedas and of the Vedangas, and friends of Brahmadatta, as they had been in their preceding births. One was named *Pantchala* (or *Pantchica*): it was he who, in the various transmigrations, had been the fifth; the sixth was called then *Candarica*. Brahmadatta had been the seventh. Pantchala, learned in the Rig-veda, was a great Atcharya;[6] Candarica possessed two

[6] A spiritual teacher

Vedas, the Sama and the Yadjour. The king, son of Anouha, had the privilege of knowing the language of all beings. He cultivated the friendship of Pantchala and of Candarica. Delivered, like common men, to the empire of the senses and the passions, on account of what they had done in their preceding births, they nevertheless knew how to distinguish the requirements of duty from desires & from luxury.

The excellent prince Anouha, after having crowned king the virtuous Brahmadatta, animated by devotion, entered on the way which leads to heaven. Brahmadatta married the daughter of Devala, called *Sannati*, and who owed this name to the respect which she inspired. Her father had instructed her himself in the great science of devotion, and her virtue was such that she was destined to be born only once on the earth.

The four friends, who had followed Pantchala, Candarica, and Brahmadatta to Campilya, were born into a family of Brahmans very poor. These four brothers were named *Dhritiman, Soumanas, Vidwan* and *Tatwadarsin*; profound in the reading of the Vedas, and penetrating all the secrets of nature, they united all the knowledges which they had gathered in their preceding existences. Happy in the exercise of their devotion, they wished still to go and perfect themselves in solitude. They told it to their father, who cried out: "It is to fail in your duty to abandon me thus. How can you quit me, leaving me in poverty, taking away from me my children who are my only riches, and depriving me of their services" These Brahmans replied to this disconsolate father: We are (about) to give you the means of coming out of this state of poverty. Hear these words: they will procure you great riches. Go find the virtuous king Brahmadatta, repeat them to him before his counsellors.

Happy at hearing you, he will give you lands and riches, he will crown at last all your desires. Go; and be satisfied." Then they told him certain words, and after having honored him as their spiritual master, they gave themselves only to the practice of the Yoga, and obtained (their) final emancipation.[7]

The son of Brahmadatta was Vibhradja himself, born again; animated by piety, and covered with glory, he was named *Viswaksena*. One day Brahmadatta, his soul content and happy, was walking in a wood with his wife: he resembled Indra accompanied by Satchi. This prince heard there the voice of an ant: it was a lover who sought to bend his mistress by his tender language. In picking up the answer of the passionate lover, and thinking of the littleness of this being, Brahmadatta could not help laughing out loud. Sannati appeared offended at it, and blushed. Her resentment went so far as to make her refuse to eat: her husband wished in vain to appease her. She replied to him with a bitter smile: "O prince, you have laughed at me, I can no longer live". The king told her the truth such as it was. She was unwilling to believe it, and replied to him with wounded feelings: "O prince, that is not in nature. What man can know the language of the ants? unless it is an effect of the favor of a god recompensing the good actions of a preceding life, or the fruit of a great penitence, or the result of a supernatural science. O king, if it is true that you have this power, if you know the language of all beings, deign to communicate to me your knowledge, or let me die, as truly cursed by you."

Brahmadatta was touched by the tender complaints of the queen: he had recourse to the protection of Narayana, lord of all beings. Abstracted and fasting

[7] That is, they died to be born no more on earth.

for six nights, he adored him: then this glorious prince, in a vision, perceived the god, who is the love of all nature, and who said to him: "Brahmadatta, tomorrow morning thou shalt have good fortune". Thus spoke the god, and disappeared.

In the meanwhile the father of the four Brahmans having learned from his children the mysterious words which they had communicated to him, regarded himself as sure of his object. He sought a moment when he might meet the king with his counsellors, and could not for some time find the moment to make him hear the words which he had to say to him. Narayana had rendered his oracle; the king, satisfied with his answer, had performed the ablution of his head, and mounted upon a chariot all shining with gold, was reentering into the city. The chief of the Brahmans, Candarica, was holding the reins of the horses, and the son of Babhravya was bearing the chowri[8] and the royal fan. "This is the moment," said the Brahman to himself, and immediately he addresses these words to the king and (to) his two companions: "The seven hunters of the country of Dasarna, the stags of mount Calandjara, the geese of Sarodwipa, the swans of Manassa were anciently in Couroukchetra[9] Brahmans instructed in the Vedas: in this long voyage why then do you remain behind?" At these words Brahmadatta was struck dumb, as well as his two friends Pantchala and Candarica. Seeing the one let fall the reins and the standard, and the other the royal fan, the spectators and courtiers were struck with astonishment. In a moment, the king elevated upon the car with his two companions, recovered his senses and continued his route. But all three recalling to mind the borders of the sacred lake,

8 A fly-flap made of the tail of a Tartary cow
9 A part of India.

recovered also at the same time their ancient sentiments of devotion. They loaded with riches the Brahman, giving him precious stones and other presents.
Brahmadatta yielded his throne to Viswaksena, and
caused him to be crowned king: as for him, he retired
into the forest with his wife. There the pious daughter of Devala, Sannati, happy to give herself only to
devotion, said to her husband: "O great king, I knew
very well that you were acquainted with the language
of the ants; but by feigning anger, I wished to warn
you that you were in the chains of the passions. We
are going now to follow the sublime route which is
the object of our desires. It is I who have reawakened
in you this love of devotion which was there only
drowsy". The prince was charmed at this discourse
of his wife; and by means of devotion, to which he
consecrated himself with all the might of his soul he
entered into that superior way to which it is difficult
to arrive.

Candarica, animated by the same zeal, was as able
in the science of the *Sankhya* as in that of the *Yoga*,
and purified by his works, he obtained perfection and
the mysterious union with God.

Pantchala labored to explain the rules of the holy
law, and applied himself to develop all the precepts of
pronounciation; he was master in the divine art of
devotion, and by his penitence he acquired a high
glory.

# Appendix

## Διαλογος

Δεκιος – – – – – – – – – – Clarke. Manlius. S.
Κατων – – – – – – – – – – Thoreau. David. H.

Δεκιος    Ὁ Καισαρ σε χαιρειν διακελευεται.

Κατων    Ει δυνατον ην φιλους εμου σφακτους χαιρειν
διακελευεσθαι, τουτο κεχαρισμενον αν ἐίη. Ου την
προσαγορευειν βουλην χρη;

Δεκιος    Προς σε λεγειν αφικνουμαι. Ὁ Καισαρ τα πραγματα
σοι κακως εχειν αισθανεται· και δε αυτῳ σε μεγα
ποιουντι μελει της σης σωτηριας.

Κατων    Το αυτο εμοι και τῃ Ρωμῃ ειμαρμενον εστι· ει ὁ
Καισαρ εμε σωζειν βουλεται κελευε αυτον ουτην
πατριδα πορθειν· συ μεν φρασαι τουτο τῳ
αυτοκρατορι, και εμε δυσχεραινειν τον βιον ὁν αυτος
διδοναι εχει.

Δεκιος    Ἡ Ρωμη και ἡ βουλη εκδοτους τῳ Καισαρι εαυτους
ποιουσι· Οι αρχοντες και οι ἡγεμονες, των αυτου
νικων των τε θριαμβων αυτον εμποδιζοντες, ετελευτων.
Δια τι προς τον Καισαρα κατατιθεναι χαριν φευγεις;

Κατων    Σος λογος αυτος τουτο διακωλυει.

Δεκιος    Ὠ Κατων, κελευομαι προσφιλως σε των σων
βουλευματων αποτρεπειν. Τον επικειμενον σοι κινδυνον
διασκοπει τον τε ολεθρον εν τῳ νυν απειλουντι σοι.
Πλειστων τιμων παρα των πολιτων απολαυσεις ει μονον
προσχωρειν προς τε τον Καισαρα κατατιθεναι χαριν
βουλῃ. Ἡ Ρωμη χαρει και σε ὑπερτατον βροτων
αναβλεψει.

Κατων    Αλις των τοιουτων· ου προσδοκαν τον βιον επι
τοιοισδε εμοι προσηκει.

Δεκιος   Ὁ Καισαρ τας σας αρετας γνωριζει, διοτι την σην
σωτηριαν πολλου τιμα· αυτῳ επιστελλε επι ποσῳ
δεξαιτ' αν σε ὁμολογιας τε εκτιθετι

Κατων   Κελευε μεν αυτον τους λοχους διαπεμπειν την δε τῃ
δημοκρατιᾳ ελευθεριαν. αποδιδοναι, και τα
πεπραγμακα αναφερειν προς το συγκλητον, τουτων
πεπραγμενων, εγω προς αυτον φιλιαν πραξω.

Δεκιος   Ὦ Κατων, παντες την σην σοφιαν αγαν επαινουσι.

Κατων   Κελευε μεν αυτον, εμης φωνης ου φιλουσης τους εν
κακοις αλοντας απολυειν και ἁμαρτηματα καλλυνειν,
εγωγε επι το βημα αυτου χαριν αναβησομαι και τον
δημον πεισω αυτῳ ἁμαρτηματα συγγινωσκειν.

Δεκιος   Τῳ νικωντι ταδε επη πρεπει.

Κατων   Ὦ Δεχιε· ταυτα τα επη Ρωμαιῳ πρεπει.

Δεκιος   Τι εστι Ρωμαιος τῳ Καισαρι εχθρος.

Κατων   Μειζων του Καισαρος, ὁ φιλος της αρετης εστι.

Δεκιος   Μιμνησκου ἱνα τοπου· Ουτι κηζειναι, μικρης βουλης
προεδρευειν. Ουκ νυν εν τῃ αγορᾳ, παντων των
Ρωμαιων επιψωνουντων, δημηγορεις.

Κατων   Αυτον τουτο δια μνημης εχειν χρη ὁς ἡμας δευρο
αγει: Το του Καισαραρ ξιφος την της Ρωμης βουλην
ωλεγωσε. Φευ· ἡ τουδε νικη και ἡ ευτυχια σε τα
ομματα εκστατικον εξαπατουσι· ει αυτον καλως
σκοπεις, μεμολυσμενος φονῳ, προδοσιᾳ, θεοσυλιᾳ,
και μιασμασι ὡν την μνημην μονην θαμβων φανησεται,
συνοιδα εμαυτῳ δυστανῳ και εχθετῳ κακοις φαινομενῳ,
αλλα προς των θεων ομνυμι ὁτι εχαιων μυριαδων
κοσμων προσφερομενων, ουκ ὁδε Καισαρ ειην.

Δεκιος   Τοι αυτην αποκρισιν τῳ Καισαρι ὁ Κατων αποπεμπει,
αντι παντων των αυτου ευμενων προνοιων της σε
φιλιας εκουσιως προσφερομενης;

Κατων   Αυτου προνοια ὑβριστικη και ματαια εστιν. Ὦ
ὑπερηφανε ανερ· ὁι θεοι εμου προνοιαν εχουσι· ει
ὁ Καισαρ την μεγαλοψυχιαν επιδεικνυναι βουλεται,

δει αυτον προνοιαν τωνδε εμων φιλων εχειν, και ευ
χρησθαι τη δυναστεια κακως ειλημενη

Δεκιος Δια την σην αδαματην καρδιαν επιλανθανει σεθνητον
οντα. Εισπιπτεις τον σον ολεθρον. Αλις των
τοιουτων· οτε απαγγελλω πως ταυτη ή πρεσβεια
διαπραττεται πασα η Ρωμη δακρυα χυζει.

The Cliffs–a Cenotaph.

Siste qui conscendis!
Hîc,
Filius Naturae,
TAHATTAWAN, Sachimaupan,*
Extremus Indorum,
Venatus, hoc rivo piscatus est.
Per agros, prata, collesque, regnavit,
At si famae credendum est,
Manus non longas habuit.
Homo, Princeps, Christianus,
Quamvis incultus non indeploratus.
In moribus scilicet austerus et sine levitate;
Sermone grandis, venustus, imo etiam modicus!!!
Integritate fortitudineque explorata praeclarus.

———

Hoc Scopulum ejus cenotapium esto.
Indi, eheu! Ubique gentium sunt?
"Wehquetumah,–onk–kuttinnumoush–penowohtcáog–
wutche–kꝏkompuhchasuash,–kah–aongkóe–an–
ohkeꝏg–wutche–kutahto–onk." Psalm, 2. 8.
Sculptum A. D. 1836.

* "Sachimaupan; he that was prince here. This expression they use, because they abhor to mention the dead by name: and therefore, if any man bear the name of the dead, he changeth his name; and if any stranger accidentally name him, he is checked; and if any wilfully name him, he is fined: and amongst states, the naming of their dead Sachims is one ground of their wars."
R. Williams' Key into the Language of the Indians of N. E.

———

# Editorial Appendix

# Notes on Illustrations

Page of *The Prometheus Bound*        following page 152

Thoreau revised and corrected his translation of *The Prometheus Bound* in his own copy of the January 1843 number of the *Dial*. This page shows several of his changes.–Special Collections, Morris Library, Southern Illinois University at Carbondale.

Page of *The Seven Against Thebes*

The only complete version of Thoreau's translation of *The Seven Against Thebes*, HM 13193, is a rough draft manuscript at the Huntington Library. This page contains examples of the kinds of revisions and alternative readings that are characteristic of the manuscript.–The Huntington Library.

First page of HM 13204

HM 13204 contains draft translations of all of the odes that appeared in "Fragments of Pindar" and many of those that appeared in "Pindar." It is also the source for parts of four odes published in this volume as "Pindaric Odes From HM 13204." On this page Thoreau names his source, "Thiersch's Ed. 2nd Vol," and interlines many of the Greek words he is translating, a practice he also followed in the early drafts of *The Prometheus Bound.*–The Huntington Library.

First page of "The Transmigrations of the Seven Brahmans"

The manuscript of "The Transmigrations of the Seven Brahmans," bMS Am 278.5.12 (1) at the Houghton Library, is a fair copy that Thoreau later revised in pencil. The first page shows the kinds of revisions he made throughout.–Houghton Library, Harvard University.

Pr. There's no unwillingness, but I hesitate to vex thy mind.

Io. Care not for me more than is pleasant to me.

Pr. Since you are earnest, it behoves to speak; hear then.

Ch. Not yet indeed; but a share of pleasure also give to me.
First we'll learn the malady of this one,
Herself relating her destructive fortunes,
And the remainder of her trials let her learn from thee.

Pr. 'T is thy part, Io, to do these a favor,
As well for every other reason, and as they are sisters of thy
father.
Since to weep and to lament misfortunes,
There where one will get a tear
From those attending, is worthy the delay.

10. I know not that I need distrust you,
But in plain speech you shall learn
All that you ask for; and yet e'en telling I lament
The god-sent tempest, and dissolution
Of my form — whence to me miserable it came.
For always visions in the night moving about
My virgin chambers, enticed me
With smooth words; "O greatly happy virgin,
Why be a virgin long? is permitted to obtain
The greatest marriage. For Zeus with love's dart
Has been warmed by thee, and wishes to unite
In love; but do thou, O child, spurn not the couch
Of Zeus, but go out to Lerna's deep
Morass, and stables of thy father's herds,
That the divine eye may cease from desire."
With such dreams every night
Was I unfortunate distressed, till I dared tell
My father of the night-wandering visions.
And he to Pytho and Dodona frequent
Prophets sent, that he might learn what it was necessary
He should say or do, to do agreeably to the gods.
And they came bringing ambiguous
Oracles, darkly and indistinctly uttered.
But finally a plain report came to Inachus,
Clearly enjoining him and telling,
Out of my home and country to expel me,
Discharged to wander to the earth's last bounds,
And if he was not willing, from Zeus would come
A fiery thunderbolt, which would annihilate all his race.
Induced by such predictions of the Loxian,
Against his will he drove me out,
And shut me from the houses; but Zeus' rein
Compelled him by force to do these things.
Immediately my form and mind were
Changed, and horned, as you beheld, stung
By a sharp-mouthed fly, with frantic leaping
Rushed I to Cenchrea's palatable stream,
And Lerna's source; but a herdsman born-of-earth

Page of *Prometheus Bound*

Page of *The Seven Against Thebes*

Fragments of Pindar

Thiersch's Ed. 2nd Vol p 216

First at Artemisium
The children of the Athenians laid the shining
Foundation of freedom,
And at Salamis and Mycalae,
And in Plataea making it firm
As adamant.

First page of HM 13204

The world is founded upon the sraddha.

# The Transmigrations of the Seven Brahmans.

The divine eye, which Sanatcoumara had given me, made me perceive the seven Brahmans, of whom he had spoken to me, unfaithful to their sacred rules, and yet attached to the worship of the Pitris. They bore names conformable to their works: they were called Vagdouchta, Crodhana, Hinsa, Pisouna, Cavi, Swasrima and Pitrivarttin: they were sons of Cosica, and disciples of Gargya. Their father (happening to die), they commenced the prescribed ceremonies under the direction of their master. By his order they guarded his foster cow, named Capila, who was accompanied by her calf already as large as she. On the way, the sight of this magnificent cow, who supplied all the wants of Gargya, tempted them: hunger impelled them, their reason was blinded; they conceived the cruel and mad project of slaying her. Cavi and Swasrima endeavored to prevent them from it. What could the

(12,1)

First page of "The Transmigrations of the Seven Brahmans"

# Acknowledgments

ALTHOUGH individual contributions to this volume by the staff of *The Writings of Henry D. Thoreau* are recorded in Editorial Contributions, I would like to give special thanks to William L. Howarth and Elizabeth Hall Witherell, as well as to Thomas Blanding, Carolyn Kappes, Joseph J. Moldenhauer, and Leonard Neufeldt. Without their professionalism and expertise the editing of this volume could never have taken place. In addition, the following present and former members of the Textual Center staff helped prepare *Translations*: Claire Badaracco, Sarah Louisa Dennis, Kristin Fossum, Rebecca Larson, Nora W. Mayo, Mark R. Patterson, George Ryan, and Marsha Shankman.

Indispensable financial support has come from the National Endowment for the Humanities and the National Council of Teachers of English, as well as from Princeton University, the University of Pennsylvania, and the University of California, Santa Barbara.

The following libraries have generously granted permission to refer to, quote, and publish unique manuscript and printed material in their collections: Special Collections, Morris Library, Southern Illinois University at Carbondale; The Huntington Library, San Marino, California; Houghton Library, Harvard University; Harvard University Archives, Harvard University; The Pierpont Morgan Library, New York; Yale University Library, Yale University; Concord Antiquarian Museum, Concord, Massachusetts; Henry W. and Albert A. Berg Collection, The New York Public Library, Astor, Lenox and Tilden Foundations; Department of Special Collections, Mugar Memorial Library, Boston University; Rare Book and Manuscript Library, Columbia University; The Scheide Library, Princeton, New Jersey. In addition, research facilities were provided over the years by the Harvard College Library; the University and Pembroke College libraries, Cambridge; and Firestone Library, Princeton University.

A number of passages and some information in the Introduction also appeared in an earlier form in two journals and a scholarly paper. For permission to reproduce this material I would like to thank Mrs. Anne McGrath and The Thoreau Lyceum with regard to a note first published in *The Concord Saunterer;* Joel A. Myerson and G. K. Hall, Inc., for material from an article in *Studies in the American Renaissance: 1980;* and Walter Harding, Secretary of The Thoreau Society, Inc., for permission to cite opinions first expressed in a paper delivered before the Society at the Ninety-Fifth Annual Convention of the Modern Language Association of America (Houston, Texas, December 29, 1980).

Finally, I am grateful for generous contributions of time, expertise, and good will by the following individuals: Emmett L. Bennett, Mina Bryan, Harold Cannon, George Hendrick, Robert N. Hudspeth, John Leipold, Patrick McCarthy, Margaret Neussendeufer, and Robert F. Renehan. In addition, I wish to thank those who, over the years of work on this volume, have provided professional advice of a more general sort as well as warm friendship: the Rev. and Mrs. Timothy B. Cogan, whose hospitality and kindness never failed; Jonathan Arac, Carlos Baker, Elizabeth Billington Fox, Carol Kay, and T. P. Roche, Jr., who encouraged me at Princeton; Colin Wilcockson and Ian Jack of Pembroke College in the old Cambridge; and in the new, Herschel Baker, Walter Jackson Bate, Warner Berthoff, Morton Bloomfield, G. Blakemore Evans, James Engell, Alan Heimert, John Hildebidle, and Joel Porte, whose aid was particularly important in the later stages of my work. At the University of Pennsylvania, my colleagues, Hennig Cohen, Robert Lucid, Robert Regan, and Ralph Rosen provided generous personal and

# Introduction

THIS volume of *The Writings of Henry D. Thoreau* presents the texts of all of Thoreau's literary translations. "Literary translations" are substantial, independent works conceived for an audience even if not published. This definition excludes quotations of translated foreign language material in Thoreau's other published works, since these are neither independent nor of substantial length. Passages Thoreau translated into English in his *Journal* or commonplace books are also excluded, since they were intended for his personal use rather than for presentation to the public as literary exercises.

*Translations* includes seven works.[1] Four were published in the *Dial,* a Transcendentalist periodical, during 1843 and 1844: *The Prometheus Bound* of Aeschylus (January 1843), selections from the *Anacreontea* (titled "Anacreon"; April 1843), selections from the odes of Pindar (titled "Pindar"; January 1844), and "Fragments of Pindar" (April 1844). Three survive only in manuscript: a group of Pindaric odes (ca. 1843), *The Seven Against Thebes* of Aeschylus (1843-1844), and "The Transmigrations of the Seven Brahmans" (1849-1851).

---

[1] "The Preaching of Buddha," a translation of passages from two articles published by Eugène Burnouf in *La Revue Indépendante* in April and May 1843 ("Fragments des Prédications de Buddha," April 25, 1843, 231-242; "Considérations sur l'Origine du Bouddhisme," May 25, 1843, 520-534) appeared anonymously in the January 1844 number of the *Dial* (4:391-401). It has been attributed to Thoreau since George Willis Cooke's, " 'The Dial'; an Historical and Biographical Introduction with a List of the Contributors" (*Journal of Speculative Philosophy* 19 [July 1885]:225-265). However, in " 'The Dial' and Corrigenda," pp. 322-323 of the same issue of the *Journal of Speculative Philosophy,* Cooke states that "the extracts made from 'The White Lotus of the Good Law' [the name given to the source in the *Dial*] were by Miss E. P. Peabody, and translated from Burnouf."

An Appendix to this volume includes two college compositions in the classical languages: Διαλογος (1835), and "The Cliffs—a Cenotaph" in Latin (1836). While not translations as defined above, these two pieces demonstrate the strength of Thoreau's early interest in classical languages and literatures, and the extent of his classical language training, and are more appropriately included in *Translations* than in another volume in this series.

HISTORY OF THE TEXTS

*The Prometheus Bound*

An entry for November 5, 1839, in Thoreau's *Journal* contains a plot summary of *The Prometheus Bound* that includes a translation of about fifty lines from the play.[2] However, he does not seem to have begun translating it in its entirety until the autumn of 1842. The two surviving drafts of the

---

[2] The translation in *Journal 1: 1837-1844,* ed. Elizabeth Hall Witherell et al. (Princeton: Princeton University Press, 1981), pp. 82-85, corresponds to this text of *The Prometheus Bound* as follows:

| Journal 1 | Translations |
|---|---|
| 82.35-36 | 3.22-25 |
| 83.4-6 | 4.29-34 |
| 83.9-13 | 8.16-24 |
| 83.18-21 | 13.18-22 |
| 83.29-84.13 | 23.28-24.28 |
| 84.17-19 | 34.25-29 |
| 84.22-33 | 36.7-26 |
| 84.37-39 | 53.23-26 |
| 85.25 | 31.11-12 |

Although the excerpts in *Journal 1* vary in wording from the later versions, Thoreau apparently had reference to these passages in translating the entire play. On "14" of HM 926 he wrote a note to himself to "see J no 1" for twenty-two lines he had already translated (*Journal 1,* 83.29-84.13, near the end of the first manuscript volume of the *Journal;* 23.28-24.28 in *Translations*). He did so to avoid having to copy them out again. The twenty-two lines appear in the second surviving draft and as Thoreau first copied them they are identical to the *Journal* version. Moreover, with minor exceptions all of the other *Journal* excerpts closely resemble the parallel passages in HM 926, the earliest surviving full manuscript draft.

tragedy both appear to come from this period. The first and less polished of them is now at the Huntington Library, San Marino, California (HM 926).[3] It can be dated because Thoreau followed his usual practice of recycling used sheets as scrap paper, and wrote his translation of *The Prometheus Bound* directly over or beside existing text.[4] Much of this earlier material dates from the spring or early summer of

---

[3] For a physical description of HM 926, see the headnote on p. 235.

[4] The existing text is as follows:

"2"  List of topics for "Natural History of Massachusetts." [In April 1842 Emerson gave Thoreau the volumes of reports that he reviewed in this essay, which was published in the July 1842 issue of the *Dial*.]

"3"  Pages "101-102" of a manuscript volume in the Morgan Library (MA 608). [Labelled "Paragraphs &c., Mostly Original" by H.G.O. Blake, this volume was transcribed in 1842 and is called "Transcripts, 1840-1842" in *Journal 1* (pp. 403-429; see pp. 618-619 for information on dating). Some of the original material on the leaf, a reflection on the Hindu scriptures, appears in *Journal* entries dated August 7, 1841 (*Journal 1*, p. 317) and March 23, 1842 (*Journal 1*, p. 387). Thoreau must have filled this leaf in MA 608 after March 1842 and removed it from the manuscript volume even later than that.]

"4"  Draft of "Natural History of Massachusetts."

"5"  Six lines in an early hand on the subject of the "beneficial tendency of knowledge."

"6"  Lines quoted from Wordsworth's "Peter Bell." [These lines appear in "A Walk to Wachusett," which Thoreau drafted in August 1842 and published in the *Boston Miscellany* in January 1843.]

"7"  List of topics and page numbers in *The Laws of Menu*, and Thoreau's name and "Concord" as an address in Margaret Fuller's hand. [Emerson had intended to include excerpts from *Menu* in the first issue of the *Dial* in July 1842 (see *The Journals and Miscellaneous Notebooks of Ralph Waldo Emerson*, ed. William H. Gilman and J. E. Parsons [Cambridge, Mass.: Harvard University Press, 1970], 8:484). They did not appear until January 1843, when Thoreau prepared this "Ethnical Scripture" himself. Early versions of some passages appear in MA 608 (*Journal 1*, pp. 419-425, passim). This leaf cannot be connected with a known Fuller letter, and so offers no clues to the dating.]

"8"  Draft of "Natural History of Massachusetts."

"14"  Draft of "To the Mountains in the Horizon." [Thoreau worked on versions of this poem from May 2, 1841 (*Journal 1*, p. 307), until 1849 when it appeared in *A Week* (see *A Week on the Concord and Merrimack Rivers*, ed. Carl F. Hovde, William L. Howarth, and Elizabeth Hall Witherell; historical introduction by Linck C. Johnson [Princeton: Princeton University Press, 1980], pp. 163-165); one version begins "A Walk to Wachusett."]

In addition, an unnumbered leaf located between pages numbered "22" and "23" contains the first page of a letter dated October 10, 1842, from Thoreau to Isaiah Williams.

1842, providing a *terminus a quo*. The latest dated piece of existing text is a draft of the beginning of a letter of October 10, 1842, to Isaiah Williams. The text of this letter occupies the first page of a folio, the other three leaves of which Thoreau used for *The Prometheus Bound*. Therefore, Thoreau probably began the translation sometime in the summer or early autumn of 1842, and continued to work on it until at least October 10.

The second *Prometheus Bound* manuscript, now at the Houghton Library, Harvard University (bMS Am 278.5.15), adopts many of the revisions Thoreau made in the first surviving version.[5] It also bears a closer relationship to the final printed text and must have followed soon after HM 926, in late October or November 1842. Yet while it is closer to the *Dial* translation, the Houghton manuscript is still a fairly early version. At least one more draft may have preceded the printer's copy that Emerson reported receiving on December 13, 1842.[6]

Later, Thoreau corrected and revised *The Prometheus Bound* in his own copy of the January 1843 *Dial* (pp. 363-386). This corrected *Dial*[7] provides the copy-text for the present edition of the play. Since the variants between *Dial* and corrected *Dial* do not seem to be pointed toward excerption or inclusion in another work, they are adopted as revisions. There is, in addition, no evidence that Thoreau intended any republication, despite the favorable reception of the printed version.[8]

---

[5] For a physical description of bMS Am 278.5.15, see the headnote on p. 235.

[6] Ralph Waldo Emerson to Charles Stearns Wheeler, Concord, December 13, 1842; cited in Joel Myerson, *The New England Transcendentalists and the "Dial": A History of the Magazine and Its Contributors* (Rutherford, N.J.: Fairleigh Dickinson University Press, 1980), p. 86.

[7] Now in Special Collections at the Morris Library, Southern Illinois University at Carbondale.

[8] Myerson, *The New England Transcendentalists and the "Dial,"* p. 248, n. 44.

The edition of Aeschylus Thoreau used for his *Journal* excerpts from *The Prometheus Bound* is not known.[9] He does not identify it, the excerpts are too short to allow such a determination on the basis of stylistic characteristics, and there is no external evidence of his having read a particular edition. He may have used the edition in Emerson's library that was probably the source later for his full translation: Aeschylus, *Tragœdiae: Ad exemplar accurate expressae, Editio stereotypa,* [ed. G. H. Schaefer] (Leipzig: Tauchnitz, 1819).[10] It could also have been one of the several editions in the Harvard College Library.[11] However, a careful comparison of Schaefer's edition both with Thoreau's English and with the Greek of the Oxford Classical Text edition[12]

[9] The discussions that follow on the sources of Thoreau's translations first appeared in part in two articles by Kevin P. Van Anglen: "A Note on Thoreau and Æschylus," *Concord Saunterer* 12 (Spring 1977):11, and "The Sources for Thoreau's Greek Translations," in *Studies in the American Renaissance: 1980,* ed. Joel Myerson (Boston: Twayne, 1980), pp. 291-299.

[10] See Walter Harding, *Emerson's Library* (Charlottesville: University Press of Virginia, 1967), p. 5. Although no editor's name appears on the title page, André Wartelle, in his *Bibliographie Historique et Critique d'Eschyle et de la Tragédie Grecque, 1518-1974* (Paris: Société d'Édition "Les Belles Lettres," 1978), pp. 40, 46, identifies this text as a reprint of G. H. Schaefer's edition, printed by Tauchnitz in 1812.

[11] Editions of Aeschylus' tragedies in the Harvard College Library before 1842 included the following: Thomas Stanley (London: Jacob Flesher, 1663); Christian G. Schütz (Halae: Johannes Jacob Gebauer, 1782-1794); an 1800 reissue of Schütz, also by Gebauer; Friedrich H. Bothe (Leipzig: Weidmann, 1805); Richard Porson's 1806 two-volume edition published at Glasgow, London, and Oxford by Foulis, Payne, et al.; a revision of Stanley by Samuel Butler (Cambridge, Eng.: Cambridge University Press, 1809-1816); Bishop Charles J. Blomfield (Cambridge, Eng.: John Smith for the University Press, 1819) and another reissue of Schütz (London: G. and W. B. Whittaker, 1823). In addition, T. D. Woolsey's edition of *The Prometheus of Æschylus, with Notes, for the Use of Colleges in the United States* (Boston: James Munroe, 1837) was also in the Harvard Library, and was part of a series favored by the faculty for classroom use. The 1806 Porson edition was preceded in 1795 by Porson's earlier revision of Stanley's seventeenth-century edition. This was the text upon which the Schaefer edition available to Thoreau was based.

[12] Aeschylus, *Septem Quae Supersunt Tragoedias,* ed. Denys Page (Oxford: Clarendon Press, 1972).

reveals that in the *Dial* version of the play he follows Schaefer's textual readings almost without exception. These include incidental features, such as punctuation, capitalization, spelling of proper names, and forms of notation for metrically deficient lines and lacunae. They also include such substantive aspects of the Greek as the ascription of speeches, the order and metrical division of individual lines, and variant readings of the text. A comparison of the way these features are treated in the other editions of Aeschylus available to Thoreau with the way they are treated in Schaefer's edition demonstrates that the latter is the most likely basis for Thoreau's translation.[13]

### "Anacreon"

Although this translation is entitled "Anacreon" in the *Dial,* two running heads are used there: "Anacreon" for the prose introductory material and "Anacreontics" for the poems themselves. No drafts of the introductory prose survive, but

[13] Schaefer is also the source for Thoreau's translation of *The Seven Against Thebes,* although in this case he may have used an 1817 printing (see p. 170). The editor has compared both *The Prometheus Bound* and *The Seven Against Thebes* with both printings and found no differences. The principal instance of Thoreau's translation diverging from both the 1817 and the 1819 printings occurs in *The Seven Against Thebes,* and is discussed in Textual Note 102.20-21. In addition, two other categories of divergence should be noted. First, Thoreau's translation of *The Prometheus Bound* consistently marks scene division in the original by giving the list of characters that will appear in the scene that follows. This is standard practice in most of the editions of the Aeschylus that were available to Thoreau in the Harvard College Library, but is not done (except for the first scene, at 3.21) in either the 1817 or 1819 printing of the Schaefer edition. Whether Thoreau added such scene divisions in his translation on the basis of his reference to some specific edition of *The Prometheus Bound,* or whether he was following the common practice of his day, is unknown. Secondly, the number and placement of asterisks on or between lines of text as a sign of metrically deficient or textually dubious lines in the original sometimes differs slightly between Thoreau's two Aeschylean translations and the 1817 and 1819 printings of the Schaefer edition. Again, it is possible that this results from his reference to other editions.

in his *Journal* for December 1838 (*Journal 1,* pp. 62, 65), Thoreau translated three of the poems: the "Ode to the Cicada," "Return of Spring," and "Cupid Wounded." He quoted the first two in "Natural History of Massachusetts,"[14] but only the last is found in the *Dial* translation of April 1843, which includes ten other complete poems or substantial portions thereof (pp. 484-490). Two relevant stages of the text follow the *Dial* publication: the corrected *Dial,* and versions of the article incorporated into both the first and second editions of *A Week on the Concord and Merrimack Rivers* (1849, 1868).

Thoreau's intention in revising this article is important to the choice of copy-text. The definition of a literary translation in this volume excludes Thoreau's English versions of "Ode to the Cicada" and "Return of Spring" because they appear only as quotations in another work or as part of *Journal* entries. Since Thoreau included "Cupid Wounded" in his *Dial* piece, however, the 1838 *Journal* version is pre-copy-text for that poem. The uncorrected *Dial* provides the copy-text for this translation because all but one of Thoreau's alterations in the corrected *Dial* serve to fit the article into the context of *A Week.* That one alteration, in which Thoreau has changed his translation of a Greek quotation in the prose introduction, has been accepted (see Textual Note 56.14).

Because the versions in *A Week* are post-copy-text, variants between those versions and the *Dial* versions are not automatically adopted. In two cases, variants are emended into the present text, however: one of the variants corrects an error (see Textual Note 58.8) and another clarifies a change in speaker in one of the poems (see Textual Note 58.25).

All of the poems in "Anacreon" are from a group of Greek lyrics known collectively as the *Anacreontea.* Although Thoreau accepted them as the work of Anacreon himself,

---

[14] *Dial* 3 (July 1842):23, 24. See Textual Note 56.32-33 for texts.

# 166 INTRODUCTION

they are now held to be the product of his Hellenistic imi-
tators. These poems (which largely survive in manuscript
in the Palatine Anthology) were first published in a one-
volume edition in 1554 by Henricus Stephanus (Henri Es-
tienne), who provided a Latin commentary and translation.
They then went through many editions, often being published in conjunction with the work of other Greek lyric
poets. The edition Thoreau used for his *Journal* translations
of the "Ode to the Cicada," "Return of Spring," and "Cupid
Wounded" is unknown, but it may have been the 1560 edition of Stephanus that is listed in the Harvard College Library catalogue published in 1830.[15] This book is composed
of a volume of Pindar's odes and a volume of the Greek lyric
poets, bound as one. Although there is no record that Thoreau borrowed it, this edition was at least available to him in
December 1838.

For his *Dial* translation, however, Thoreau used an edition
printed in 1598 at the Commelin Press in Heidelberg which
was also composed of two volumes bound as one. As with
the 1560 edition, the first volume contains Pindar; the second, Thoreau's source, is a collection of a number of Greek
lyric poets titled *Carminum Poetarum novem, lyricæ poeseωs
principum, fragmenta*. It reprints with small changes the
text of the *Anacreontea* as found in the 1554 edition, along
with Stephanus' notes and Latin translation from that edition
and additional notes by M. Aemilius P. Fr. Portus.[16] In the

[15] *A Catalogue of the Library of Harvard University in Cambridge,
Massachusetts,* 3 vols. (Cambridge, Mass.: E. W. Metcalf, 1830), 2:646.

[16] The first volume of the 1598 edition is Pindar, *Olympia, Pythia,
Nemea, Isthmia. Græce & Latine,* [ed. and trans. Henricus Stephanus],
comm. M. Aemilius P. Fr. Portus (Heidelberg: Commelin, 1598). For
reproductions of the title pages and sample pages from each volume,
see Kenneth W. Cameron, "Thoreau's Two Books of Pindar," *Emerson
Society Quarterly* 38 (1965):96-112.

To reiterate the relationships between the editions that Thoreau used
or might have used and the first edition, Stephanus was both editor and
publisher of the *editio princeps* (Lutetiae, 1554) of the *Anacreontea*; the
Greek text is followed by his Latin notes and translation. The 1560

same April 1843 number in which "Anacreon" appeared it is listed as one of the books brought from England by Bronson Alcott and Charles Lane for the Fruitlands library.[17] On February 12, 1843, Emerson had written Thoreau from New York regarding this issue of the magazine, which Thoreau was editing for him. Among other questions about contributions, he asked whether Thoreau planned to include any Greek translations.[18] In his response, Thoreau mentions that he had brought back from Charles Lane's "the Minor Greek Poets, and will mine there for a scrap or two" (*Correspondence*, p. 88). This is almost certainly a reference to the Com-

---

collection in the Harvard College Library has a general title page listing the contents of the book as a whole (the odes of Pindar, and lyric poems by Alcaeus, Sappho, Stesichorus, Ibycus, Anacreon, Bacchylides, Simonides, and Alcman), and a separate title page for the second of the two volumes, the *Carminum Poetarum novem,* whose contents are substantially the same as those of the second volume of the 1598 Commelin edition. The text of the *Anacreontea,* which is in the second volume of the 1560 and 1598 editions, is substantially the same in both of those editions as it is in the *editio princeps.* Although Stephanus is listed as editor-publisher and the date of publication is given, neither title page of the 1560 edition gives the place of publication. According to modern Harvard Library records, it was published in Geneva; however, according to Douglas E. Gerber (*A Bibliography of Pindar, 1513-1966, Philological Monographs of the American Philological Association,* no. 28, [{Cleveland}: Case Western Reserve University Press, 1969], p. 8), it was published in Paris.

Gerber notes that Fabricius records the 1598 Commelin edition as a "mera repetitio primae Stephanianae" ("an uncorrupt reprint of the first edition of Stephanus"). Although the 1598 edition adopts the physical format of the 1560 edition, Fabricius is almost surely referring to the text, notes, and translation of the 1554 edition of the *Anacreontea.*

[17] "Catalogue of Books," *Dial* 3 (April 1843):548. The publication date for the Commelin reprint of Stephanus listed there is 1597 and not 1598. This is due to the confusing bibliographical format of the book. Printed as two volumes in one, it has two title pages, both of which give the date of publication as 1598. But two of the prefatory pieces for each volume are dated, and these show that the book was set gradually during late 1597, with additions at each stage.

[18] *The Correspondence of Henry David Thoreau,* ed. Walter Harding and Carl Bode (New York: New York University Press, 1958; Westport, Conn.: Greenwood Press, Inc., 1974), pp. 86-88.

melin edition of Pindar and the Greek lyric poets.[19] In October 1848 Bronson Alcott presented Thoreau with the Fruitlands copy of this book, which is now in the collection of the Concord Antiquarian Museum.[20] This copy not only has use marks for most of the *Anacreontea* translated in the *Dial*, but a close comparison of Thoreau's English and the Greek of this text shows it to be the source of his translation.

## The Seven Against Thebes

Thoreau's second Aeschylean translation is *The Seven Against Thebes*, which exists only in a complete rough draft at the Huntington Library (HM 13193). Several brief *Journal* quotations suggest that Thoreau was reading the play as early as the end of January 1840,[21] but there is no evidence that he began to translate the entire work until after he had done *The Prometheus Bound*. In the same February 15, 1843, letter in which he reports his borrowings from Charles Lane, he goes on to tell Emerson that "the translation of the Æschylus I should like very well to continue anon, if it should be worth the while" (*Correspondence,* p. 88). There is no external evidence that this refers to *The Seven Against Thebes*. However, the surviving manuscript of the play was written a few months later, in the summer of 1843, when Thoreau was living on Staten Island with the William Emersons.[22]

[19] Although Thoreau may be referring to another anthology listed in Lane's "Catalogue," "Wintertoni Poetæ Minores Graeci. Graece et Latine. Cantabrigiæ. 1677" (p. 548), no *Anacreontea* appear in this collection.

[20] The Fruitlands copy is inscribed: "Henry D. Thoreau / from his friend / A. Bronson Alcott / Concord, October, 1848."

[21] Thoreau twice quotes brief descriptions of shields held by the champions involved in the fighting in *The Seven Against Thebes,* first in an entry of January 29, 1840 (*Journal 1,* p. 106) and again in a passage dating from July and August 1840 (*Journal 1,* p. 165). See footnote 11 for possible sources of these earlier translations.

[22] For a physical description of HM 13193, see the headnote on p. 245. The leaves of this manuscript are numbered consecutively in pencil from "1" to "39"; text other than that of this draft of *The Seven Against Thebes* is all in pencil:

"2-4"    Surveys or plans for a garden.
"13a"    Draft of letter to Lidian Emerson (recipient's copy dated May 22, 1843).

Its date is established by the drafts of two letters over which he wrote his translation of the play. The first is a fragment of a long letter to Lidian Emerson that Thoreau recycled a quarter of the way through his translation. The recipient's copy is dated May 22, 1843. The second is a rough draft of a letter to the New York editor, J. L. O'Sullivan, on the manuscript leaf paged "24." Responding on August 1 to O'Sullivan's letter of July 28 (*Correspondence,* p. 130), Thoreau offered the *Democratic Review* "a translation—(in the manner of Prometheus Bound in the Dial which you may have seen)." It is not known whether Thoreau completed and sent this letter. However, on August 6 he wrote his mother that he had been translating Greek poetry (*Correspondence,* p. 132), and the next day he wrote Emerson announcing that he had "made a very rude translation of The Seven Against Thebes—" (Berg Collection, New York Public Library; cf. *Correspondence,* p. 133). This "very rude" version may be HM 13193.[23]

O'Sullivan did not publish *The Seven Against Thebes* and nothing more is known of Thoreau's attempts to publish it. On September 14, 1843, Thoreau wrote Emerson complaining about his lack of success in the New York publishing world—including O'Sullivan's paper. He then notes that he

---

"14"   Surveying notes.
"24"   Draft of letter to J. L. O'Sullivan (August 1, 1843).

[23] The dated material in HM 13193 provides a *terminus a quo,* but it is impossible to put a close limit on the completion of the work. Whether Thoreau would have described this translation as "very rude" is also difficult to know; his other translations provide the only standards for comparison, and Thoreau does not characterize them. Physical features—primarily the amount and kind of revision—and the literal, gnomic nature of the translation both indicate that the surviving manuscript of *The Seven Against Thebes* is a rough draft, but it is not as rough as the manuscript version of the odes of Pindar, HM 13204 (see the third illustration, following p. 151), which is written in pencil and sprinkled with Greek words and phrases. HM 13193 does not have the characteristics of a first draft—the omission of five lines after 104.11 and of a word after 107.32-33 (see Textual Notes 104.11 and 107.32-33) may be copying errors—and so could be a version that followed the "very rude translation."

has "not prepared any translations for the Dial, supposing there would be no room—though it is the only place for them" (Department of Special Collections, Mugar Memorial Library, Boston University; cf. *Correspondence*, p. 139), perhaps confirming the frustration of his efforts to have them brought out in the *Democratic Review*.

Thoreau's source for this translation, as for *The Prometheus Bound*, is Aeschylus' *Tragœdiae: Ad exemplar accurate expressae, Editio stereotypa* edited by Schaefer and published at Leipzig by Tauchnitz. Thoreau may have brought Emerson's copy of the 1819 printing, which he used in translating *The Prometheus Bound*, with him to Staten Island. The Mercantile Society Library in Manhattan seems to have had a copy of the 1817 printing, but there is no evidence that Thoreau used this library until late August.[24]

## "Pindar," "Fragments of Pindar," and "Pindaric Odes From HM 13204"

"Pindar" and "Fragments of Pindar" can be traced directly to Emerson's enthusiasm for Thoreau's abilities as a translator. He wrote to Thoreau on July 20, 1843, that Charles Newcomb of Brook Farm had:

expressed his great gratification in your translations & said that he had been minded to write you & ask of you to translate in like manner—Pindar. I advised him by all means to do so. But he seemed to think he had discharged his conscience. But it was a very good request. It would be a fine thing to be done since Pindar has no adequate translation no English equal to his fame. Do look at the

[24] On August 29, Thoreau wrote his mother that "The Mercantile Library—ie its librarian—presented me with a stranger's ticket for a month—" (Pierpont Morgan Library; cf. *Correspondence*, pp. 135-136). As noted in footnote 10, the 1819 Aeschylus published by Tauchnitz is identified by Wartelle as a reprint of G. H. Schaefer's 1812 Tauchnitz edition. Although Wartelle (pp. 44-45) lists no new printing by Tauchnitz in 1817, Yale University Library owns an 1817 edition (Lipsiae: Sumtibus et Typis Caroli Tauchnitzii) and the *Catalogue of the Mercantile Library in New York* (New York: Edward O. Jenkins, 1844) includes an entry under "Æschylus" for "Tragœdiæ [Græcè.] 12°. Lipsiæ. 1817."

book with that in your mind, while Charles is mending his pen. (Rare Book and Manuscript Library, Columbia University; cf. *Correspondence,* pp. 126-127)

In the same August 7 letter to Emerson in which he mentioned his completion of *The Seven Against Thebes,* Thoreau replied to this suggestion, noting that "Pindar too I have looked at, and wish he was better worth translating." "However," he added later in the letter, "I have not done with Pindar yet" (*Correspondence,* p. 133). Indeed he had not, for a draft of nearly 500 lines of Pindar's poetry survives in manuscript at the Huntington Library (HM 13204). This draft dates from some time between early August and late fall 1843. Nevertheless, Emerson still had not received a final version of the translation on October 25 (*Correspondence,* p. 149), and a *Journal* entry of November 9, in which Thoreau commented on the importance Pindar attaches to fame (*Journal 1,* p. 487), suggests that the work was still on his mind. In the January 1844 *Dial* (pp. 374-390), a selection of Pindar's odes finally appeared. This was followed in the April number (pp. 513-514) by "Fragments of Pindar." According to a headnote by the editor, these had inadvertently been omitted from the January issue.

The Huntington manuscript, which has all the characteristics of an early draft,[25] does not represent Thoreau's final choice of material for the *Dial.* In many cases the manuscript and the *Dial* contain different lines from the same ode, and even when the same lines appear in both, the translations often differ in wording and in the order of words and lines. About half of the material in "Pindar" and all of the selections in "Fragments of Pindar" appear in draft in HM 13204,[26]

---

[25] It contains pencilled, often cancelled and fragmentary translations of a different selection of Pindar's poetry than later appeared in the *Dial.* In addition, words from the Greek text are frequently interlined along with one or more English equivalents, suggesting that these are rough, working notes rather than anything approaching a finished translation. For a physical description of the manuscript, see the headnote on p. 261.

[26] See the headnotes on pp. 261 and 265.

along with unpublished lines from odes that are represented in the *Dial* and selections from four odes that are not represented.

Copy-text for "Pindar" and "Fragments of Pindar" is Thoreau's corrected *Dial*; though Thoreau later included excerpts from these two pieces as quotations in *A Week*, his revisions of "Pindar" in the corrected *Dial* do not serve to prepare it for this use (as do his revisions of "Anacreon," for which uncorrected *Dial* is copy-text). Because they are quotations, the versions in *A Week* are post-copy-text. There are no substantive variants between the *Dial* and *A Week* versions of the excerpt from "Fragments of Pindar." There are, however, two substantive variants between the *Dial* and *A Week* versions in the portions of "Pindar" that appear in *A Week*. These are accepted as revisions reflecting Thoreau's final intention for the translation itself. All other variants between · the two versions of "Pindar" occur in punctuation and capitalization and serve to incorporate the excerpts into *A Week* as a quotation.

As noted, the *Dial* articles contain at least some portion of all but four of the odes represented in Thoreau's manuscript draft.[27] These four odes are included in this edition as "Pindaric Odes From HM 13204" because they are translations of separate Pindaric poems not found elsewhere. None of the other manuscript material is included, however, because the *Dial* selections represent Thoreau's final decisions as to the manner and extent of his translation of these odes. To print the passages translated in HM 13204 in preference to those in the *Dial,* or to conflate the two, would violate Thoreau's final choice of what portions of these other poems he wished to present to the public.

On the first page of his rough-draft manuscript, Thoreau notes that the source for his Pindaric translations is Friedrich

[27] A fifth ode not included in either *Dial* article is cancelled in HM 13204; for the text of it, see p. 267.

Thiersch's two-volume edition with notes and facing-page German translation (Leipzig: Gerhard Fleischer, 1820).[28]

## "The Transmigrations of the Seven Brahmans"

Thoreau translated "The Transmigrations of the Seven Brahmans" at least six years after he made the other translations in this volume. Only one manuscript version survives (bMS Am 278.5.12 [1] at the Houghton Library). It is a fair copy in ink, later revised in pencil.[29] Thoreau's source for this piece is S. A. Langlois' two-volume French translation of the *Harivansa* (Paris and London: Oriental Translation Fund, 1834-1835), part of an ancient Indian epic, the Mahābhārata. The story Thoreau translates appears in the twenty-first through twenty-fourth lectures of the *Harivansa* (the two volumes contain 261 lectures altogether). He omits the title of each lecture and material at the beginning of lecture 21, early in 23, and at the end of 24. The omitted passages, as well as several omitted footnotes, link these lectures to the story told in the *Harivansa*. Thoreau also adds several explanatory notes of his own that summarize information given in earlier lectures (see Textual Note 135.32). He borrowed a copy of Langlois' translation from the Harvard College Library on September 11, 1849.[30] There is no firm evidence for dating, and Thoreau could have translated the piece any time thereafter.[31] However, the record of his bor-

---

[28] Ethel Seybold, *Thoreau: The Quest and the Classics* (New Haven: Yale University Press, 1951), p. 97, incorrectly identifies the edition of Pindar Thoreau used as the 1598 Commelin Press edition, cited in full in footnote 16.

[29] For a physical description of bMS Am 278.5.12 (1), see the headnote on p. 269.

[30] See Kenneth W. Cameron, *Emerson the Essayist: An Outline of His Philosophical Development Through 1836 with Special Emphasis on the Sources and Interpretation of "Nature,"* 2 vols. (Raleigh, N.C.: Thistle Press, 1945), 2:195.

[31] Sometime during this period, perhaps soon after borrowing the *Harivansa*, Thoreau copied other extracts from it—none of which appears in "The Transmigrations of the Seven Brahmans"—in a commonplace

rowings from the Harvard College Library suggests that during the fall and winter of 1849 and the spring of 1850 he
was especially interested in Oriental religion and literature,
and passages in his *Journal* indicate that the interest extended into early summer 1851.[32]

## Appendix

The Appendix contains two compositions by Thoreau, one
in Greek and one in Latin, dating from his undergraduate
days.[33] The first, Διαλογος, was delivered by Thoreau and
his Harvard classmate, Manlius Stimson Clarke, as a Junior
Exhibition on Monday, July 13, 1835. It survives in Thoreau's hand,[34] bound in *Exhibition and Commencement Performances, 1834-35,* in the Harvard University Archives (HUC

book now in the Berg Collection of the New York Public Library (pp.
"151" to "161").

[32] Cameron, *Emerson the Essayist*, 2:195. In a *Journal* passage dated
May 6, 1851, Thoreau used some of the extracts he had copied in his
commonplace book; on June 26, 1851, he wrote, "It is unavoidable, the
idea of transmigration; not merely a fancy of the poets, but an instinct
of the race" (*The Writings of Henry David Thoreau*, 20 vols., ed. Bradford
Torrey and Francis Allen [Boston: Houghton, Mifflin & Co., 1906], 8:190-
191, 271).

[33] Thoreau's course work at Harvard included eight terms of Latin and
eight of Greek. Composition in those languages is described as part of
the classics curriculum in the reports of the Latin and Greek Depart-
ments to the Overseers of the College. See Kenneth W. Cameron, *Thoreau's Harvard Years: Materials Introductory to New Explorations, Record of Fact and Background* (Hartford, Conn.: Transcendental Books,
1966), Part I, 3-11.

[34] While Διαλογος is not signed, a comparison of the Greek hand in
which it was written with later examples of Greek in Thoreau's *Journal*
demonstrates that he inscribed the manuscript. Moreover, a comparison
of Thoreau's signature on this document with examples of his formal
hand in 1836 confirms that he is the writer. Clarke's part in the composition of Διαλογος is not known.

For a brief description of the origins of the system of public exhibitions
at Harvard, see Samuel Eliot Morison, *Three Centuries of Harvard:
1636-1936* (Cambridge, Mass.: Harvard University Press, 1936), pp. 89-
90. In *Thoreau's Harvard Years*, Part I, 15, Cameron summarizes the
College Records on the Exhibition of July 13. Thoreau and Clarke each
received $25.

6834.37). The second, "The Cliffs—a Cenotaph," is an epitaph honoring the Indian chief Tahattawan, who had lived near Concord. It appears in the "Index Rerum," a notebook at the Huntington Library (HM 945, folio 39).[35] It is dated at the bottom simply "A.D. 1836." The closest preceding dated entry was written on April 14, 1836, and the entry on the next folio page, made in Cambridge, is dated January 15, 1837. Kenneth W. Cameron has suggested a date "*circa* December 21, 1836—that is, during a Christmas vacation from college."[36]

### STYLE AND INTELLECTUAL BACKGROUND

The texts·in this volume span the early part of Thoreau's career, from his undergraduate days to a year or two past the publication of *A Week on the Concord and Merrimack Rivers* in 1849. This decade and a half was one of rapid intellectual change for Thoreau, during which he struggled to find literary forms and styles appropriate to his emerging romantic sensibility.[37] Indeed, Thoreau was as much a literary experimenter as anything else during the 1830s and 1840s. At one time or another he tried his hand at translation,

[35] For physical descriptions of both of these manuscripts, see the headnote on p. 277.

[36] Kenneth W. Cameron, "Thoreau's Early Compositions in the Ancient Languages," *Emerson Society Quarterly* 8 (1957):20.

[37] Daniel Walker Howe, *The Unitarian Conscience, Harvard Moral Philosophy, 1805-1861* (Cambridge, Mass.: Harvard University Press, 1970); William R. Hutchison, *The Transcendentalist Ministers: Church Reform in the New England Renaissance* (New Haven: Yale University Press, 1959); and Lawrence Buell, *Literary Transcendentalism: Style and Vision in the American Renaissance* (Ithaca, N.Y.: Cornell University Press, 1973), pp. 1-139, provide the best accounts of the intellectual world of Boston Unitarianism and the rise of Transcendentalism from it. See Sherman Paul, *The Shores of America: Thoreau's Inward Exploration* (Urbana: University of Illinois Press, 1958), especially pp. 1-89 on Thoreau's intellectual development during the 1830s. William Howarth, *The Book of Concord: Thoreau's Life as a Writer* (New York: Viking, 1982), describes Thoreau as a literary stylist and writer at work, especially in his *Journal*.

the "ethnical scripture," the literary excursion, poetry of several idiosyncratic sorts, and transcendental biography.[38] The patchwork quality of *A Week,* which collects many of his earlier writings, suggests the variety as well as the mixed success of this experimentation.[39] It would be wrong to conclude from this, however, that Thoreau's translations are just experiments, divorced from his broader interests and achievements. They are "literary exercises"[40] in a serious sense, and represent some of his earliest attempts to explore issues that would engage him in his later, more mature writings. These were his fascination with primitive religion and mythology, and his connected interest in the nature and origins of language. In his translating, as later in *Walden* and *The Maine Woods,* Thoreau pursued these concerns as a means of defining the task confronting the American poet.

One clear source of Thoreau's interest in translation was his lifelong reading about primitive religion and literature. Perhaps more than any other American romantic writer, he accepted a primitivist rather than a cyclical or progressive view of human history.[41] For him, therefore, the earliest

[38] Both the "ethnical scripture" in nineteenth-century America and Thoreau's contribution to the genre are discussed by Roger Chester Mueller, "The Orient in American Transcendental Periodicals (1835-1886)" (Ph.D. diss., University of Minnesota, 1968). Buell, pp. 188-207, gives an exceptionally lucid account of Thoreau and the literary excursion, while Elizabeth Hall Witherell, "The Poetry of Henry David Thoreau: A Selected Critical Edition" (Ph.D. diss., University of Wisconsin, 1979), is the fullest discussion of Thoreau the poet. There is no adequate treatment as yet of Thoreau's Transcendental biographies of Raleigh and Carlyle.

[39] The relationship of *A Week* to the rest of Thoreau's writings is discussed by Buell, pp. 208-238, and Paul, pp. 191-233. For the history of the text of the book, see *A Week,* pp. 433-543.

[40] Walter Harding and Michael Meyer in *The New Thoreau Handbook* (New York: New York University Press, 1980), p. 35, so describe Thoreau's *Prometheus Bound,* but in a pejorative sense.

[41] The best summary of concepts of history in international romanticism remains M. H. Abrams, *Natural Supernaturalism: Tradition and Revolution in Romantic Literature* (New York: W. W. Norton & Company, 1971).

poets were primitive bards whose mythology represented a higher vision of the truth than that provided by the poets and philosophers of later ages. As he wrote of Homer in the January 1844 *Dial* in which his "Pindar" also appeared:

There are few books which are fit to be remembered in our wisest hours, but the Iliad is brightest in the serenest days, and imbodies still all the sunlight that fell on Asia Minor. No modern joy or ecstasy of ours can lower its height or dim its lustre; but there it lies in the east of literature, as it were the earliest, latest production of the mind. . . . The mythological system of the ancients, and it is still the only mythology of the moderns, the poem of mankind, interwoven so wonderfully with their astronomy, and matching in grandeur and harmony with the architecture of the Heavens themselves, seems to point to a time when a mightier genius inhabited the earth. But man is the great poet, and not Homer nor Shakspeare; and our language itself, and the common arts of life are his work. Poetry is so universally true and independent of experience, that it does not need any particular biography to illustrate it, but we refer it sooner or later to some Orpheus or Linus, and after ages to the genius of humanity, and the gods themselves.[42]

Thoreau saw the simplicity and unalloyed truthfulness of a Homer as a point of contact with the primitive world and its prelapsarian purity of vision. The ancient bard was a seer into the nature of things whose soul assumed literally sublime proportions:

Ossian reminds us of the most refined and rudest eras, of Homer, Pindar, Isaiah, and the American Indian. In his poetry, as in Ho-

[42] "Homer. Ossian. Chaucer." in *Early Essays and Miscellanies,* ed. Joseph J. Moldenhauer and Edwin Moser, with Alexander C. Kern (Princeton: Princeton University Press, 1975), pp. 156-157. This passage suggests that Thoreau may have in mind the so-called "Homeric Question"—the controversy over whether the *Iliad* and the *Odyssey* were written by a single poet, or instead represent a collection of folk poetry. This controversy was one of the major issues in late eighteenth- and early nineteenth-century classical scholarship, and is reflected in the sources on Greek antiquity Thoreau read at Harvard. For a summary of the history of the "Homeric Question," see J. A. Davison, "The Homeric Question," in *A Companion to Homer,* ed. Alan J. B. Wace and Frank H. Stubbings (London: Macmillan & Co., Ltd., 1962), pp. 234-265.

mer's, only the simplest and most enduring features of humanity
are seen, such essential parts of a man as Stonehenge exhibits of
a temple; we see the circles of stone, and the upright shaft alone.
The phenomena of life acquire almost an unreal and gigantic size
seen through his mists. Like all older and grander poetry, it is
distinguished by the few elements in the lives of its heroes. They
stand on the heath, between the stars and the earth, shrunk to the
bones and sinews. The earth is a boundless plain for their deeds.
They lead such a simple, dry, and everlasting life, as hardly needs
depart with the flesh, but is transmitted entire from age to age.
There are but few objects to distract their sight, and their life is as
unincumbered as the course of the stars they gaze at.[43]

As both these passages imply, Thoreau's interest in ancient poetry and mythology had roots in something other
than mere antiquarianism. It was instead part of the broader
Transcendentalist impulse to assert the importance of poetry
in the *modern* world. For like Emerson in "The Poet," Thoreau held that a true bard is representative of man in all his
capacities: a namer, doer, and sayer whose poetic "myths"
have a special capacity for embodying the truth. Like Emerson he also found that modern literature had largely neglected its duties and become artificial and derivative; as a
result one had to go further back in history to find poets who
had this representative quality. The poetry of antiquity was
chiefly valuable, therefore, not for its own sake, but because
it provided inspiration for the possibility of poetry at the
present time. Indeed, throughout his life Thoreau "tried to
recover for himself the original conditions in which the early
creators of the great myths found themselves. Of almost
equal importance was Thoreau's perception that the 'original
conditions' surrounding the creation of myth were not so
much social, cultural, or historical as they were personal or
individual. The myth-making poet was neither helped nor
hindered by the times in which he lived; he had only to place
himself in a simple and original relation to nature. 'Wood,
water, earth, air are [now] essentially what they were; only

[43] "Homer. Ossian. Chaucer." in *Early Essays*, p. 158.

society has degenerated. This lament for a golden age is only a lament for golden men,' Thoreau wrote in his journal. If conditions were right for the individual—whatever the condition of society—then myth would arise naturally from nature to be expressed by the poet."[44]

As this suggests, the Greeks were the most famous but by no means the only people who possessed myth-making poets. Like the other Transcendentalists, Thoreau also found the voice of the true bard in American Indian poetry, the ancient Scandinavian sagas, and the Hindu and Chinese books of wisdom.[45] Each of these "primitive" cultures might inspire the modern poet to assume a representative stature for his own age. The Hindu scriptures were especially important in this regard because they comprised the oldest literature yet found. They were, as such, literally a divine revelation for Thoreau; as he says in *A Week,* "The reading which I love best is the scriptures of the several nations, though it happens that I am better acquainted with those of the Hindoos, the Chinese, and the Persians, than of the Hebrews, which I have come to last. Give me one of these Bibles, and you have silenced me for a while" (*A Week,* pp. 71-72). Similarly, a little later in *A Week* Thoreau strikes the same note in order to characterize Sir William Jones's edition of *The Laws of Menu:*

It seems to have been uttered from some eastern summit, with a sober morning prescience in the dawn of time, and you cannot read

[44] Robert D. Richardson, Jr., *Myth and Literature in the American Renaissance* (Bloomington: Indiana University Press, 1978), pp. 90-91.

[45] The best general guide to Transcendentalist views of primitive culture is Richardson, although he exaggerates the relative importance of Greek as opposed to other ancient mythologies. For Thoreau and the Indians, see Robert F. Sayre, *Thoreau and the American Indians* (Princeton: Princeton University Press, 1977); for a full list of Thoreau's Indian Notebooks, see William L. Howarth, *The Literary Manuscripts of Henry David Thoreau* ([Columbus]: Ohio State University Press, 1974), pp. 294-301; and for Thoreau's interest in the Orient, Arthur Christy, *The Orient in American Transcendentalism: A Study of Emerson, Thoreau, and Alcott* (New York: Columbia University Press, 1932), pp. 185-233.

a sentence without being elevated as upon the table-land of the Ghauts. It has such a rhythm as the winds of the desert, such a tide as the Ganges, and is as superior to criticism as the Himmaleh mountains. Its tone is of such unrelaxed fibre, that even at this late day, unworn by time, it wears the English and the Sanscrit dress indifferently, and its fixed sentences keep up their distant fires still like the stars, by whose dissipated rays this lower world is illumined. (*A Week*, p. 149)

As in his comments on Greek poetry, Thoreau suggests here that even so pure and ancient a revelation as that of the Hindus is not primarily valuable for its own sake. Rather, it must inspire men to find their own revelation today: "Every sacred book, successively, has been accepted in the faith that it was to be the final resting-place of the sojourning soul; but after all, it was but a caravansary which supplied refreshment to the traveller, and directed him farther on his way to Isphahan or Bagdat. Thank God, no Hindoo tyranny prevailed at the framing of the world, but we are freemen of the universe, and not sentenced to any cast" (*A Week*, p. 148). It is through emulating the creators of the ancient "scriptures," in other words, that the poet himself becomes a representative man and creates a mythology of his own— in Thoreau's case, a specifically American mythology—by which his generation might discover its true self once more. Indeed, it was his concern for his own time and place that prompted Thoreau to ally America's disappearing primitives with the other peoples at the dawn of time. As Robert Sayre says of *A Week:*

In "Sunday" Thoreau combines his classical and savage perspectives on early America. "It was a quiet Sunday morning, with more of the auroral rosy and white than of the yellow light in it, as if it dated from earlier than the fall of man, and still preserved a hea-thenish integrity." The dawn is Homeric rather than Christian. But mixed with the rosy-fingered dawn is the "white," which warns us of the coming white man, "pale as the dawn," while the "heathenish integrity" refers to both the Indians and the pagan Greeks and Romans. . . . And so the day describes the conflict between, on the one hand, the savage ages of Homer, epic poets, and American Indians, who were all hunters, warriors, and representatives of natural religion, and, on the other, the modern ages of Christianity, farmers, and a civilized poetry.[46]

Thoreau's decision to become a translator was part of this continuing search for the "heathenish integrity" of the primitive bard. His earliest introduction to contemporary scholarship on "primitive" literatures took place in connection with his training in the Classics—the same context out of which his Greek translations arose. Well versed in Latin and with a good start in Greek even before he entered Harvard in 1833, Thoreau continued to study these languages during his time in Cambridge.[47] Ethel Seybold's summary of his classical studies in college suggests his range of reading as an undergraduate:

Thoreau went through the regular classical course at Harvard—two years of Latin and three years of Greek grammar; two years of the study of Greek and Roman antiquities; the reading in Greek of the crown orations of Aeschines and Demosthenes, Xenophon's *Anabasis,* Sophocles' three Theban plays, and Euripides' *Alcestis,* and in Latin of Horace's *Odes, Satires,* and *Epistles,* selections from Livy, the *Medea* of Seneca, Cicero's *De claris oratoribus* and *De*

[46] Sayre, pp. 31-32.

[47] For Thoreau's study of the ancient languages in preparation for college, see Kenneth W. Cameron, *Young Thoreau and the Classics: A Review* (Hartford, Conn.: Transcendental Books, 1975). His undergraduate classical studies are detailed in Seybold, *Thoreau: The Quest and the Classics,* especially pp. 23-26, and Anthony John Harding, "Thoreau and the Adequacy of Homer," *Studies in Romanticism* 20 (1981):317-332. For a more general discussion of his education, see Christian P. Gruber, "The Education of Henry Thoreau, Harvard 1833-1837" (Ph.D. diss., Princeton University, 1953), especially pp. 117-148. Class lists, reading lists, etc., from Thoreau's undergraduate years are reproduced by Cameron in *Emerson the Essayist,* 2:191-208, and *The Transcendentalists and Minerva: Cultural Backgrounds of the American Renaissance with Fresh Discoveries in the Intellectual Climate of Emerson, Alcott and Thoreau,* 3 vols. (Hartford, Conn.: Transcendental Books, 1958), 2:359-360, 425-432. As these suggest, his training in practical translation and in original composition in foreign languages was thorough.

*officiis,* and Juvenal's properly expurgated *Satires*—without showing any special interest until he reached his junior year and Homer. Then we find him supplementing Felton's *Iliad,* which was used at Harvard, with the scholarly Heyne edition, reading Hobbes's seventeenth-century English translation of the *Iliad* and the *Odyssey,* and expressing his enthusiasm over Homer to a friend.[48]

To be educated in the Classics at early nineteenth-century Harvard meant more than language training, composition in the original, and reading in the standard authors, however. It was also an education in a distinctly romantic view of the world of classical antiquity. During the years before the Civil War, Cambridge was the center of a series of changes in American classical studies, largely due to the presence on its faculty of the German-educated Edward Everett and George Ticknor, as well as Thoreau's own Greek teacher, C. C. Felton. One of the most important of these changes was a new emphasis on Greek (as opposed to Latin) literature, and its interpretation in the light of contemporary European classical scholarship. Much of this scholarship was openly primitivist in orientation and partook of the Hellenism so widespread in the late eighteenth and early nineteenth centuries.[49] For example, one of the secondary works assigned to students of Thoreau's generation was Henry Nelson Coleridge's *Introductions to the Study of the Greek Classic Poets,* a book which not only strongly influenced Thoreau's own view of Homer,[50] but also reinforced the attitude toward the Greeks

[48] Seybold, pp. 23-24.

[49] Two good surveys of the Classics in nineteenth-century America are Daniel Walker Howe, "Classical Education and Political Culture in Nineteenth-Century America," *Newsletter: Intellectual History Group* 5 (1983):9-14, and Meyer Reinhold, *Classica Americana: The Greek and Roman Heritage in the United States* (Detroit, Mich.: Wayne State University Press, 1984), especially pp. 174-220. For the influence of Everett, Ticknor, and Felton, see Morison, *Three Centuries of Harvard,* pp. 224-238. For the parallel rise of Hellenism in Britain, see Richard Jenkyns, *The Victorians and Ancient Greece* (Cambridge, Mass.: Harvard University Press, 1980), and Frank M. Turner, *The Greek Heritage in Victorian Britain* (New Haven: Yale University Press, 1981).

[50] Anthony John Harding, and Seybold, pp. 24, 96, both discuss the

then prevalent at Harvard. Coleridge held that the poet of the Homeric age "was preeminently . . . a teacher" who "possessed all the knowledge of men and things which was then attainable," and whose "vocation consisted in pleasing and instructing all classes of society, and the natives of various islands or provinces through which he wandered."[51] His medium was not "Latin—the voice of empire and of war, of law and of the state," but "Greek—the shrine of the genius of the old world; as universal as our race, as individual as ourselves; of infinite flexibility, of indefatigable strength, with the complication and the distinctness of nature herself; to which nothing was vulgar, from which nothing was excluded; . . . at once the variety and picturesqueness of Homer, the gloom and the intensity of Æschylus; not compressed to the closest by Thucydides, not fathomed to the bottom by Plato, not sounding with all its thunders, nor lit up with all its ardors even under the Promethean touch of Demosthenes!"[52] The ancient Greek poet exploited his uniquely malleable language by telling the stories of his national mythology, a collection of religious wisdom that Coleridge defended as "the secular Bible of mankind."[53] Moreover, the Greek myths had this almost scriptural status because they fulfilled a definition of the function of poetry akin to that of the American Transcendentalists:

---

importance of Coleridge's book in Thoreau's intellectual growth. He borrowed the book from the Harvard College Library on September 15, 1836; see Cameron, *Emerson the Essayist,* 2:193. Richardson, pp. 90-137, discusses Thoreau's reading in mythological treatises and the importance of individual mythological systems in his writing.

[51] Henry Nelson Coleridge, *Introductions to the Study of the Greek Classic Poets. Designed Principally for the Use of Young Persons at School and College. Part I* (London: John Murray, 1830), p. 109.

[52] H. N. Coleridge, p. 34.

[53] H. N. Coleridge, p. 70. See Richardson, pp. 9-33, on the contemporary controversy over the truth of pagan mythology. See Anthony John Harding, p. 322, on Thoreau's rejection of the doctrine of national mythology in favor of an approach to primitive tales more in keeping with the Emersonian doctrine of the poet.

Poetry is the convergence, nay, the identity, of all other species of knowledge; it creates the Individual to stand as the symbol of the Universal, the Finite for the Infinite; it has to do not with men, but man; it is addressed to the great republican heart of the civilized world, and must therefore speak in the all-pervading language of essential human nature. No poet can be a great poet, but as being inclusively a naturalist and a historian in the light as well as the life of genuine philosophy. All other men's worlds are the Poet's chaos. His Imagination must be all compact; that is, all his powers of every sort must be concentered into one, before his pen will be able to give to the airy forms of things unknown

"A local habitation and a name."

His is that most wondrous and alchemic power which extracts and purifies and compounds the material drugs supplied by learning and research, and waves over them the wand of its enchantment, till, in the crisis of mental projection, they glance out embodied and transfigured into eternal images of Light.[54]

Thoreau read and did a report on Coleridge's book during his senior year, and it served as one of his earliest introductions to the idealism of its author's more famous uncle, Samuel Taylor. (Thoreau's college theme opens, in fact, with a long quotation from the book on the distinction between the Fancy and the Imagination that paraphrases the *Biographia Literaria* itself.[55]) The younger Coleridge's work is also typical of the other books on primitive Greek mythology and poetry Thoreau read during his last year in Cambridge. Even the text of the *Iliad* he used expressed similar, if more reserved sentiments.[56] This edition, by C. C. Felton, described the Homeric age as one in which, "though raised consid-

[54] H. N. Coleridge, pp. 111-112.

[55] "Introductions to The Study of the Greek Classic Poets. By Henry Nelson Coleridge . . . Part I" in *Early Essays,* pp. 50-51.

[56] C. C. Felton, ed., ʹΟΜΗΡΟΥ ʹΙΛΙΑΣ. *The Iliad of Homer, From the Text of Wolf. With English Notes and Flaxman's Illustrative Designs* (Boston: Hilliard, Gray, 1833). This book was required reading at Harvard; for Thoreau's ownership of it, see Walter Harding, "A New Checklist of the Books in Henry David Thoreau's Library," in *Studies in the American Renaissance: 1983,* ed. Joel Myerson (Charlottesville: University Press of Virginia, 1983), p. 167.

erably above barbarism, the marks of primitive simplicity
were still discernible."[57] Although not quite as much a primitivist as Coleridge, Felton also declared that the Greek language's power as a medium for poetry lay in its primitive
simplicity: "There is a certain point in the progress of every
people, when their language is most fitted for poetical composition. It is when they have risen above the state of barbarism to a condition of refinement, yet uncorrupted by luxury, and before the intellectual powers have been given much
to speculative philosophy. Then the rudeness of language is
worn away, but the words are still used in their primitive
meanings." For Felton "such was the condition of our own
noble language in the time of Elizabeth" and "such was the
condition of the Greek language in the age of Homer." The
Homeric dialect was a natural, full language that "had attained a descriptive force, a copiousness, and harmony, which
made it a fit instrument to express the immortal conceptions
of poetry. Its resources were inexhaustible. For every mood
of mind, every affection of the heart, every aspect of nature,
it had an appropriate expression, and the most delicate im-
agery. Its words and sentences are pictures; in such living
forms do they bring the thing described before the reader's
eye. The metrical harmony of the Iliad has never been equalled.
The verse flows along freely and majestically, more like the
great courses of Nature, than any invention of man."[58]

Similarly, Friedrich von Schlegel's *Lectures on the History of Literature,* which Thoreau borrowed at about the
same time as the Coleridge book,[59] defends Greek mythology
as the basis for poetry, and praises the primitive simplicity
of the earliest Greeks and their language. Schlegel declares
that "in all countries it has been the fate and progress of

[57] Felton, p. vii.

[58] Felton, pp. viii-ix.

[59] Thoreau borrowed the first volume of Schlegel on September 5,
1836, and the second volume on October 3 of that year; see Cameron,
*Emerson the Essayist,* 2:193.

poetry to begin with the wonderful and the sublime, with
the mysterious majesty of the gods, and the elevated character of the heroic times,—and ever afterwards to descend
lower and lower from this lofty flight—to approach nearer
and nearer to the earth—till at last it sinks—never to rise
again—into the common life and citizenship of ordinary
men."[60] The Homeric poems had this prelapsarian quality
because they dealt with "the mysterious majesty of the gods,
and the elevated character of the heroic times."[61] Like Coleridge, Schlegel saw this as the reason why the earliest Greek
poets had a significance beyond their own culture and why
they should stand as a model for the aims of poetry in the
modern world.[62] The *Iliad* and the *Odyssey* unfold a universal pattern of heroism; subject to neither mere national
prejudice nor the artificiality of literary tradition, "there
breathes throughout" both

poems a freer spirit, a sensibility more open, more pure, and more
universal—alive to every feeling which can make an impression on
our nature, and extending to every circumstance and condition of
the great family of man. A whole world is laid open to our view in
the utmost beauty and clearness, a rich, a living, and an evermoving
picture. The two heroic personages of Achilles and Ulysses, which
occupy the first places in this new state of existence, embody the
whole of a set of universal ideas and characters which are to be
found in almost all the traditions of heroic ages, although nowhere
else so happily unfolded or delineated with so masterly a hand.[63]

In Schlegel's view, this heroic spirit also permeates the
poetry of the authors Thoreau himself translated. The aris-

[60] Frederick Schlegel, *Lectures on the History of Literature, Ancient
and Modern*, 2 vols. (Philadelphia: Thomas Dobson and Son, 1818), 1:46.

[61] Schlegel, 1:68-77, discusses Homer as a primitive mythopoeic bard.

[62] Schlegel was in the forefront of the German romantic attempt to
revise and reapply the myths of antiquity. See Richardson, pp. 119 and
165-168, on Schlegel's impact on Thoreau and Hawthorne, who both
followed his view that literature in the modern world should reinterpret
and recast the mythology of primitive folk cultures. See also Abrams,
pp. 65-70.

[63] Schlegel, 1:33.

tocratic poetry of Pindar, for example, consists of "festival
songs [which] can scarcely be called lyric poems." Rather,
"they are heroic or epic poems composed in celebration of
particular events," describing "the graceful repose of high-
born lords, who in peaceful times, and surrounded by happy
dependents, passed a careless life in chivalric pastimes and
contests; or listened, among the society of congenial friends,
to the songs of illustrious poets, and the celebration of their
heroic ancestors."[64] Similarly, Aeschylus' plays fit into this
class of heroic poetry, for he too was concerned with the life
of gods and heroes, the mythology of the Greeks. In *The
Prometheus Bound* (as in Homer) the national religion of a
people became universal and

assumed a new, a peculiar, a characteristic appearance. He has not
been contented with the representation of individual tragical events:
Throughout all his works there prevails an universal and perpetual
recurrence to a whole world of tragedy. The subjection of the old
gods and Titans—and the history of that lofty race being subdued
and enslaved by a meaner and less worthy generation—these are
the great points to which almost all his narrations and all his ca-
tastrophes may be referred. The original dignity and greatness of
nature and of man, and the daily declension of both into weakness
and worthlessness, is another of his themes. Yet in the midst of the
ruins and fragments of a perishing world, he delights to astonish
us now and then with a view of that old gigantic strength—the spirit
of which seems to be embodied in his Prometheus—ever bold and
ever free—chained and tortured, yet invincible within.[65]

During the first few years after his graduation Thoreau
continued his reading in classical scholars like Schlegel and
Coleridge, supplementing them with such general critics of
"primitive" poetry as Herder and Madame de Staël. His *Journal* for the late 1830s bespeaks the influence of this reading,
since it is filled with entries exploring the nature of early
Greek poetry, heroism, and mythology. For the young Thoreau Greek myth continued to embody a higher, yet more

[64] Schlegel, 1:41-42.          [65] Schlegel, 1:43-44.

elementary vision of the truth, "the stuff that gods are made of," however much some might call it "a poet's fancy" (*Journal 1*, p. 33). The *Iliad* was the greatest monument of this simple and primitive culture, a poem which "like a natural sound . . . has reverberated to our days. Whatever in it is still freshest in the memories of men—was most childlike in the poet" (*Journal 1*, p. 31). This primitivist reading of early Greek literature clearly lies behind Thoreau's earliest versions of his translations. The fifty-line *Journal* fragment of *The Prometheus Bound,* for instance, begins with the following stock comment on Aeschylus:

—There was one man lived his own healthy Attic life in those days. The words that have come down to us evidence that their speaker was a seer in his day and generation. At this day they owe nothing to their dramatic form, nothing to stage machinery, and the fact that they were spoken under these or those circumstances; All display of art for the gratification of a factitious taste, is silently passed by to come at the least particle of absolute and genuine thought they contain. The reader will be disappointed, however, who looks for traits of a rare wisdom or eloquence—and will have to solace himself, for the most part, with the poet's humanity—and what it was in him to say.— He will discover that, like every genius, he was a solitary liver and worker in his day. (*Journal 1*, p. 82)

Like Coleridge and Schlegel, Thoreau here characterizes Aeschylus as a true primitive, who owes nothing to artifice or the benefits of "civilization." He is mere poetic "humanity" itself, a representative man for his primitive age who looked into the rude, unhandselled nature of things. Yet the translated excerpts from the play that follow this passage are presented not to illustrate the superiority of antiquity but as proof of the possibility of living just such an "Attic life" today. Here as elsewhere Thoreau sought not to worship the past but to put it to present use in inspecting the facts of life: "Genius must ever take an equal start, and all the generations of men are virtually at a stand-still, for it to come and consider of them." A contemporary poet must do as the

ancient bards had done, and be "a seer in his day and generation." As he goes on to say with Emersonian wit, "Let
the seer bring down his broad eye to the most stale and
trivial fact—and he will make you believe it a new planet in
the sky." The story of Prometheus is, therefore, more than
an occasion for antiquarian reverence; it must be pondered
seriously in order to test its current worth: "As to criticism,
man has never to make allowance to man—there is naught
to excuse—naught to bear in mind. All the past is here
present to be tried, let it approve itself if it can" (*Journal 1*,
p. 82).

This habitual attitude toward the Greeks and the value of
their mythology can also be seen in a *Journal* entry containing one of Thoreau's earliest translated portions of *The
Seven Against Thebes*. He once again opens with a conventional description of the Greeks as primitives endowed with
a language of special power—a passage that summarizes
Coleridge's *Greek Classic Poets* on national character: "The
Greeks, as the Southerns generally, expressed themselves
with more facility than we in distinct and lively images, and
as to the grace and completeness with which they treated
the subjects suited to their genius they must be allowed to
retain their ancient supremacy. . . . The Greeks were stern
but simple children in their literature. We have gained nothing by the few ages which we have the start of them. This
universal wondering at those old men is as if a matured
grown person should discover that the aspirations of his
youth argued a diviner life than the contented wisdom of
his manhood" (*Journal 1*, pp. 105-106).[66] Aeschylus is a
prime example of this primitive, childlike simplicity before
the truth of things, the ability of his countrymen to front a
fact poetically in all its starkness. While "the Greeks had no
transcendent geniuses like Milton and Shakespear," whose

[66] Compare this passage with Coleridge, pp. 25-28, and with Thoreau's
own paraphrase in "Greek Classic Poets," *Early Essays*, pp. 51-52.

achievement was the result of a tradition of high culture ("whose merit only posterity could fully appreciate"), nonetheless they had this seer representative of their time and place:

Aeschylus had a clear eye for the commonest things. His genius was only an enlarged common sense.

He adverts with chaste severity to all natural facts. His sublimity is Greek sincerity and simpleness—naked wonder which mythology had not helped to explain.

Tydeus' shield had for device

>          "An artificial heaven blazing with stars;
>          "A bright full moon in the midst of the shield,
>          "Eldest of stars, eye of night, is prominent. . . .

He is competent to express any of the common manly feelings. If his hero is to make a boast, it does not lack fullness—it is as boastful as could be desired—he has a flexible mouth, and can fill it readily with strong round words—so that you will say the man's speech wants nothing—he has left nothing unsaid, but he has actually wiped his lips of it.

Whatever the common eye sees at all and expresses as best it may—he sees uncommonly and describes with rare completeness— The multitudes that thronged the theatre could no doubt go along with him to the end. . . .

Aeschylus was undoubtedly alone and without sympathy in his simple reverence for the mystery of the universe. (*Journal 1*, pp. 106-107)

Here as in the *Journal* fragment from *The Prometheus Bound*, however, Aeschylus' representative quality makes him not so much the object of hero-worship as an inspiration for the poets of contemporary Europe and America. "The social condition of genius is the same in all ages" (*Journal 1*, p. 107) and despite all the disadvantages of the modern world, poetry is still possible. Even in nineteenth-century America, "a rugged and uncouth array of thought, though never so modern, may rout them [Homer and the rest] at any moment. It remains for other than Greeks to write the literature of the next century" (*Journal 1*, p. 106).

Finally, Thoreau's typical stance toward antiquity can also be seen in the *Journal* passage in which he first translated three of the *Anacreontea*. There he invoked "Truth's speaking trumpet" as "the sole oracle—the true Delphi and Dodona—which kings and courtiers would do well to consult—nor will they be balked by an ambiguous answer. . . . as often as they have gone gadding abroad to a strange Delphi—and her mad priestess—they have been benighted—and their age Dark or Leaden" (*Journal 1*, p. 63). As this suggests, the true spirit of ancient Greece can be found at any time and in any place: those eras in which truth is abandoned "are garrulous and noisy eras—which no longer yield any sound—but the Grecian, or *silent* and melodious, Era, is ever sounding in the ears of men" (*Journal 1*, p. 63). Yet here it was the unique silence or solitude of the ancient Greek poet that impressed Thoreau: "Aeschylus was undoubtedly alone and without sympathy in his simple reverence for the mystery of the universe" (*Journal 1*, p. 107). Furthermore, the sheer difficulty of recovering that Attic silence in the modern age almost overwhelmed Thoreau at this point in his career: "It were vain for me to interpret the Silence—she cannot be done into English— For six thousand years have men translated her, with what fidelity belonged to each, still is she little better than a sealed book" (*Journal 1*, p. 64). As he says at the end of this passage, all one can do for now is "go on—like those Chinese cliff swallows, feathering our nests with the froth—so they may one day be bread of life to such as dwell by the sea shore" (*Journal 1*, p. 64).

Despite these momentary misgivings, however, Thoreau did go on to translate the silence of the primitive bard into English. His finished translations in the *Dial* (like the slightly later "Transmigrations of the Seven Brahmans") also arose from his interest in ancient poetry and mythology. During the early 1840s, when he was working on the Greek translations, he continued to express sentiments in his *Journal* like those accompanying the earlier fragments of Aeschylus and the *Anacreontea*. The following entirely conventional declaration on the nature of early Greek poetry, made in September 1841, sums up his feelings during this period:

> In the youth of poetry men love to praise the lark and the morning—but they soon forsake the dews and skies—for the nightingale and evening shades. Without instituting a wider comparison I might say that in Homer there is more of the innocence and serenity of youth, than in the more modern and moral poets. The Iliad is not sabbath but morning reading—and men cling to this old song, because they have still moments of unbaptized and uncommitted life which give them an appetite for more. There is no cant in him—as there is no religion—we read him with a rare sense of freedom and irresponsibleness, as though we trod on native ground, and were autochthones of the soil.
>
> Through the fogs of this distant vale we look back and upward to the source of song—whose crystal stream still ripples in the clear atmosphere of the mountain's side, and casts a silver gleam afar. (*Journal 1*, p. 332)

This tribute to Homer as a primitive, autochthonous bard at the clear headwaters of the literary tradition is typical of Thoreau's views at the time of his Greek *Dial* translations. In addition, it was written in the very year he first seriously studied the most primitive literature of them all: the ancient Sanscrit scriptures. This was an event whose impact on Thoreau's intellectual development was extraordinary, having "the force of a revelation."[67] The Hindu sages henceforth joined Homer and the American Indians as Thoreau's "morning reading." An early version of the powerful tribute to *The Laws of Menu* in *A Week* already cited (pp. 179-180), for example, appeared in the *Journal* on August 6, 1841, and was transcribed in a revised form sometime during the following year.[68] Furthermore, in its transcribed form its purpose is clearly to illustrate the proposition that "the Bráh-

[67] Richardson, p. 100.

[68] The original *Journal* entry is on p. 316 of *Journal 1* and the later transcription is on pp. 425-426.

men is the ideal man," possessed of higher religious knowledge than that of Thoreau's New England contemporaries.
At the same time, Thoreau also here struck a typically hope-
ful note, admitting the primacy of the Hindu sages, while
maintaining the possibility of a new, American revelation.
The "sublime passages" of *The Laws of Menu* "address what
is most abiding and deepest in human nature. . . . They
belong to the noontide of the day the midsummer of the
year. When the snow has melted and the waters evaporated
in the spring—still their truth speaks fresh and fair amid
the drought. They are not new they are not old, but wherever
the sun shines or the night broods they are true" (*Journal
1*, p. 427). A revelation like that of the Brahmans is still
available in the rough, simple wisdom of the American fron-
tier, the liminal stretches of the spirit which Thoreau himself
inhabited: "In solitude and silence whether in England or
Arkansas their old dynasty and dispensation begins
again There is an orientalism in the most restless
pioneer The farthest west is the farthest east. . . . They
harmonize with the fragrance of decayed pine leaves in sul-
try weather— The very locusts and crickets of a summer
day are but later or earlier glosses on the Dherma Sástra of
the Hindoos—a continuation of the sacred code. In the New
England noontide I have discovered more materials of Oriental history than the sanscrit contains or Sir W. Jones has
unlocked" (*Journal 1*, p. 427). Indeed, in November 1843—
when he was in the very midst of his Pindaric translations
for the *Dial*—he made the same point with regard to the
potency of the Greek and American languages:

We must look to the west for the growth of a new literature—
manners—architecture &c  Already there is more language there,—
which is the growth of the soil,—than here—good Greekish words
there are in abundance—good because necessary & expressive—
"diggings" for instance—  If you anylyze a Greek word you will not
get anything simpler truer more poetical—  And many others also
which now look so raw slang-like and colloquial when printed an-

other generation will cherish and affect as genuine American and standard. Read some western stump speech and though it be awkward and rude enough—there will not fail to be some traits of genuine eloquence or some original and forcible statement which will remind you of the great orators of antiquity. I am inclined to read the stump speeches of the west already rather than the Beauties of our atlantic orators. (*Journal 1*, p. 481)

Thoreau's contributions to the *Dial* itself are dominated by this interest in the languages and literatures of antiquity. Counting "Chinese Four Books" and "Hermes Trismegistus" (which are possibly the result of his collaboration with Emerson),[69] twenty-nine pieces by Thoreau appeared during the magazine's four-year existence. Of these, fifteen are short lyric poems and three others ("Natural History of Massachusetts," "A Winter Walk," and "Herald of Freedom") treat natural history or politics. All the rest—by far the bulk of Thoreau's writing for the *Dial*—are manifestations of his engagement with primitive cultures. Four are translations which appear in this volume (*The Prometheus Bound*, "Anacreon," "Pindar," and "Fragments of Pindar"), and another four are Thoreau's excerpts from contemporary English translations of ancient Oriental religious writings (the "ethnical scriptures"). These are "The Laws of Menu," the "Sayings of Confucius," and the two pieces of uncertain authorship just mentioned. Finally, "Aulus Persius Flaccus" and the remaining two essays ("Homer. Ossian. Chaucer." and "Dark Ages") are generally concerned with ancient poets and poetry, and the possibility of similar poetry in the modern world. As noted above, "Homer. Ossian. Chaucer." is about the decline of poetry since ancient times; in it, Thoreau compares Ossian as well as "Homer, Pindar, Isaiah, and the American Indian" to the sublimity of Stonehenge, and praises

[69] For a discussion of the authorship of "Chinese Four Books" and "Hermes Trismegistus" see *Early Essays*, pp. 385-386 and 390, respectively. On the authorship of "The Preaching of Buddha" see footnote 1; Thoreau's contributions to the *Dial* are listed in Myerson, *The New England Transcendentalists and the "Dial*," p. 314.

"the mythological system of the ancients" as "the only my-thology of the moderns, the poem of mankind."[70] Civilized verse, even that of Chaucer, represents a falling off from the true primitive power of a Homer or an Ossian:

We cannot escape the impression, that the Muse has stooped a little in her flight, when we come to the literature of civilized eras. Now first we hear of various ages and styles of poetry, but the poetry of runic monuments is for every age. The bard has lost the dignity and sacredness of his office. He has no more the bardic rage, and only conceives the deed, which he formerly stood ready to perform. . . . The poet has come within doors, and exchanged the forest and crag for the fireside, the hut of the Gael, and Stonehenge with its circles of stones, for the house of the Englishman. No hero stands at the door prepared to break forth into song or heroic action, but we have instead a homely Englishman, who cultivates the art of poetry. We see the pleasant fireside, and hear the crackling fagots in all the verse. The towering and misty imagination of the bard has descended into the plain, and become a lowlander, and keeps flocks and herds. Poetry is one man's trade, and not all men's re-ligion, and is split into many styles. It is pastoral, and lyric, and narrative, and didactic.[71]

Yet here too, Thoreau's sense of declination is not absolute. There is still hope for a poetry of real power and spiritual insight in the modern world. "Compared with this simple, fibrous life, our civilized history" may indeed appear "the chronicle of debility, of fashion, and the arts of luxury. But the civilized man misses no real refinement in the poetry of the rudest era. It reminds him that civilization does but dress men. It makes shoes, but it does not toughen the soles of the feet. It makes cloth of finer texture, but it does not touch the skin. Inside the civilized man stands the savage still in the place of honor. We are those blue-eyed, yellow-haired Saxons, those slender, dark-haired Normans."[72] This inter-nal savagery in man awaits only an effort of the will to man-

[70] "Homer. Ossian. Chaucer." in *Early Essays*, p. 157.
[71] "Homer. Ossian. Chaucer." in *Early Essays*, pp. 162-163.
[72] "Homer. Ossian. Chaucer." in *Early Essays*, p. 159.

ifest itself and reverse the flow of history. As Thoreau says in his other essay for the *Dial*, "Dark Ages," the light which enlightens men still shines as it did for the ancient Greeks. One must only turn one's eye (in the Emersonian sense) to see, and one will realize that the darkness of the past "is not so much a quality of the past, as of tradition. It is not a distance of time but a distance of relation, which makes thus dusky its memorials. What is near to the heart of this generation is fair and bright still. Greece lies outspread fair and sunshiny in floods of light, for there is the sun and daylight in her literature and art. Homer does not allow us to forget that the sun shone—nor Phidias, nor the Parthenon. Yet no era has been wholly dark. . . . Always the laws of light are the same, but the modes and degrees of seeing vary. The gods are partial to no era, but steadily shines their light in the heavens, while the eye of the beholder is turned to stone. There was but the eye and the sun from the first. The ages have not added a new ray to the one, nor altered a fibre of the other."[73]

Similarly, Thoreau translated "The Transmigrations of the Seven Brahmans" at a time when he was particularly active in pursuing his interest in primitivism. The index for Thoreau's *Journal* during the years 1848-1850 suggests this. It includes entries on "Savage Eloquence," "Old Epic," "Mod. Hindoo Literature," "Hindoo & Englishman," and the "Greeks & Hindoos."[74] Although not all the *Journal* for this period survives, the parts that do demonstrate that Thoreau's broader aim was still to recover the eloquence and vision of the primitive bard. In a passage on the Tahitians, for example, he contrasts the language of primitives and that of civilized

[73] "Dark Ages," in *Early Essays*, pp. 145-146.

[74] This index will be printed in *Journal 3: 1848-1851*, ed. Mark R. Patterson, William Rossi, and Robert Sattelmeyer (Princeton: Princeton University Press, in preparation). It is part of the manuscript of the 1848-1850 journal, HM 13182, at the Huntington Library in San Marino, California. The passages quoted range in date from after July 30, 1848, to October 1849.

men, striking the same note as in his earlier comments on the Greeks: "How much of nature & vigor of true action and eloquence must there be in the speech of every wild man. We carefully preserve a few phrases used by our generals in time of battle but think of the harangues of savage warriors Our public speaking is comparatively tame."[75] Moreover, Thoreau continued to assert the higher truth of primitive mythology, a theme which had appeared in his writings as early as his undergraduate days:

The fragments of fables handed down to us from The remotest antiquity in the mythologies and traditions of all nations would seem to indicate that the life of Christ his divine preeminence & his miracles are not without a precedent in the history of mankind.— Brahma  Indeed such lives are but the epochs in history though ancient and mod. hist. or as they should both be called mod. hist may not be able to span the interval between two such epochs or eras. All the gods that are worshipped have been men—but of the true God of whom none have conceived—all men combined would hardly furnish the germ.[76]

This *Journal* entry is an early version of the sentiments which so scandalized the public in *A Week*. For all their religious unorthodoxy, however, Thoreau's views here are not very different from his general comments on primitive cultures during the preceding decade. Modern man and religious opinion have declined from the higher vision of antiquity; at the same time, there is still a chance for man to reform. If he will return to the elemental and contemplative vision of the Greeks and Hindus, he may approach the godhead in his own way and for his own generation. Moreover, this *Journal* passage also resembles its predecessors in that its aim is to establish a more general definition of the nature of the poet-prophet. Adopting Emersonian terms, Thoreau goes on to contrast those men in whom "the eye is the predominant feature," whom he calls "seers," with those whose ears predominate. These are the poets, who

[75] HM 13182.        [76] HM 13182.

hear all that is said though they appear to give no heed.

The eyes are quick but their glances may be detected  The ears do not betray their attention.

The former observe the signs of the future—the others hear the strains of the muse.—  Of the former you shall not say that they are ignorant for they have seen—nor of the latter that they are ignorant for they have heard.[77]

The Hindu sages themselves combined both these functions because they had a contemplative openness toward the divine which bridged the gap between the active role of the imagination and the passive role of the understanding. As Thoreau put it in a slightly later passage in the *Journal:*

The Hindoos by constitution possess in in a wonderful degree the faculty of contemplation—they can speculate—they have imagination & invention & fancy. The western man thinks only with ruinous interruptions & friction—his contemplative faculty is rusty & does not work. He is soon aground in the shallows of the practical—  It gives him indigestion to think. His cowardly *legs* run away with him—but the Hindoo bravely cuts off his legs in the first place. To him his imagination is a distinct & honorable faculty as valuable as the understanding or the legs—  The legs were made to transport it—& it does not merely direct the legs. How incredibly poor in speculation is the western world!—  one would have thought that a drop of thought & a single afternoon would have set afloat more speculations—

What has Europe been *thinking* of these two thousand years. A child put to bed half an hour before its time would have invented more systems—would have had more theories set afloat would have amused itself with more thoughts. But instead of going to bed and thinking Europe has got up and gone to work, and when she goes to bed she goes to sleep. We cannot go to bed & think as children do  The Yankee cannot sit but he sleeps

—I have an uncle who is obliged to sprout potatoes on sundays to keep him awake. The Hindoo thinks so vividly & intensely that he can think sitting or on his back—far into a siesta  He can dream awake.[78]

This passage, from about the same time as his translation of "The Transmigrations of the Seven Brahmans," strikes a

<hr>

[77] HM 13182.          [78] HM 13182.

familiar note of declination. In the context of the rest of the *Journal* for these years, however, it is once more a call to action rather than to despair. For Thoreau "the contemplations of the Indian sages have" done more than "aided the intellectual development of mankind."[79] Like the elemental simplicity of Homer and Aeschylus, their writings are chiefly valuable because of the inspiration they provide for modern man. Even in the nineteenth century,

> as it were we see the shore slope upward *over* the Alps & the Ural mountains & the Caucasus & Himaloo chain.
> *Ex oriente lux* may still be the motto of scholars, for though Greece & Rome politically have passed away, that source of light is not yet exhausted. The western world has not yet derived from the east all the light which it is destined to receive.[80]

Taken in context, therefore, his translation of "The Transmigrations of the Seven Brahmans" is another manifestation of Thoreau's effort to recapture the vision of the primitive bard for his contemporaries. Indeed, this story from the *Harivansa* is itself about the possibilities for spiritual renewal and change through contemplation. As such, it represents one more instance of Thoreau's continuing search for "the chaunt of the Indian muse," a voice that could be heard as readily in the nineteenth as in any earlier century, and as easily on the banks of the Merrimack as on those of the Ganges or the Aegean.

As the preceding discussion suggests, the works in this volume are intimately connected with a romantic, "primitivist" view of antiquity and ancient literature—a view Thoreau first picked up from his undergraduate reading at Harvard, and which became one of the dominant themes of his own writing in the 1840s. His translations therefore stand as one more instance of the truth of Reuben Brower's observation that:

[79] HM 13182.        [80] HM 13182.

Translations—exactly because of the peculiar conditions of their manufacture—are of special interest to a critic of poetry; for they show him in the baldest form the assumptions about poetry shared by readers and poets. To paraphrase Collingwood, [every translation, like] every poem is an unconscious answer to the question: "What is a poem?" But the question is never the same question, any more than the question "What is a man?" is the same question when asked in 1200 or 1600 or 1900. . . . For instance, a study of English translations of Homer along with the writings of contemporary literary theorists should show us vividly the continuous evolution among English readers of their definition of poetry and their historical picture of ancient Greece.[81]

Thoreau's translations, in other words, reveal his assumptions both about the nature of the poet's calling in the nineteenth century, and about the nature of poetry in antiquity. They stem equally from his view of Homer and Aeschylus and the Sanscrit writers as primitive bards, and from the need he felt for the modern poet to imitate their purity of vision and language. The translations perform this double

[81] Reuben Brower, *Mirror on Mirror: Translation, Imitation, Parody* (Cambridge, Mass.: Harvard University Press, 1974), p. 161. Eric A. Havelock, in "The *Aeneid* and Its Translators," *Hudson Review* 27 (1974):338-370, has undertaken just this sort of study with regard to the great English translations of the classical epics. He shows that Gavin Douglas' fifteenth-century Scots version of the *Aeneid* tells us a great deal about his chivalric literary culture and its relative lack of perceived cultural distance from classical antiquity. So do the very different sixteenth-century *Aeneid*s of Surrey, Phaer, and Stanyhurst, which bespeak the impact of humanist scholarship, rhetorical theory, and literary nationalism on Elizabethan poetry. Dryden's *Aeneid* and Pope's translations of Homer provide some of the most revealing evidence we have about English neoclassicism and its attitude toward Greece and Rome; and in the twentieth century the great modernist imitations of Homer, Virgil, and Petronius suggest that translation can be stretched either to subvert or to reaffirm the centrality of the original text. In Pound's *Cantos I* and *II* or Eliot's *The Waste Land* classical originals are reshaped in response to modernist assumptions about myth and the role of poetry in the modern world that are surprisingly like those of Thoreau and his contemporaries. Nor is this phenomenon limited to poetry. As F. O. Matthiessen demonstrated long ago, the style of translated prose also suggests much about the age in which it was written. See his *Translation: An Elizabethan Art* (Cambridge, Mass.: Harvard University Press, 1931).

function in more than a general way, however. In addition
to their broader connection with his reading in and writing
about "primitive" cultures, these works represent, in their
very style, Thoreau's adherence to commonplace romantic
assumptions about the art of translation, as well as to a more
specifically Transcendentalist linguistic tradition.

In considering the options available to him as a translator,
for instance, Thoreau was almost surely familiar with the
Restoration and early eighteenth-century distinction among
three basic strategies of translation: *metaphrase, paraphrase,* and *imitation.*[82] A *metaphrase* attempts to reproduce
the syntax, sounds, and word order of the original, even at
the cost of violating accepted canons of grammatical and
literary correctness in English. The translator's aim is to hew
his English as close as possible to the style of the foreign
text. Browning's versions of Greek tragedy are the most famous nineteenth-century examples of this strategy. The
opening lines of his translation of Aeschylus' *Agamemnon*
give a good sense of the virtues and shortcomings of this
approach:

[82] Dryden's "Preface" to *Ovid's Epistles* is the *locus classicus* of this
distinction. See John Dryden, *Poems, 1649-1680,* ed. Edward Niles Hooker
et al., vol. 1 of *The Works of John Dryden* (Berkeley: University of
California Press, 1956), 109-119. Dryden's scheme is presented here
merely as an historically relevant device for elucidating Thoreau's practice as a translator.

Recent studies of the history and theory of translation are: F. Guenth-
ner and M. Guenthner-Reutter, eds., *Meaning and Translation: Philo-
sophical and Linguistic Approaches* (New York: New York University
Press, 1978); L. G. Kelly, *The True Interpreter: A History of Translation
Theory and Practice in the West* (Oxford: Basil Blackwell, 1979); Peter
Newmark, *Approaches to Translation* (Oxford: Pergamon Press, 1981);
and George Steiner, *After Babel: Aspects of Language and Translation*
(London: Oxford University Press, 1975). Ezra Pound's "How to Read,"
in *Literary Essays of Ezra Pound,* ed. T. S. Eliot (New York: New
Directions, 1954), pp. 15-40, and Hugh Kenner's introduction to Pound's
*Translations,* enl. ed. (New York: New Directions, 1963), are also useful.
Steiner, pp. 236-295, contains an especially good discussion of Dryden,
Goethe, and other theorists of translation from the Renaissance on, and
Kelly provides a good introduction to the history of this genre.

*Warder:* The gods I ask deliverance from these labours,
    Watch of a year's length whereby, slumbering through it
    On the Atreidai's roofs on elbow,—dog-like—
    I know of nightly star-groups the assemblage,
    And those that bring to men winter and summer
    Bright dynasts, as they pride them in the æther
    —Stars, when they wither, and the uprisings of them.
    And now on ward I wait the torch's token,
    The glow of fire, shall bring from Troia message
    And word of capture: so prevails audacious
    The man's-way-planning hoping heart of woman.[83]

As a literal, word-for-word rendition of the Greek, this translation generally succeeds. But whether it equally well represents the style of the original for the English-speaking reader is debatable. For instance, the unnatural syntax and stiltedness of Browning's English have been criticized by many as vitiating the sense of excitement and expectation found in this scene in the original. Indeed, as A. E. Housman showed, this overly scholarly, literal approach is open to devastating parody.[84]

*Paraphrase,* on the other hand, is the predominant mode

---

[83] *The Works of Robert Browning,* centenary ed. (London: Smith, Elder & Co., 1912), 8:299. For a particularly illuminating discussion of this and some other English translations of the play, see Brower, *Mirror on Mirror,* pp. 159-180. See also Peter Green's trenchant piece, "Some Versions of Aeschylus. A study of tradition and method in translating classical poetry," in his *Essays in Antiquity* (Cleveland and New York: The World Publishing Co., 1960), pp. 185-215.

[84] In his "Fragment of a Greek Tragedy," first published in *The Bromsgrovian* (June 1883), Housman's chorus provides the following pastiche of metaphrastic translations of Greek tragic style:

> *Chorus:* O suitably-attired-in-leather-boots
>     Head of a traveller, wherefore seeking whom
>     Whence by what way how purposed art thou come
>     To this well-nightingaled vicinity?
>     My object in enquiring is to know,
>     But if you happen to be deaf and dumb
>     And do not understand a word I say,
>     Then wave your hand, to signify as much.

Gavin Ewart, ed., *The Penguin Book of Light Verse* (London: Allen Lane, 1980), p. 380.

of translating. The translator largely maintains the sense of the original, but aims to find English stylistic (and sometimes substantive) equivalents for its literary devices and manner. He seeks, in other words, to avoid the shortcomings of metaphrase by recreating the *effect,* not just the literal sounds and word order, of the original for the English reader. Good modern examples are Robert Fitzgerald's Homeric and Virgilian translations and Richmond Lattimore's versions of Greek tragedy. Paraphrase contrasts sharply with the third strategy, *imitation,* perhaps best known from its popularity in the eighteenth century. Johnson's "London" and "The Vanity of Human Wishes" are two famous examples. Johnson took a pair of Juvenalian satires and adapted them to his own moral concerns and the circumstances of his times. In the process, he imbued them with his more serious, yet sympathetic attitude toward human corruption and futility. The general outline of the Latin poems remains, as do individual scenes and phrases, but both in manner and matter Johnson reworked them into something new and independent. Similarly, T. S. Eliot's *The Family Reunion* might be considered a later example of the imitation (albeit a very loose one). It retains the essential structure and characterization of its Aeschylean model, *The Eumenides,* but skews the story in the direction of a different, Christian resolution.

Metaphrase, paraphrase, and imitation form a traditional spectrum of approaches to the problems confronting a translator, against which Thoreau's translations can be placed.[85] In terms of this spectrum they represent either very conservative paraphrase or outright metaphrase. The *Dial* versions of *The Prometheus Bound,* Pindar, and Anacreon, and "The Transmigrations of the Seven Brahmans" for example, are conservatively paraphrastic: Thoreau is fairly faithful to the syntax, diction, and sounds of his originals yet largely—

[85] For some of the specific problems in translating Latin, Greek, and a number of other languages, see Reuben A. Brower, ed., *On Translation* (Cambridge, Mass.: Harvard University Press, 1959), pp. 11-133.

with the exception of a number of passages in *The Prometheus Bound*—avoids stilted literalism. His aim is accuracy of literary effect as well as accuracy to the literal forms of the texts before him—a strategy that makes his English hew close to the Greek and French, but not too close. In the early manuscript drafts of *The Prometheus Bound* and Pindar as well as in the surviving manuscript of *The Seven Against Thebes,* his approach is different. In these cases Thoreau is metaphrastic. He retains the syntax, word order, and stylistic devices of the original much more often than in the finished *Dial* translations, and frequently ranks alternative English translations for specific Greek words and phrases above and below his initial translation of a line. Sometimes even the original Greek words are also interlined with the English. Comparing the two *Prometheus Bound* drafts to the final *Dial* text suggests, moreover, that Thoreau had a work pattern as a translator. He moved gradually away from the initial metaphrase of the manuscript translations toward the final, very conservative paraphrase of the *Dial* versions. In each successive version he still sought to convey the matter and manner of the Greek; at the same time he polished his English and tried to avoid the excesses of literalism.

Thoreau's style as a translator suggests that he had two goals in mind. First, he sought to reproduce the substance and style of the original text as closely as possible. Yet while he clearly felt the attractions of an "intertextual" literalism, he wanted to avoid falling into the unimaginative, self-defeating literalism of a Browning. He therefore took care to revise his finished translations from the point of view of their status as literary works in English, which had to reproduce the stylistic effects of the foreign language original for a modern, nineteenth-century American or English audience. This double aim can be seen in a number of ways in the works collected here. For example, Thoreau's concern for accuracy manifests itself in his faithfulness to the specific editions of the classical authors he used. Early nineteenth-century editions of Aeschylus, Pindar, and the *Anacreontea* often differ textually both among themselves and from those in general circulation today. Thoreau's English follows his sources very closely—so closely that it helps identify which contemporary editions he used. Indeed, he was so alert to the scholarly aspects of Greek textual editing that in a number of instances his Pindar translation was influenced by the *apparatus criticus* of Thiersch's edition.[86] A comparison of modern Greek editions with the sources Thoreau actually used in the 1840s also emphasizes this detailed fidelity. In many cases words or phrases that would be mistranslations of the Oxford Classical Text or Teubner editions are actually accurate renderings of the older editions Thoreau used. This fidelity to sources extends to substantive matters (such as wording, phrasing, and the ascription and order of speeches) as well as to accidental features (like spelling and capitalization). Similarly, accidental peculiarities in the French of "The Transmigrations of the Seven Brahmans" are also reproduced in Thoreau's English.

At the same time, Thoreau's interest in his translations as English literary works in their own right is suggested by a careful study of the surviving manuscripts. He reworked individual words and phrases to find the most satisfactory translation and was often undecided about particular cases until a very late stage in the process.[87] A comparison of the two early drafts of *The Prometheus Bound* with the *Dial* version illustrates this pattern particularly well. The second and third versions are almost complete revisions of their

[86] For examples of Thoreau's indebtedness to his sources, see Van Anglen, "The Sources for Thoreau's Greek Translations," in *Studies in the American Renaissance: 1980,* pp. 291-299. In part his concern with accuracy and classical textual criticism reflects the impact of the new German scholarship on Harvard College at this time.

[87] Thoreau's multiple unresolved variants, in which he ranked alternative translations either vertically or horizontally without making a final choice among them, are the clearest evidence in the manuscripts of his careful method as a translator. See pp. 223-224.

predecessors, a fact bespeaking Thoreau's seriousness and commitment to their literary quality. His Pindaric translations show similar care and deliberation. Furthermore, Thoreau's choice of Pindaric odes and sections of odes for translation is radically different in the manuscript version versus the *Dial* version. His plan for this translation was clearly, therefore, a deliberate one which underwent radical revision long before it came under Emerson's editorial scrutiny.

Of course, Thoreau was not entirely successful in achieving both these aims. In the classical translations he occasionally misunderstood his source or mistook one Greek word for another on the basis of a false derivation—something that rarely occurs in his translation of "The Transmigrations of the Seven Brahmans" from the French. Similarly, Thoreau's very conservatism as a translator often made his English inelegant and wooden, even in the finished translations in the *Dial*. Yet despite these lapses, Thoreau's translations often succeed in terms of his own goals. His *Prometheus Bound,* for instance, frequently picks up the force and concision, the spareness, of Aeschylus' Greek, conveying the density and gnomic quality of the original. Similarly, in the Pindaric poems, Thoreau's conservative paraphrase helped him capture their most elusive yet central quality: an intense metaphoric unity. Because of this, Reuben Brower considered Thoreau "the nineteenth-century writer who it seems might have best shown English readers the harmony of Pindar."[88]

---

[88] Brower, *Mirror on Mirror,* pp. 52-53. In "The Transmigrations of the Seven Brahmans" Thoreau's method of translation is somewhat different. As in the Greek translations, he is faithful to the text in front of him in many respects (e.g., peculiarities of punctuation, capitalization, etc.). Yet in this case he felt less constrained to translate his source fully and literally. He translates only portions of the *Harivansa,* leaving out sentences and occasional paragraphs, and he also paraphrases and abridges the notes. There are a number of possible reasons for this. Because he was translating it at second-hand, from French rather than the original Sanscrit, Thoreau may have accorded the *Harivansa* a lower literary status than the two Aeschylean tragedies or the Greek lyric poetry. How-

Whether his translations succeed or fail, Thoreau's achievement can be measured against the strategy of conservative paraphrase that he employed. This strategy was not Thoreau's alone, but represents the literary assumptions of his time in a number of ways. For one thing, it comes very near the Transcendentalist ideal of what a good translation should be. Reviewers for the *Dial* habitually praised the "fidelity" and "faithfulness" of translators to the literal meaning of their sources. In her review of a translation of Michelangelo's sonnets, for example, Margaret Fuller wrote that "fidelity must be the highest merit of these translations; for not even an Angelo could translate his peer."[89] Another *Dial* reviewer held that "translators have been long in learning that it is safe to be literal."[90] Paradoxically, however, these reviewers valued fidelity precisely because they saw translation as a foredoomed effort. As S. G. Ward noted of a contemporary translation of Dante:

We took up this book, not a little prejudiced; for who with the deep music of the original ringing in his ears, but must view the best translation with some aversion? And verily were all the world acquainted with originals, translators would stand but a poor chance, if indeed they could under such circumstances exist. A translation is neither more nor less than a paraphrase, only in a different language; and this is the only answer to give to those who insist that if there be any meaning in a poet, it can be translated, that the thought cannot escape if the words are rendered by equivalents. But let any one paraphrase Shakspeare, and see what work he will make of it. Hence is a translator's in one respect the most ungrateful

---

ever, it is more likely that his cuts were intended simply to make the story told in "The Transmigrations of the Seven Brahmans" complete in itself without reference to the *Harivansa* as a whole.

[89] [Margaret Fuller], review of *Michael Angelo, considered as a Philosophic Poet, with Translations,* by John Edward Taylor, *Dial* 1 (January 1841):401. For attribution of authorship, see Myerson, *The New England Transcendentalists and the "Dial,"* p. 292.

[90] Review of *Egmont, a Tragedy in five acts. Translated from the German of Goethe, Dial* 2 (January 1842):395. Attributed by Myerson, *The New England Transcendentalists and the "Dial,"* p. 295, to either Margaret Fuller or Elizabeth Palmer Peabody.

of all literary tasks. Yet is it one of the most honorable and most useful, for few can go to the fountain heads, and none can go to them all; and without the labors of conscientious translators, not the Bible only, but our Plato and Æschylus would be sealed books to most of us.[91]

For the Transcendentalists, the very inadequacy of translation demanded that the translator remain as faithful to the original as possible. Yet this emphasis on literal fidelity to an original did not preclude a concern for other values. On the contrary, the Transcendentalists combined it with an emphasis on the literary quality of a translation as a work in its own right. Like Thoreau, they preferred close paraphrase to metaphrase. Theodore Parker, for instance, praised C. C. Felton (under whom Thoreau himself learned to translate Homer) for his "singular fidelity" as a translator of German. But Parker also praised "his version" as "uncommonly idiomatic and fresh," adding that "it reads like original English."[92] Similarly, in the review just cited S. G. Ward also endorsed the style of translating for which Thoreau strove:

We believe the time is past, when a distinction can be made between a free and a literal translation of a great work. A translation must be literal, or it is no translation. And if the translator cannot be free and literal at once, if he cannot learn to move freely and gracefully in his irons, he is wanting in a prime requisite. It is in vain to speak of translating in the spirit of an original, without confining one's self too closely to the text. You may thus produce as good a work as Pope's Homer, but no translation.[93]

[91] [S. G. Ward], "Translation of Dante," review of *The first ten Cantos of the Inferno of Dante newly translated into English verse,* by T. W. Parsons, *Dial* 4 (January 1844):286. For attribution, see Myerson, *The New England Transcendentalists and the "Dial,"* p. 301.

[92] [Theodore Parker], "German Literature," review of *Specimens of Foreign Standard Literature,* edited by George Ripley, Vol. VII, VIII, and IX, containing German Literature, translated from the German of Wolfgang Menzel, by C. C. Felton, *Dial* 1 (January 1841):339. For attribution, see Myerson, *The New England Transcendentalists and the "Dial,"* p. 292.

[93] [Ward], p. 290.

As these comments from the *Dial* suggest, for the Transcendentalists "fidelity" was a complex concept. It meant close attention to the literal meaning of the original, yet it also meant something other than the exact and uninspired literalism of a Browning. Like the German romantics, who may have influenced them,[94] Fuller and Parker sought to define translation as an essentially spiritual act, an effort at identifying with the genius inherent in the language of the source. Such an identification meant that one must aim not just at a literal accuracy with regard to the forms of the foreign language text, but also at a recreation of the spirit and effect of the source text in one's own language. As Wilhelm von Humboldt put it, "fidelity" in a translation "must be aimed at the real nature of the original, not at its incidentals. . . ."[95] Or as A. W. Schlegel wrote, "Literalness is a long way from fidelity. Fidelity means that the same or similar impressions are produced, because these are the essence of the matter."[96] The Transcendentalists, in other words, followed Goethe in demanding an "interlinear version" of the original which was a close translation but not a mere schoolboy crib. Rather, such an "interlinear version" was one "in which the translator penetrates to the essence of the

[94] Because so much of the commentary on translation by German romantics occurs in the context of prefaces or incidental comments in the course of other writings, it is not always easy to trace the specific indebtedness of the New England Transcendentalists to the Germans in these matters. Fuller and the others quoted here were, however, heavily influenced by contemporary German thought in general: see Stanley M. Vogel, *German Literary Influences on the American Transcendentalists* (New Haven: Yale University Press, 1955), especially pp. 61-163; and Henry A. Pochmann, *German Culture in America: Philosophical and Literary Influences, 1600-1900* (Madison: University of Wisconsin Press, 1957), pp. 153-255.

[95] Wilhelm von Humboldt, [From the "Einleitung," *Aeschylos' Agamemnon metrisch übersetzt*], trans. in André Lefevere, *Translating Literature: The German Tradition from Luther to Rosenzweig* (Amsterdam: Van Gorcum, Assen, 1977), p. 42.

[96] August Wilhelm Schlegel, [From the *Geschichte der klassischen Literatur*], trans. in Lefevere, p. 52.

original through close imitation of language use,"—a mimetic act that parallels and recreates the "experience and temperament" of the source text while at the same time reproducing the specific forms on the printed page.[97]

Thus, the comments of the *Dial* critics strongly resemble those of many contemporary German commentators on translation in asserting the impossibility of translation—it is for them, as much as for Fuller and the rest, an attempt, an approach, that involves both closeness to the original and a simultaneous transfer of its effect in terms of one's own language and cultural experience.[98] In such a process, as Schleiermacher notes, the result should be neither too free nor too literal, but "faithful" to both spirit and letter.[99] While it is not known whether Thoreau read any of the leading German sources on the theory and practice of translation, his own comments on the art of translating are very similar to those of his fellow contributors to the *Dial*. Translation at best provides an inadequate version of the original. Faced with the inherent impossibility of the task, the translator cannot help but feel a sense of frustration:

Those who have not learned to read the ancient classics in the language in which they were written must have a very imperfect knowledge of the history of the human race; for it is remarkable that no transcript of them has ever been made into any modern tongue, unless our civilization itself may be regarded as such a transcript. Homer has never yet been printed in English, nor Æschylus, nor Virgil even,—works as refined, as solidly done, and as beautiful almost as the morning itself; for later writers, say what we will of their genius, have rarely, if ever, equalled the elaborate beauty and finish and the lifelong and heroic literary labors of the ancients.[100]

[97] Kelly, *The True Interpreter*, pp. 92-93.

[98] See particularly Friedrich Schleiermacher, ["Ueber die verschiedenen Methoden des Uebersezens"], trans. in Lefevere, pp. 66-89.

[99] Schleiermacher, trans. in Lefevere, pp. 75-76.

[100] *Walden*, ed. J. Lyndon Shanley (Princeton: Princeton University Press, 1971), p. 103.

As his reference to classical poetry in this passage suggests, however, Thoreau's views on the problems of translation, unlike those of the other Transcendentalists, were decisively influenced by his more general views on "primitive poetry." The ancient poets are here once again Thoreau's "morning reading," and their stories illustrate the "heroic literary labors" of antiquity. He once more characterizes the language of the Greeks as more potent and spiritually significant than modern English, and it is in this linguistic decline that the true difficulty of translation lies:

The student may read Homer or Æschylus in the Greek without danger of dissipation or luxuriousness, for it implies that he in some measure emulate their heroes, and consecrate morning hours to their pages. The heroic books, even if printed in the character of our mother tongue, will always be in a language dead to degenerate times; and we must laboriously seek the meaning of each word and line, conjecturing a larger sense than common use permits out of what wisdom and valor and generosity we have. The modern cheap and fertile press, with all its translations, has done little to bring us nearer to the heroic writers of antiquity. They seem as solitary, and the letter in which they are printed as rare and curious, as ever. It is worth the expense of youthful days and costly hours, if you learn only some words of an ancient language, which are raised out of the trivialness of the street, to be perpetual suggestions and provocations. (*Walden*, p. 100)

The portrait of the ancient Greek poet here is a familiar one: a prescient bard wrapped in solitude, writing "in a foreign language dead to idle & degenerate times".[101] Because modern man lives in just such times, the translations of the modern age have difficulty conveying this superior language of antiquity. The language of Homer, like that of the Hindu sages or the American Indians, is one "which we must be born again in order to speak" (*Walden,* p. 101), a tongue which after the fall or "lapse of ages a few scholars *read,* and a few scholars only are still reading it" (*Walden,* p. 101).

[101] *Journal 2: 1842-1848,* ed. Robert Sattelmeyer (Princeton: Princeton University Press, 1984), p. 169.

Furthermore, if the translator is to have even limited success he must do as Thoreau did in his English versions of Aeschylus and the rest: he "must laboriously seek the meaning of each word and line" in order to conjecture that "larger sense than common use permits out of what wisdom and valor and generosity we have" (*Walden*, p. 100). Like the modern poet he must imitate the primitive bard not only in the *substance* of his vision, but in his *language* as well.

It is, therefore, in regard to the nature of language (and especially primitive language) that Thoreau's translations most decisively suggest his broader assumptions about poetry and the nature of the translator's task. For, as a number of scholars have shown, the Transcendentalists were intensely interested in the nature and origins of language.[102] The intellectual roots of this interest range from European idealism and the neoplatonism of Thomas Taylor to more indigenous New England controversies over the interpretation of scripture. In general, however, the Transcendentalists agreed that words and the sounds of words were imbued with spiritual significance—a view which had its two most famous literary expressions in Emerson's *Nature* and

[102] See Philip F. Gura, "Elizabeth Palmer Peabody and the Philosophy of Language," *ESQ*, n.s., 23 (1977):154-163; "Thoreau's Maine Woods Indians: More Representative Men," *American Literature* 49 (1977):366-384; and most recently, *The Wisdom of Words: Language, Theology, and Literature in the New England Renaissance* (Middletown, Conn.: Wesleyan University Press, 1981). See also John B. Wilson, "Grimm's Law and the Brahmins," *New England Quarterly* 38 (1965):234-239; and Michael West, "Scatology and Eschatology: The Heroic Dimensions of Thoreau's Wordplay," *PMLA* 89 (1974):1043-1064; "Charles Kraitsir's Influence upon Thoreau's Theory of Language," *ESQ*, n.s., 19 (1973):262-274; *"Walden's* Dirty Language: Thoreau and Walter Whiter's Geocentric Etymological Theories," *Harvard Library Bulletin* 22 (1974):117-128. Two recent broader studies of language theory in the mid-nineteenth century are Mason I. Lowance, Jr., *The Language of Canaan: Metaphor and Symbol in New England from the Puritans to the Transcendentalists* (Cambridge, Mass.: Harvard University Press, 1980), especially pp. 247ff.; and John T. Irwin, *American Hieroglyphics: The Symbol of the Egyptian Hieroglyphics in the American Renaissance* (New Haven: Yale University Press, 1980).

the etymology of *labor* in the "Spring" chapter of *Walden*. As such, the Transcendentalist position represented a rejection of the "counter" theory of language proposed by Locke. However much he might agree with Locke in other ways,[103] Thoreau joined his colleagues in rejecting the notion that words are arbitrary, shifting designations for the things they name, bearing no inherent or necessary relation to the world of experience. Like the others, Thoreau also adhered to an anti-Lockean primitivist theory of the origins and development of language. This was one of the central features of the linguistic tradition stretching back beyond Horne Tooke to the Port Royalists and, ultimately, to Plato.[104] Scholars in this tradition posited a linguistic fall of man away from an original, universal language, a *fall* at Babel paralleling man's spiritual fall in Eden.[105] Primitive peoples, because they were closer to man's original universal language, spoke a more potent and spiritually significant tongue, in which words corresponded to the things they named. Language then progressively degenerated through history along with man's capacity for unmediated spiritual experience, and civilized words came to have an arbitrary and artificial relationship to their counterparts in the natural world. They fell away, in other words, from their primordial capacity to fulfill Emerson's definition of language in *Nature:*

1. Words are signs of natural facts.
2. Particular natural facts are symbols of particular spiritual facts.
3. Nature is the symbol of spirit.

[103] Although not entirely satisfactory with regard to Emerson, Joel Porte's *Emerson and Thoreau: Transcendentalists in Conflict* (Middletown, Conn.: Wesleyan University Press, 1966) remains the best guide to Thoreau's essentially Lockeian epistemology.

[104] Hans Aarsleff, *The Study of Language in England, 1780-1860* (Princeton: Princeton University Press, 1967), provides a good summary of part of this tradition.

[105] The many layers of meaning in American romantic conceptions of "the fall of man" can be seen in Emerson's case as well; see B. L. Packer, *Emerson's Fall: A New Interpretation of the Major Essays* (New York: Continuum, 1982), especially pp. 85-147.

As Emerson goes on to say, "It is not words only that are emblematic; it is things which are emblematic"; and it is only among primitives that the connection between the two is habitually made:

Because of this radical correspondence between visible things and human thoughts, savages, who have only what is necessary, converse in figures. As we go back in history, language becomes more picturesque, until its infancy, when it is all poetry; or, all spiritual facts are represented by natural symbols. The same symbols are found to make the original elements of all languages. It has moreover been observed, that the idioms of all languages approach each other in passages of the greatest eloquence and power. And as this is the first language, so is it the last. This immediate dependence of language upon nature, this conversion of an outward phenomenon into a type of somewhat in human life, never loses its power to affect us. It is this which gives that piquancy to the conversation of a strong-natured farmer or back-woodsman, which all men relish.[106]

Recent scholarship has shown how deeply Thoreau was influenced by this view of language. Michael West and Philip Gura, for example, have concentrated on the ways in which *Walden* attempts to return to a primitive level of experiencing nature through a reform of nineteenth-century English. By shaping his words backward etymologically toward their purer roots in Greek and other ancient languages, Thoreau sought to reunite words and the things they name. In doing so, he followed Emerson's *dictum* that "the corruption of man is followed by the corruption of language. . . . But wise men pierce this rotten diction and fasten words again to visible things; so that picturesque language is at once a commanding certificate that he who employs it, is a man in alliance with truth and God."[107] Thoreau himself said as

---

[106] Ralph Waldo Emerson, *Nature* in *Nature, Addresses, and Lectures,* ed. Robert E. Spiller and Alfred R. Ferguson, vol. 1 of *The Collected Works of Ralph Waldo Emerson* (Cambridge, Mass.: Harvard University Press, 1971), 17-20.
[107] Emerson, *Nature, Addresses, and Lectures,* p. 20.

much in "Walking" when he noted the connection between the natural, the primitive, and the linguistically pure:

> Where is the literature which gives expression to Nature? He would be a poet who could impress the winds and streams into his service, to speak for him; who nailed words to their primitive senses, as farmers drive down stakes in the spring, which the frost has heaved; who derived his words as often as he used them,—transplanted them to his page with earth adhering to their roots; whose words were so true and fresh and natural that they would appear to expand like the buds at the approach of spring, though they lay half smothered between two musty leaves in a library,—aye, to bloom and bear fruit there, after their kind, annually, for the faithful reader, in sympathy with surrounding Nature.[108]

It is this view of the poet and his role (to recover the primitive purity of words) that is behind the culminating definition of *labor* in the "Spring" chapter of *Walden*. There Thoreau employs the peculiar linguistic theories of Dr. Charles Kraitsir to reverse both the spiritual *fall* or *lapse* of man (through the metaphor of the grub in metamorphosis to a butterfly) and his linguistic fall (through the press of the English words back into antiquity, toward their roots in primitive Greek):

> the earth expresses itself outwardly in leaves, it so labors with the idea inwardly. The atoms have already learned this law, and are pregnant by it. The overhanging leaf sees here its prototype. *Internally,* whether in the globe or animal body, it is a moist thick *lobe,* a word especially applicable to the liver and lungs and the *leaves* of fat, ($\lambda\varepsilon i\beta\omega$, *labor, lapsus,* to flow or slip downward, a lapsing; $\lambda o\beta o\varsigma$, *globus,* lobe, globe; also lap, flap, and many other words,) *externally* a dry thin *leaf,* even as the *f* and *v* are a pressed and dried *b.* The radicals of lobe are *lb,* the soft mass of the *b* (single lobed, or B, double lobed,) with a liquid *l* behind it pressing it forward. In globe, *glb,* the guttural *g* adds to the meaning the capacity of the throat. The feathers and wings of birds are still drier and thinner leaves. Thus, also, you pass from the lumpish grub in the earth to the airy and fluttering butterfly. The very globe continually transcends and

---

[108] "Walking," in *Excursions and Poems,* vol. 5 of *The Writings of Henry David Thoreau* (Boston: Houghton Mifflin, 1906), 232.

translates itself, and becomes winged in its orbit. (*Walden,* pp. 306-307)

As we have seen, however, Thoreau did not have to wait until his introduction to Kraitsir in order to begin developing a Transcendentalist view of language. Even as an undergraduate his reading in mythology and classical scholarship introduced him to the notion that primitive languages were more expressive and potent than those of civilized ages. H. N. Coleridge had praised Greek for having the "infinite flexibility" and "indefatigable strength" of nature itself. Felton and Schlegel also praised it and as early as December 1839 (some five years before he encountered Kraitsir) Thoreau wrote the following passage, obviously with Emerson's *Nature* in mind:

> The state of complete manhood is virtue—and virtue and bravery are one— This truth has long been in the languages. All the relations of the subject are hinted at in the derivation and analogies of the Latin words *vir* and *virtus;* and the Greek αγαθος and αριστος. Language in its settled form is the record of men's second thoughts; a more faithful utterance than they can momentarily give. What men say is so sifted and obliged to approve itself as answering to a common want, that nothing absolutely frivolous obtains currency in the language. The analogies of words are never whimsical and meaningless, but stand for real likenesses— Only the ethics of mankind, and not of any particular man give point and vigor to our speech. (*Journal 1,* p. 92)

Similarly, in August 1841 Thoreau wrote the first version of his later declaration in *A Week* that "there are other, savager, and more primeval aspects of nature than our poets have sung. It is only white man's poetry. Homer and Ossian even can never revive in London or Boston. And yet behold how these cities are refreshed by the mere tradition, or the imperfectly transmitted fragrance and flavor of these wild fruits. If we could listen but for an instant to the chaunt of the Indian muse, we should understand why he will not exchange his savageness for civilization. Nations are not whimsical. Steel and blankets are strong temptations; but the Indian does well to continue Indian" (*A Week,* p. 56).[109]

Thus, Thoreau's interest in the purity of primitive language preceded any specific debt to Kraitsir or other contemporary linguists. It was part of a more general response to the literature of the Greeks, Hindus, and other primitives that took shape very early in his career. The relatively literal style of his translations suggests, moreover, that passages like the derivation of *labor* in *Walden* were not his first attempt to bring "the chaunt of the Indian muse" to Concord, if not London or Boston. For as we have seen, the translations themselves were composed in the context of his primitivist view of Greek and Sanscrit language and literature. In shaping his English as closely as possible to the more potent poetry of his originals, he was therefore pressing his degenerate language back toward its original roots in the universal language of primitive man. Just as the vowels and syllables of *labor* pressed back past the *lapse* and *fall* in the "Spring" chapter of *Walden,* so the English of Thoreau's *Prometheus Bound* or "Pindar" sought to recapture those "savager, and more primeval aspects of nature than our poets have sung."

By staying close to the language of the Greeks and (albeit via a French translation) the Sanscrit scriptures—as by studying American Indian languages—Thoreau tried to recover the clearer insight of these bards into the nature of things. As the preceding survey of contemporary linguistic theory suggests, this insight was recoverable precisely because of the relationship of primitive language to the unmediated experience of the ancient bard. The very simplicity and elemental vision of an Aeschylus were reflected in the language of *The Prometheus Bound* and *The Seven Against Thebes.* By translating these plays so as to recreate both the letter and the stylistic effect of the original for the modern reader, Thoreau was trying to remake his own English into

[109] For the earlier version of this passage, see *Journal 1,* p. 321.

something more emblematic of the true relationship of words and natural facts. Furthermore, because of his philosophical differences with Emerson, Thoreau was especially aware that the word *translation* itself embodied the true relationship of signifier and signified in antiquity. For its Latin root, *translatio,* comes from the verb *transfero* and means first, the turning of one language into another; and second, a movement from one spiritual state to another, as in the phrase, "the translation of a saint." This pun is by no means fortuitous, but is itself one of the most significant of the "radical roots" of words. Thus *translation* contains within itself the very promise of rebirth by which true writing becomes a spiritual act. As Thoreau showed in his derivation of *labor* in the "Spring" chapter, the press of words *back* into linguistic antiquity parallels the metamorphosis of the grub into a butterfly. As a result, "the very globe continually transcends and translates itself, and becomes winged in its orbit."

Thoreau's translations, therefore, mirror two strands of Transcendentalist thought: an abiding interest in the nature and origins of language, and a more general primitivism. As such, they are by no means anomalies or oddities, the results of a hidebound education and outdated literary tastes. Rather, they form part of a broader pattern in Thoreau's career and the history of Transcendentalism. For they are among his earliest attempts to restore the English language and American vision to something like their prelapsarian state. Stylistically and thematically they seek to address the same issues as his later *mythopoesis* in "Walking" and "Wild Apples," or his sojourns in *A Week* and *The Maine Woods*. Like *Walden* they proclaim the possibility of poetry even in the nineteenth century. Thus, when the headnote to *The Prometheus Bound* announced that Thoreau's was a translation "in which fidelity to the text, and to the best text, is what is mainly attempted" (p. 3), it was doing more than commenting upon his penchant for accuracy. It was also suggesting something about the deepest literary values of this man and the group to which he belonged. In matter and manner Thoreau's literary translations affirmed the central Transcendentalist position: that poetry is *promethean* or prospective, not *epimethean* or retrospective. It is a means of recovering an uncivilized, savage and bardic perspective on things, a way to reverse the damaging effects of history and the dead weight of the past. Just as in his punning in *Walden* or his reversal of the Fall in *A Week,* through his translations Thoreau sought to regenerate the American language by confronting it with the rougher, more natural tongue of the Greeks and Hindus—an attempt to recover for his contemporaries the emblematic relationship between words and the things they name. It is in that relationship, finally, that he sought himself to become a latter-day bard, a writer of heroic tales, a teacher of America's "poor scholars." Thoreau's translations are an early and tentative first step toward the themes of his mature writings, that new day which would soon dawn.

## THEORY OF COPY-TEXT

*Translations,* like other volumes in *The Writings of Henry D. Thoreau,* is an "unmodernized . . . eclectic or critical text."[110] Editing of this volume began under the sponsorship of the Center for Editions of American Authors and continued under that of the Committee on Scholarly Editions, both agencies of the Modern Language Association of America. The editorial theory and practice employed here conform in general to the standards of these organizations. The editor shares final responsibility for the editorial process with the Editorial Board and editorial staff of *The Writings of Henry D. Thoreau.* Since previous volumes in the Princeton Edition have explained the theoretical basis upon which the writings are

[110] *Early Essays,* p. 305.

edited,[111] only a brief definition of terms and essential editorial procedures will be given here. Joseph J. Moldenhauer's discussion of copy-text theory in his introduction to *Early Essays and Miscellanies*[112] is particularly comprehensive.

In an "eclectic or critical text," the surviving document over which the author exercised greatest control—the "copy-text"—is emended by the editor to represent the author's final intentions. If the author prepared the work for printing, copy-text will ideally be the printer's copy. If the printer's copy is lost, the descending order of preferred copy-texts is usually: a set of corrected proofs for the first edition, a copy of the first edition with authorial corrections, the first edition itself. For a work that was not printed, the latest surviving manuscript is the copy-text. By careful emendation of the copy-text, the editor produces a text which is a more accurate reflection of the author's intentions than any single documentary version. Sources for emendations include the author's working manuscripts and those printed forms of the text demonstrably or probably under the author's control. Such forms of documentation are, on the basis of their chronological relationship to the copy-text, called either "pre-copy-text" or "post-copy-text." In addition, a few emendations must rest upon the judgment of the editor.

A text is composed of two kinds of elements. The words, which carry most of the discursive meaning, are often referred to in editorial theory as "substantives." The features of a text's appearance that may or may not affect its discursive meaning—spelling, paragraphing, punctuation, word-division, capitalization, typography, and design—have been called "accidentals." These other features almost inevitably receive less attention from the author as well as the printer than the words in a text. Because reprintings and resettings

[111] Editorial principles for the *Journal* differ from those for works prepared for or presented to an audience—lectures, essays, books, letters. See *Journal 1*, pp. 628-632.

[112] *Early Essays*, pp. 305-308.

multiply the possibilities for the imposition of press house-styles and for other kinds of corruption, the accidentals of the copy-text are usually accepted as the most reliable. Both substantives and accidentals, however, may be emended from other versions that are demonstrably authorial.

## EDITORIAL PRINCIPLES

### Printed Copy-Texts

Printer's copy does not survive for any of the four translations published in Thoreau's lifetime: *The Prometheus Bound,* "Anacreon," "Pindar," and "Fragments of Pindar." All four appeared in the *Dial.* Thoreau's own copy of the *Dial,* with his corrections and revisions in the pieces he contributed, provides copy-text for *The Prometheus Bound,* "Pindar," and "Fragments of Pindar." Copy-text for "Anacreon" is the original, uncorrected *Dial* version. Pre-copy-text forms of these pieces include manuscript drafts and *Journal* and commonplace book versions. Post-copy-text forms of "Anacreon," "Pindar," and "Fragments of Pindar" appear in the first two editions of *A Week on the Concord and Merrimack Rivers* (1849, 1868) (for details of pre- and post-copy-text forms for each translation see the headnotes on pp. 235, 241, 261, 265).

This edition presents the final state of each text as a translation. Changes Thoreau made in order to incorporate part or all of a translation as a quotation in *A Week* are not accepted. However, changes that correct, clarify, or revise his translation itself are accepted as emendations (see Textual Notes 56.14, 58.8, 58.25, 119.28, 119.32).

The headnote preceding each of the *Dial* translations is accepted in this edition. Since the headnote to "Anacreon" was included in *A Week,* it must be authorial. The headnotes to *The Prometheus Bound* and the two Pindar pieces may have been supplied by Emerson, but in the absence of firm evidence of this they are accepted as Thoreau's.

Such details of the printed texts as running heads, relative type sizes of prose and poetry, and titles are considered design features and are adapted to the series design of the Princeton Edition. Notices of termination—Thoreau's initials and rules at the close of each piece—have been silently omitted. Footnotes have been moved to appropriate positions when necessary. The original pagination, printer's signatures, and smudges are disregarded; broken yet still legible letters and punctuation marks are treated as though they were unbroken. In "Anacreon," "Pindar," and "Fragments of Pindar," rules between poems have been retained except where the end of a poem coincides with a page break in this edition. When that occurs, the Princeton Edition text follows the *Dial*'s practice of omitting the rules.

## Manuscript Copy-Texts

*The Seven Against Thebes*, the "Pindaric Odes From HM 13204," "The Transmigrations of the Seven Brahmans," Διαλογος, and "The Cliffs—a Cenotaph" exist only in manuscript, which provides copy-text for each. Pre-copy-text forms of *The Seven Against Thebes* appear in the *Journal* and "The Service" (for details see the headnote on p. 245). *The Seven Against Thebes* and "Pindaric Odes From HM 13204" are rough drafts; "The Transmigrations of the Seven Brahmans" is a fair copy corrected in pencil. Διαλογος and "The Cliffs—a Cenotaph" make up the Appendix, and are fair copies.

This edition presents the final revised version from each manuscript; that state reflects most accurately Thoreau's expectation of an audience, eventual if not immediate. He clearly hoped to publish *The Seven Against Thebes* (see p. 169); the Pindaric odes in HM 13204 were probably revised along with the other texts in that manuscript when he was preparing the material for publication but before he made his final selection; and the manuscript for "The Transmigrations of the Seven Brahmans" looks like the printer's copy that survives for several of his essays—neatly inscribed and carefully prepared with a title and footnotes (see the fourth illustration, following p. 151)—though no evidence of efforts to arrange publication has been found.

Thoreau revised and corrected in both ink and pencil, cancelling and reworking the on-line text; alterations in both media are accepted. In all three of the translations in manuscript, Thoreau also interlined alternative English equivalents of the original Greek or French without cancelling the on-line text. This is because the process of translation involves considering several alternatives for words and phrases, and often the most precise meaning is not apparent until the context is complete. Thoreau's interlined alternatives reflect his attempts to arrive at the best translation of his original. A chronological pattern in these alternative interlineations is suggested by the manuscript evidence: Thoreau usually wrote his first alternative reading immediately above the on-line reading (see Alteration 76.32), and then placed additional alternative readings either below the on-line reading (see Alteration 82.5), or above the first alternative reading (see Alteration 107.16). Occasionally, due to lack of space above the line, he placed the first alternative below the line (see Alteration 80.24). In general, this edition prints the alternative Thoreau inscribed last, using this pattern as a guide.[113] In the few cases in which several alternative readings are interlined horizontally, the reading farthest to the right is assumed to be the last one (see Alteration 138.30).

In addition, especially in "The Transmigrations of the Seven Brahmans," Thoreau used parentheses to set off parts of the on-line text. When alternative readings are interlined above parenthesized text, the interlined readings are accepted; the parentheses are considered to apply to the on-line text and are not reproduced. When Thoreau parenthesized the on-

---

[113] An examination of the three translations for which both printed and manuscript versions exist (*The Prometheus Bound* and the two Pindaric pieces from the *Dial*) reveals that Thoreau is slightly more likely to settle on the interlined reading than the reading on the line.

line text without interlining alternative readings, the parentheses are retained as representing his final, though incomplete, intention; they may express his uncertainty about a translation. In several cases in *The Seven Against Thebes,* alternative readings that are on the same line are parenthesized (see Textual Note 73.14-15). Both the readings and the parentheses are reproduced, because their arrangement on the line does not provide the kind of evidence about Thoreau's intention or the sequence of his choices that interlined alternatives do. Thoreau occasionally interlined a Greek or French phrase from his source, probably for his own reference. These are not reproduced in the text.

Peculiarities of spacing and indentation in manuscript copy-texts are silently regularized because they cannot be represented consistently in print. When Thoreau has completed a run-on line by interlining text either above or below the line, the position of the interlined material has been normalized. Thoreau's written forms of the asterisk (*, x, +) in "The Transmigrations of the Seven Brahmans" are emended to footnote numbers.

## General Principles of Emendation

The editor has identified the following texts as the sources for Thoreau's translations, and referred to them for emendations and notes:

> *The Prometheus Bound:* Aeschylus, *Tragœdiae: Ad exemplar accurate expressae, Editio stereotypa,* [ed. G. H. Schaefer] (Leipzig: Tauchnitz, 1819).
>
> *The Seven Against Thebes:* Aeschylus, *Tragœdiae: Ad exemplar accurate expressae, Editio stereotypa,* [ed. G. H. Schaefer] (Leipzig: Tauchnitz, either 1817 or 1819).
>
> "Anacreon": *Carminum Poetarum novem, lyricæ poeseωs principum, fragmenta,* [ed. and trans. Henricus Stephanus], comm. M. Aemilius P. Fr. Portus (Heidelberg: Commelin, 1598); bound with Pindar, *Olympia, Pythia,*

*Nemea, Isthmia. Græce & Latine,* [ed. and trans. Henricus Stephanus], comm. M. Aemilius P. Fr. Portus (Heidelberg: Commelin, 1598).

"Pindar," "Fragments of Pindar," and "Pindaric Odes From HM 13204": Pindar, *Werke,* ed. Friedrich Thiersch, 2 vols. (Leipzig: Gerhard Fleischer, 1820).

"The Transmigrations of the Seven Brahmans": Mahābhārata. *Harivansa,* trans. S. A. Langlois, 2 vols. (Paris and London: The Oriental Translation Fund, 1834).

The headnotes for the translations of Anacreon, Pindar, and the *Harivansa* give titles and page and line numbers in Thoreau's sources for the poems or excerpts he translated so that the interested reader can locate them more easily.

This edition does not correct Thoreau's mistranslations of his foreign language originals, nor does it regularize peculiarities of punctuation, syntax, and grammar that result when he follows his source literally. Both the source text and nineteenth-century principles of English usage have been consulted to determine when Thoreau deliberately reproduces the style of his original and when his English is in error.

Editorial treatment of misspellings and errors of punctuation depends not only on Thoreau's intention for publication, but also on the condition in which the text survives. The care with which Thoreau reviewed both proofsheets and finished copies of his published works—attested to by the many corrections in the proofsheets of *A Week* and *Walden* and in his own copies of works he published, including these pieces in the *Dial*—demonstrates his intention to conform to contemporary standards of usage in published material. In printed copy-texts (*The Prometheus Bound,* "Anacreon," "Pindar," and "Fragments of Pindar"), therefore, as well as in "The Transmigrations of the Seven Brahmans," which has all the characteristics of printer's copy, misspellings and errors of punctuation are emended.

In the case of Διαλογος, which is the text of a public performance,[114] errors of punctuation and spelling errors involving missing or incorrect letters of the Greek alphabet are corrected. However, missing accents or breathing marks are not added to Thoreau's Greek, even though they are usually considered part of the spelling of these words, because of the possibility that their omission might have been intentional. The presence or absence of breathing marks, for example, may reflect Thoreau's use of them to guide his pronunciation during the actual oral delivery of the piece at Harvard. The absence of both these features in the Greek spelling may signify a conservative retention at Harvard of the pre-nineteenth-century English practice of omitting them in school and college exercises.

In *The Seven Against Thebes* and the "Pindaric Odes From HM 13204," misspellings and errors of punctuation are not emended unless they seriously obscure the meaning. Although Thoreau did translate *The Seven Against Thebes* with a view toward publication, and it is possible to infer a general intention on his part to publish the Pindaric odes, both works survive only as rough drafts. The degree of editorial intervention that would be required to bring texts in this state to the condition of printer's copy cannot be justified by the remote intention to publish. There is no evidence of plans to publish "The Cliffs—a Cenotaph," a fair copy bound in a notebook; the only emendation occurs as a result of the different arrangements of the text in manuscript and in type (see Emendation *148.21).

The editor has referred to four dictionaries Thoreau is known to have used in order to check unusual spellings, and has emended only when the copy-text spelling is not

---

[114] The bound volume of Exhibitions in the Harvard University Archives that includes Διαλογος is one of a number of such volumes forming an official collection of these presentations over many decades, and Thoreau's manuscript shares the status of the other public records of Harvard College.

listed in any one of them.[115] Thoreau's spellings of Indian and Greek proper names are not emended to their standard modern forms. As they stand they are comprehensible, and the Greek spellings attempt to reproduce their sounds in the original.[116]

## EDITORIAL PROCEDURES

The text of the present edition is based upon transcripts typed from photocopies of the copy-texts. The typescripts of *The Seven Against Thebes,* "Pindaric Odes From HM 13204," "The Transmigrations of the Seven Brahmans," and the compositions in the Appendix were read at least four times against the photocopy and twice against the manuscripts. Obscure elements and cruxes were rechecked against the original manuscript. The *Dial* texts—*The Prometheus Bound,* "Anacreon," "Pindar," and "Fragments of Pindar"—were read against copies of that publication in the Department of Rare Books and Special Collections, Firestone Library, Princeton University, and the Harry Elkins Widener Memorial and Houghton libraries, Harvard University. Thoreau's corrections and revisions in his own copy of the *Dial,* now in Special Collections at the Morris Library, Southern Illinois University at Carbondale, were checked by an editor, and several

[115] The dictionaries consulted are Nathan Bailey's *An Universal Etymological English Dictionary,* seventeenth edition (London: T. Osborne et al., 1759); Samuel Johnson and John Walker, *Johnson's English Dictionary* (Boston: Charles Ewer and T. H. Carter, 1828); John Walker, *A Critical Pronouncing Dictionary . . . of the English Language* (New York: Collins and Hannay, 1823); and Noah Webster, *An American Dictionary of the English Language* (New York: N. and J. White, 1838). See Walter Harding, "New Checklist of the Books in Thoreau's Library," in *Studies in the American Renaissance: 1983,* pp. 151-186. Thoreau's editions of Webster and Bailey are unknown; the editor has used the editions listed to approximate those on Thoreau's shelves.

[116] The reader should note that Thoreau often follows the older convention of using a "c" rather than a "k" to transliterate the Greek *kappa.* Thus, while δίκη is normally rendered "dike" today, Thoreau follows the practice still observed by some in his time and gives it as "dice".

were rechecked by David P. Koch, Curator of Special Collections at the Morris Library. In addition, the *Dial* texts of "Anacreon," "Pindar," and "Fragments of Pindar" were compared with their later adaptations in the 1849 and 1868 editions of *A Week*.

The editor and staff members read the textual apparatus against original sources four times. They read galley, page, and revised page proof, and "blue lines"—photoprints of the film positives from which the text is printed—three times against the transcript; two more readings at each stage were provided by Princeton University Press for the text and four more readings altogether for the apparatus.[117]

In accordance with guidelines established by the Center for Editions of American Authors and continued by the Committee on Scholarly Editions, this volume has been examined by an independent textual expert, Professor Bruce Redford, Department of English, University of Chicago. In addition, Professor Glenn Most, Department of Classics, Princeton University, examined and commented upon the notes for the translations of Pindar, and Professor Ralph Rosen, Department of Classical Studies, University of Pennsylvania, reviewed the entire text.

The editorial apparatus for each translation is collected immediately following this introduction. A headnote at the beginning of each apparatus describes the circumstances and dates of Thoreau's work on the translation, and identifies the copy-text and pre- and post-copy-text forms, giving physical descriptions for manuscript material, along with both Thoreau's source text and editions previous to this one. The kinds of information reported in the apparatus following each

---

[117] The number of readings differs because the text (pp. 1-148) was set by linotype, while the front and back matter were photocomposed on a Linotron 202 using machine-readable copy produced at the Textual Center at the University of California, Santa Barbara. The new technology has eliminated several stages from the old process.

headnote vary from one translation to the next. The categories of Textual Notes, Emendations, and End-of-Line Hyphenation are used as needed. For texts edited from manuscript, Thoreau's changes are reported in a list of Alterations; for texts based on the corrected *Dial,* a list of Thoreau's Corrections and Revisions records his changes; when later printed forms are relevant, a list of Variants is provided. The entries in all of these types of apparatus are keyed to page and line number.

In textual notes, the editor explains decisions to emend or not to emend the copy-text where those decisions vary from the general principles of emendation (see pp. 224-227). Textual notes may also be used to provide amplification for entries in the list of emendations, to describe physical features of the text, to comment on some of Thoreau's decisions as a translator, and to clarify confusing passages, sometimes by providing alternative translations.

Emendations record the editor's changes in the copy-text other than those listed as silent design changes or typographical conveniences (see pp. 222, 224), and editorial judgments about possible readings. Emendations provide first the emended reading, which appears in the text of this volume, then its source (in a few cases the editor is identified at the head of the list as the source for all of the emendations), then the rejected reading, which is always from the copy-text. When the editor makes a judgment about the intended position of a word or phrase, supplies matter for the text, or changes the text's format, a description of the change may be required. An asterisk preceding an emendation indicates that it is discussed in a textual note.

Alterations report all substantive changes Thoreau made to a manuscript copy-text. The form of reporting usually describes the effects of the changes, rather than their cause. For example, "saved] safe" means that Thoreau first wrote "safe" and then altered it to "saved", but the report does not explain whether he altered by erasing or by writing over the "fe". More complex alterations, including alternative readings unresolved by Thoreau (see pp. 223-224), are reported descriptively. Alterations provide first the final reading, the result of Thoreau's alteration, which appears in the text of this volume, then either the original reading or a description of how the original reading was changed. Many alterations for *The Seven Against Thebes* and "The Transmigrations of the Seven Brahmans" report more than one change to the same word or phrase. These alterations describe the physical relationship of one word or phrase involved in the change to another, without commenting on the sequence of the changes. The interested reader may reconstruct the development of a given reading by applying to the description the editor's general conclusions about the position of alternative readings as evidence for sequence. An asterisk preceding an alteration indicates that it is discussed in a textual note.

The list of Thoreau's corrections and revisions reports all of the changes Thoreau made in his translations published in the *Dial,* by writing them in his own copy of that periodical. The abbreviations "D" and "CD" mark, respectively, the original and corrected versions of a reading. Each entry provides first the reading that appears in the text of this volume (which may or may not be the revised reading, depending on the editor's judgment about Thoreau's final intention for the translation as an independent work), then the source of that reading, then the rejected reading and its source. An asterisk preceding an entry in the list of Thoreau's corrections and revisions indicates that it is discussed in a textual note.

The table of variants records differences between relevant printed forms of a given translation, using "D" for the *Dial,* "CD" for the corrected *Dial,* and "49" and "68" for the 1849 and 1868 editions of *A Week on the Concord and Merrimack Rivers.* Each entry provides first the reading that appears in the text of this volume, then its source, then the variant reading or readings and sources. When a printed form is not listed, the reader should assume that it agrees in substantives with the reading in this volume. An asterisk preceding an entry in the list of variants indicates that it is discussed in a textual note.

The final category of apparatus is the table of end-of-line hyphenation. This records compound word division at the end of the line in the copy-texts. Every instance of a compound word hyphenated at the end of a line in the copy-text requires a judgment on the part of the editor as to the form the word or words should take in this edition. Resolution of such problems is based on Thoreau's normal construction of the word or words in question, in other places in the copy-text itself or in other of his works. When no evidence of Thoreau's usual practice exists, his dictionaries are consulted to resolve the question.[118] The form recorded in the hyphenation list is the form to which the editor has resolved each of these cases. For example, in the copy-text for "Anacreon," the word "bookshop" (55.7) appears hyphenated at the end of a line. It could be resolved either to "bookshop" or "book-shop"; it appears in this volume as one word because Thoreau habitually spelled it as one word.

Hyphenation that has been introduced in the printing of this edition is not recorded with the end-of-line hyphenation. In all but one case, the hyphen should be retained in compound words hyphenated at line-end. The exception is 63.12-13 "common- / wealth", which is one word in the copy-text.

Several conventional symbols are employed throughout the apparatus. A wavy dash ($\sim$) to the right of the square bracket stands for the same word or phrase as precedes the bracket. An inferior caret ($_\wedge$) signifies the absence of a punctuation mark. The virgule with a space on either side ( / ) represents the end of a line.

[118] For a list of these, see footnote 115.

ABBREVIATIONS USED IN TEXTUAL NOTES
AND TABLES

| | |
|---|---|
| CD | Thoreau's copy of the *Dial,* with his corrections; in Special Collections, Morris Library, Southern Illinois University at Carbondale. |
| CSmH | The Huntington Library, San Marino, California. |
| D | *The Dial: A Magazine for Literature, Philosophy, and Religion,* 4 vols. 1: (Boston: Weeks, Jordan and Company, 1841); 2: (Boston: E. P. Peabody, 1842); 3: (Boston: E. P. Peabody, 1843); 4: (Boston: James Munroe and Company, 1844). Cited by volume and page numbers. |
| ed. | Signifies a reading for which the editor's judgment is the source. |
| ICarbS | Special Collections, Morris Library, Southern Illinois University at Carbondale. |
| *Journal 1* | Henry D. Thoreau, *Journal 1: 1837-1844,* ed. Elizabeth Hall Witherell et al. (Princeton: Princeton University Press, 1981). |
| MH | Houghton Library, Harvard University, Cambridge, Massachusetts. |
| MH-UA | Harvard University Archives, Harvard University, Cambridge, Massachusetts. |
| NNPM | The Pierpont Morgan Library, New York. |
| *Reform Papers* | Henry D. Thoreau, *Reform Papers,* ed. Wendell Glick (Princeton: Princeton University Press, 1973). |
| *A Week* | Henry D. Thoreau, *A Week on the Concord and Merrimack Rivers,* in one of several editions: Boston: James Munroe and Company, 1849; Boston: Ticknor and Fields, 1868; Princeton: Princeton University Press, 1980. |

49        Henry D. Thoreau, *A Week on the Concord
          and Merrimack Rivers* (Boston: James Mun-
          roe and Company, 1849).

68        Henry D. Thoreau, *A Week on the Concord
          and Merrimack Rivers,* new and rev. ed.
          (Boston: Ticknor and Fields, 1868).

1893      Henry D. Thoreau, *The Writings of Henry D.
          Thoreau,* 11 vols. (Boston: Houghton, Mifflin
          and Company, 1893). Cited by volume and
          page number.

1906      Henry D. Thoreau, *The Writings of Henry D.
          Thoreau,* 20 vols., ed. Bradford Torrey and
          Francis Allen (Boston: Houghton Mifflin,
          1906). Cited by volume and page number.

# The Prometheus Bound.

*Headnote*

Copy-text: *Dial* 3 (January 1843):363-386, as corrected by Thoreau (ICarbS).
Pre-copy-text:
  1. CSmH (HM 926). 21 leaves numbered from "1" to "32" in the center of some pages, as follows:
    "1"   fragment of white wove, 20.3 x 20.8 cm., unlined.
    "2"   fragment of blue wove with round stationer's mark, unlined, 12.4 x 19.7 cm.
    "3"   white wove, lined, 20.3 x 15.9 cm.
    "4"   fragment of white wove, lined, 18.8 x 19.7 cm.
    "5"   fragment of white wove with oval stationer's mark, unlined, 20 x 20 cm.
    "6"   blue wove with stationer's mark of basket of flowers in circle, 25 x 20.2 cm.
    "7"   white wove, unlined, 25.4 x 20.2 cm.
    "8"   white wove, unlined, 25 x 20 cm.
    "9"   blue wove with "P. S & Co." stationer's mark, unlined, 25 x 20 cm.
    "10"  fragment of blue wove, 8 x 20.2 cm.
    "11"  fragment of blue wove, 12.6 x 19.9 cm.
    "12"  fragment of blue wove, 11.5 x 20.1 cm.
    "13"-"31"  5 folios of blue wove with "P. S & Co." stationer's mark, unlined, 25.1 x 20.2 cm.
    "32"  blue wove with "P. S & Co." stationer's mark, unlined, 25.1 x 20 cm.
  Drafted about August 1842; mounted and bound with leaves of the printed version in the Riverside Edition (1893).
  2. MH (bMS Am 278.5.15). 22 unnumbered leaves of white wove, 24.7 x 19.7 cm. Drafted September-October 1842.
Previous editions: 1893, 10:288-336; 1906, 5:337-375.
Source: Aeschylus, *Tragœdiae: Ad exemplar accurate expressae, Editio stereotypa*, [ed. G. H. Schaefer] (Leipzig: Tauchnitz, 1819), pp. 17-57.

*Textual Notes*

  3.14  (*Strength and Force.*):   Thoreau adds a translation of the eponymous names, ΚΡΑΤΟΣ ΚΑΙ ΒΙΑ in Aeschylus.

3.15 (*Vulcan.*): Thoreau adds the Latin name for this god, which does not appear in Aeschylus.

4.25 [you'll hear,]: Thoreau adds this clarifying phrase, which does not appear in Aeschylus.

7.4 Except him: I.e., Prometheus.

8.5 insult: "insult" here is an imperative, ὕβριζε in Aeschylus, not part of the direct object of "bestow" in the next line.

8.12 *foreseeing*: Thoreau here translates the Greek προμηθέως ("Prometheus"); he italicizes it, perhaps to emphasize the meaning of the central character's name.

8.15 *alone*: Thoreau adds this word, which does not appear in Aeschylus.

11.11 Who so hard-hearted: Thoreau follows Aeschylus τίς ὧδε τλησικάρδιος which omits the verb "to be."

11.21 palm: Thoreau's literal translation of Aeschylus παλάμᾳ, "with the palm" (i.e., of someone's hand), preserves the sound and synecdoche of the Greek.

11.33-12.1 till . . . release: Thoreau, like Aeschylus, infers the direct object from its context: πρὶν ἂν ἐξ ἀγρίων / δεσμῶν χαλάσῃ.

16.29 will without bits: Thoreau's literal translation of Aeschylus γνώμῃ στομίων ἄτερ, "unbridled will."

21.18 thee.: ed.; "thee" in D and CD. In Aeschylus the line ends with a period.

22.21 undaunted: HM 926, bMS Am 278.5.15; the first "u" was set upside-down in the printed text.

24.22 harnessed: CD; "has harnessed" in D. Aeschylus, both manuscript drafts, and the context support the construction "[I] harnessed."

26.20 *All arts to mortals from Prometheus.*: CD; Thoreau italicizes this line. In D, he mistranslates the line, "*All arts from mortals to Prometheus*"; Thoreau's revision follows Aeschylus πᾶσαι τέχναι βροτοῖσιν ἐκ Προμηθέως.

27.28-29 in . . . spirit: CD; "in bright / Cheerfulness the cherishing spirit" in D. CD follows Aeschylus φαναῖς / θυμὸν ἀλδαίνουσαν ἐν εὐφροσύναις, "in bright cheerfulness having fed the heart."

27.32 tormented. * * *: This line in the original is metrically deficient; Schaefer signals the deficiency with a line of six asterisks.

28.10 blind * * *: This line in the original is metrically deficient; Thoreau follows Schaefer in signalling the deficiency with three asterisks.

29.1 Image of earth-born Argus: Context and word order in Aeschylus, [τὰν] τάλαιναν οἴστρος, / εἴδωλον Ἄργου γηγενοῦς, imply that this appositive refers to "some fly" at 28.33, not "me wretched".

29.1-2 cover it earth: An imperative and vocative, following Aeschylus ἄλευ' ὦ δᾶ, "cover it, O Earth."

31.11-12 Hephaistus' the hand: CD; "Hephaistus' hand" in D. CD follows Aeschylus Ἡφαίστου δὲ χείρ.

32.19 worth: CD; "worthy" in D. The Greek phrase in Aeschylus, ἀξίαν τριβὴν ἔχει, is difficult to translate well; it means "is a worthwhile expense of time." HM 926 reads "has worthy delay"; bMS Am 278.5.15 reads "worthy delay occasions."

32.33 it is: CD; "is" in D. The accusative absolute in Aeschylus, ἐξόν, requires that a subject be expressed in the English translation.

33.18-21 Prophets . . . gods: D; "he must" written in margin of CD, with no indication of position.

34.1-2 out unwilling,: CD; "out," in D. CD reproduces the wordplay of Aeschylus ἄκουσαν ἄκων. Thoreau's caret marking insertion is written directly over the comma after D "out"; he may have intended it as a cancellation of the comma.

34.24 to say,: CD; "to say aught," in D. D is an overly literal version of Aeschylus εἰπεῖν ὅ, τι / λοιπὸν πόνων.

36.34 Mæotic: ed.; D and CD "Mœotic" is incorrect. HM 926 and bMS Am 278.5.15 both read "Maeotic."

38.1 bear: CD; "hear" in D. CD follows Aeschylus φέροις.

38.15 tyrant's power: ed.; "tyrants' power" in D. Context indicates that this phrase refers to Zeus alone. Aeschylus τύραννα σκῆπτρα means "tyrannical powers." HM 926 reads "kingly powers"; bMS Am 278.5.15 reads "Kingly sceptre" on line, with "tyrants power" interlined above.

40.7-8 flood, boundary of continents,: CD; "flood boundary of continents" in D. CD clarifies the appositive relationship of "flood" and "boundary" in Aeschylus ῥεῖθρον ἠπείρων ὅρον.

40.9-10 sun-travelled * * *: Thoreau follows Schaefer in representing a lacuna in the original Greek text by three asterisks.

41.13 colony.: ed.; "colony" in D and CD. In both of the manuscript drafts and Aeschylus the sentence ends with a period.

42.8-10 thou clearly . . . Wert called: CD; "you clearly . . . Were called" in D. In CD, Thoreau underlines "you" and writes "thou" in the right margin, then underlines "Were" and writes "t" in the left margin. His intention to alter these words is less clear than if the printed text were cancelled, but the changes are accepted because they make the form of address consistent with "soothes thee" at 42.12.

44.35    Fates * * *:    Thoreau follows Schaefer in representing a lacuna in the original Greek by asterisks; Schaefer uses five asterisks.

47.10    brings us:    CD; "brings" in D. Neither Aeschylus nor the manuscript drafts includes the pronoun.

48.10    ask'st . . . me.:    Below this line and below 50.15 in this edition a vertical space has been added between speeches where the *Dial* printer neglected to do so.

48.13    change:    ed.; "change." in D and CD. Although the order of lines 48.13 and 48.14 varies from D and CD in both Aeschylus and the manuscript drafts, neither the Greek nor the English supports the punctuation in D. Aeschylus reads:

τῆς σῆς λατρείας τὴν ἐμὴν δυσπραξίαν,
σαφῶς ἐπίστασ', οὐκ ἂν ἀλλάξαιμ' ἐγώ.

HM 926 reads:
For thy service my ill fortune
Plainly know, I would not exchange.
bMS Am 278.5.15 reads:
For Thy servitude my ill fortune
Plainly know I would not change.
(final version)

51.30-31    for, it is base for a wise man to err.:    CD; "for, it is base to err, for a wise man." in D. CD does not follow the word order in Aeschylus, σοφῷ γὰρ αἰσχρὸν ἐξαμαρτάνειν, though HM 926 and bMS Am 278.5.15 do: "for a wise man it is base to err." Thoreau may have intended to revise to "for, for a wise man it is base to err" but the mark he drew to indicate transposition extends above "to err" only.

52.3    Fire's:    ed.; "Fires' " in D and CD. πυρός is singular possessive. Though bMS Am 278.5.15 "Fires" has no punctuation, HM 926 reads "A two-edged curl of fire."

52.24    bellowing of:    CD; "bellowing" in D. CD is a more literal rendering of Aeschylus βροντῆς μύκημ' ἀτέραμνον.

52.33    there:    CD; "the" in D. CD follows Aeschylus κοὐκ ἔστι νόσος.

53.14    wreaths:    ed.; "wreathes" in D and CD. Aeschylus ἕλικες, both manuscript drafts, and the context indicate that this should be a noun, not a verb.

## Emendations

| | |
|---|---|
| 3.21 | *and*]  ed.;  and |
| 10.1 | Chorus.]  ed.;  ~∧ |
| 18.22 | Know'st]  ed.;  Knows't |

* 21.18    thee.]  ed.;  ~∧
* 22.21    undaunted]  HM 926  bMS Am  278.5.15;
           nndaunted
  27.24    remain]  HM 926  bMS Am 278.5.15;  remian
  28.30    what]  ed.;  wbat
* 36.34    Mæotic]  ed.;  Mœotic
* 38.15    tyrant's]  ed.;  tyrants'
* 41.13    colony.]  ed.;  ~∧
* 48.10    ask'st . . . me.]  *vertical space below added in this
           edition*
* 48.13    change]  ed.;  ~.
  51.30-31 man to err.]  ed.;  ~. ~ ~, (*see Textual Note 51.
           30-31*)
* 52.3     Fire's]  ed.;  Fires'
* 53.14    wreaths]  ed.;  wreathes

## Thoreau's Corrections and Revisions

  12.13    that]  CD;  ~—  D
  13.17    Gæa]  CD;  Gaea  D
* 24.22    harnessed]  CD;  has harnessed  D
* 26.20    *All arts to mortals from Prometheus.*]  CD;  *All
           arts from mortals to Prometheus.*  D
* 27.29    cherishing the]  CD;  the cherishing  D
* 31.11-12 Hephaistus' the hand]  CD;  Hephaistus' hand  D
* 32.19    worth]  CD;  worthy  D
* 32.33    it is]  CD;  is  D
* 33.18-21 Prophets . . . gods.]  D;  he must *in right
           margin*  CD
* 34.1-2   out unwilling,]  CD;  out,  D
* 34.24    to say,]  CD;  to say aught,  D
* 38.1     bear]  CD;  hear  D
  40.7     flood,]  CD;  ~∧  D (*see Textual Note 40.7-8*)
* 42.8-10  thou clearly . . . Wert called]  CD;  you clearly . . .
           Were called  D
* 47.10    brings us]  CD;  brings  D
⸱* 51.30-31 for, it is base for a wise man to err.]  CD;  for, it
           is base to err, for a wise man.  D
* 52.24    bellowing of]  CD;  bellowing  D
* 52.33    there]  CD;  the  D

## End-of-Line Hyphenation

  37.6     forsooth

# Anacreon.

## Headnote

Copy-text: *Dial* 3 (April 1843):484-490.
Pre-copy-text: For "Cupid Wounded." (61.21-62.6): NNPM MA 1302:1 (*Journal 1*, p. 65), December 23, 1838.
Post-copy-text: *A Week* 1849, pp. 236-242; *A Week* 1868, pp. 238-244 (*A Week* 1980, pp. 225-231).
Source: *Carminum Poetarum novem, lyricæ poesews principum, fragmenta*, [ed. and trans. Henricus Stephanus], comm. M. Aemilius P. Fr. Portus (Heidelberg: Commelin, 1598); bound with Pindar, *Olympia, Pythia, Nemea, Isthmia. Græce & Latine*, [ed. and trans. Henricus Stephanus], comm. M. Aemilius P. Fr. Portus (Heidelberg: Commelin, 1598).
Sources of individual poems:

| Thoreau's Title | Title and Page Number in Stephanus |
|---|---|
| 57.1-13   On His Lyre. | Εἰς λύραν. (p. 47) |
| 57.15-22   To A Swallow. | Εἰς χελιδόνα. (p. 62) |
| 57.24-58.8   On A Silver Cup. | Εἰς ποτήριον ἀργυροῦν. (pp. 54-55) |
| 58.10-17   On Himself. | Εἰς ἑαυτόν. (p. 54) |
| 58.19-59.22   To A Dove. | Εἰς πεισεράν. (pp. 51-52) |
| 59.24-35   On Love. | Εἰς Ἔρωτα. (p. 50) |
| 60.1-14   On Women. | Εἰς γυναῖκας. (pp. 47-48) |
| 60.16-24   On Lovers. | Εἰς τοὺς ἐρῶντας ᾠδάριον. (p. 73) |
| 60.26-61.5   To A Swallow. | Εἰν χελιδόνα. (p. 53) |
| 61.7-19   To A Colt. | Πῶλε Θρηϊκίη, τί δέ με (p. 77) |
| 61.21-62.6   Cupid Wounded. | Εἰς Ἔρωτα. (p. 65) |

[Anomalies in several of these titles result from both older orthographic conventions and misprints: 57.24-58.8 ἀργυροῦν would now be written ἀργυροῦν; 58.19-59.22 πεισεράν is probably a misprint for περιστεράν and 60.26-61.5 Εἰν for Εἰς. In addition, in a modern edition these Greek titles would not begin with capital letters.]

## Textual Notes

56.13   ὃ: The *Dial* and *A Week* versions are both incorrect in reading ὅ. This edition emends from Thoreau's probable source, Ralph Cudworth, *The True Intellectual System of the Universe*, ed.

Thomas Birch, 4 vols. (London: J. F. Dove, for Richard Priestly, 1820), 2:71.

    56.14 *perceive*: CD; *"understand"* in D. This change is accepted as a revision that refines Thoreau's translation rather than fitting the piece for inclusion in *A Week,* as do the other alterations to the introductory prose in his copy of the *Dial.* Cudworth translates the phrase as "that cannot be apprehended otherwise than by the flower of the mind." Thoreau may have been influenced by the translation in "The Oracles of Zoroaster" in *The Phenix* (New York: William Gowan, 1835), p. 167; it reads, "which it becomes you to understand with the flower of the mind."

    56.32-33 odes . . . 24: Thoreau's reference is to poetry in his essay, "Natural History of Massachusetts," in *Dial* 3 (July 1842):19-40. The first ode, on p. 23, has no title:

> We pronounce thee happy, Cicada,
> For on the tops of the trees,
> Drinking a little dew,
> Like any king thou singest.
> For thine are they all,
> Whatever thou seest in the fields,
> And whatever the woods bear.
> Thou art the friend of the husbandmen,
> In no respect injuring any one;
> And thou art honored among men,
> Sweet prophet of summer.
> The Muses love thee,
> And Phœbus himself loves thee,
> And has given thee a shrill song;
> Age does not wrack thee,
> Thou skilful, earthborn, song-loving,
> Unsuffering, bloodless one;
> Almost thou art like the gods.
> > > (Stephanus, Εἰς τέττιγα., p. 67)

The second, on p. 24, is called the "Return of Spring":

> Behold, how spring appearing,
> The Graces send forth roses;
> Behold, how the wave of the sea
> Is made smooth by the calm;
> Behold, how the duck dives;
> Behold, how the crane travels;
> And Titan shines constantly bright.
> The shadows of the clouds are moving;
> The works of man shine;

The earth puts forth fruits;
The fruit of the olive puts forth.
The cup of Bacchus is crowned,
Along the leaves, along the branches,
The fruit, bending them down, flourishes.

                    (Stephanus, Εἰς τὸ ἔαρ., pp. 63-64)

Earlier versions of both appear in Thoreau's *Journal*, the first in a passage written after December 15, 1838 (*Journal 1*, p. 62) and the second in an entry dated December 23, 1838 (*Journal 1*, p. 65).

57.22   heart. * * *:   Thoreau's asterisks represent the rest of the poem, which he has omitted.

57.32   wagons:   Thoreau follows the text of the *Anacreontea* ἁμάξας which is plural. "The Wagon" is one name given to the constellation Ursa Major in England.

58.8   Lyæus.:   49; "Lyæus" in D and CD. Thoreau neglected to supply the period at the end of the poem when he entered corrections in his copy of the *Dial;* it appears in the 1849 and 1868 editions of *A Week,* however. Because Thoreau's translation reorders the last four lines of this poem, the Greek is not a precise authority for including the period, but this edition emends from *A Week,* assuming its addition to be an authorial correction of the earlier error.

58.25   errand?—:   49; "errand?" in D and CD. Thoreau apparently added the dash to his translation of δέ while preparing it for inclusion in *A Week.* The speaker changes here, and Thoreau's revision is accepted as an attempt to make the change clearer.

## Emendations

* 56.13        ὁ] ed.;   ὅ
* 56.14        *perceive*]  CD;   *understand*
* 58.8         Lyæus.]   49;   ~$_\wedge$
* 58.25        errand?—]   49;   ~?$_\wedge$

## Thoreau's Corrections and Revisions

  56.3-4       we . . . to]   D;   let us   CD
  56.4-6       Anacreon . . . readers.*]   D;   the Teian poet.*   CD
* 56.14        *perceive*]   CD;   *understand*   D

## Variants

  55.6         WE]   D;   I   49   68
  55.16        We]   D;   I   49   68

| 55.19 | we believe] D; I believe 49 68 |
| 56.3-4 | we ... to] D; let us 49 68 |
| 56.4-6 | Anacreon ... readers.*] D; the Teian poet.* 49 68 |
| * 56.14 | *perceive*] CD; *understand* D |
| 56.30-31 | sensual.] D; *followed in 49 by* ¶Perhaps these are the best that have come down to us. *followed in 68 by* ¶These are some of the best that have come down to us. |
| 56.32-34 | *The following ... to us.] D; *lacking* 49 68 |
| * 58.8 | Lyæus.] 49; ~∧ D |
| * 58.25 | errand?—] 49; ~?∧ D |

## End-of-Line Hyphenation

| 55.7 | bookshop |

# The Seven Against Thebes.

## Headnote

Copy-text: CSmH (HM 13193). 21 leaves, numbered by Thoreau in pencil in the center of each page of the translation from "1" to "39" as follows:

"1"-"12"    3 folios of white wove "Ames," 24.7 x 19.7 cm.
"13"    fragment of blue wove, lined, 18.3 x 19.8 cm.
"14"-"15"    1 leaf of blue wove, lined recto, unlined verso, 25.1 x 19.6 cm.
"16"-"19"    1 folio of white wove "Ames," 24.7 x 19.7 cm.
"20"-"30"    3 folios of white wove, 25.4 x 20 cm.
"31"-"38"    2 folios of white wove "Ames," 24.7 x 19.7 cm.
"39"    1 leaf of white wove "Ames," 24.7 x 19.9 cm.

Probably drafted summer or fall 1843.

Pre-copy-text: For 79.33-80.1: NNPM MA 1302:2 (*Journal 1*, p. 106), January 29, 1840; for 90.1-6: NNPM MA 1718 (*Journal 1*, p. 165), July & August 1840, and "The Service," NNPM MA 607 (*Reform Papers*, p. 3), July 1840.

Previous editions: L. M. Kaiser, "Thoreau's Translation of *The Seven Against Thebes*," *Emerson Society Quarterly*, no. 17 (4th Quarter 1959):3-28 (also published separately, with the same title, by The Emerson Society, Drawer 1080, Hartford, Conn.).

Source: Aeschylus, *Tragœdiae: Ad exemplar accurate expressae, Editio stereotypa*, [ed. G. H. Schaefer] (Leipzig: Tauchnitz, either 1817 or 1819), either pp. 67-115 or pp. 59-98.

## Textual Notes

63.4  Scout.: "Messenger ? Scout." in the manuscript; Aeschylus ΑΓΓΕΛΟΣ ΚΑΤΑΣΚΟΠΟΣ means "Messenger-Scout." Because Thoreau settled on "Scout" or "Sc" in the text of the play, the editor emends to "Scout" here.

63.15  (eye)lids: Aeschylus βλέφαρα can be translated as either "eyes" or "eyelids." Thoreau's parentheses allow for both possibilities.

63.25  Cadmeans: As in the manuscript; Aeschylus closes the sentence with a period.

63.30  vigor (firmness): Alternative loose translations for Aeschylus βλάστημον, which is better translated "growth."

65.5-6  who will not loiter by the way I trust: Aeschylus πέποιθα μὴ ματᾷν ὁδῷ means "who, I believe, are not loitering along the way."

65.7-8   And . . . treachery.:  Followed by a vertical line that divides the first scene from the second. Thoreau did not mark similar divisions elsewhere in the play.

65.36   battle:  As in the manuscript; Aeschylus closes the sentence with a period.

66.11   Host:  Thoreau cancels "Host" but does not supply an alternative translation for στρατός; "Host" is restored in this edition.

66.31-32   from the stern—:  Thoreau mistranslates Aeschylus πρυμνόθεν, "to its roots" or "utterly," apparently mistaking it for πρύμνηθεν, "from the stern," "from behind."

66.34-67.2   spending . . . Cadmus:  Aeschylus Ἑλλάδος / φθόγγον χέουσαν, καὶ δόμους ἐφεστίους· / ἐλευθέραν δὲ γῆν τε καὶ Καδμου πόλιν is the object of μή . . . ἐκθαυνίσητε ("do not eradicate") at 66.31. These lines, the punctuation of which is uncertain, are more accurately translated "[do not destroy] the hearths and homes, the free land and city of Kadmus, speaking the tongue of Hellas."

67.23   Resounds above:  Thoreau mistranslates Aeschylus βοᾷ, "with a shout," apparently mistaking it for a form of the verb βοάω, "to reverberate or make a loud noise."

71.25-26   I feared hearing:  Aeschylus ἔδεισ᾽ ἀκού- / σασα can also be translated "I was afraid when I heard."

72.14   gods.:  "gods," in the manuscript; in Aeschylus the sentence ends with a period. Attribution of speakers for lines 72.12-17 is ambiguous; Thoreau may have used a comma to reflect his uncertainty.

72.23   Do . . . ill:  μή μοι θεοὺς καλοῦσα βουλεύου κακῶς· is more clearly translated "Please do not, when you call on the gods, ask their counsel badly." Broken type in Schaefer's edition causes βουλευου to appear as βουλειου.

73.14-15   (greatly) . . . (excessively):  Alternative translations for Aeschylus ὑπερφοβοῦ, "to fear greatly."

75.16-17   nor do . . . Ismenus:  The guardian deities preside at Ismenus as well as at Dirce's fountains and other locations.

76.2   and, and:  Thoreau's literal translation of the double conjunction τε καὶ; it is more commonly translated "both . . . and."

76.6   [EXIT ETEOCLES]:  Thoreau adds this stage direction in pencil; it does not appear in Schaefer's edition.

77.9   Ogygian:  ὠγυγίαν in Aeschylus; Thoreau's capitalization emphasizes that the Greek word is derived from the name of Ogyges, the legendary first king of Greece.

79.5 messengers: Here and for 83.26 "enemys", 85.17 "mans", 96.29 "others", 101.7 "messengers", and 101.12 "others", Aeschylus gives the singular possessive; for 102.10 "fathers", the situation is more complicated (see Textual Note 102.10). The editor has not emended in any case.

79.11 lot: As in the manuscript; in Aeschylus the sentence ends with a period.

79.14-15 does not permit to pass: In Aeschylus as in Thoreau's translation, the direct object "Tydeus and his army" is understood rather than expressed.

79.16 victims: Aeschylus σφάγια can also be translated "omens"; the entrails of the sacrificial animals have indicated where Tydeus should attack.

81.7 dice: Aeschylus ἐν κύβοις refers to dice used in gambling. Elswhere in this translation, "dice" is Thoreau's transliteration of δίκη, "justice."

82.2 a device: "an device" in the manuscript. The editor emends to "a" to complete Thoreau's alteration from "an emblem".

82.29 prompt . . . very: Thoreau follows the word order of Aeschylus κεἰ στόμαργός ἐστ' ἄγαν; a less literal translation is "very prompt with his tongue."

83.16-18 And . . . gate—: Aeschylus ἵππους δ' ἐν ἀμπυκτῆρσιν ἐμβριμωμένας / δινεῖ, θελούσας πρὸς πύλαις πεπτωκέναι can also be translated "And the horses, chafing in their bridles / He whirls, [horses] wishing to fall against the gate."

84.26 them, angry: "them angry" in the manuscript. The emendation is based on Aeschylus τώς νιν Ζεὺς νεμέ- / τωρ ἐπ- ίδοι κοταίνων, which makes it clear that it is Zeus who is angry.

85.7 (his): Thoreau adds this word, which does not appear in Aeschylus.

85.16 looking fear: Aeschylus φόβον βλέπων, "looking like fear itself," is a traditional epithet for Ares.

85.17-18 to be guarded: "to guarded" in the manuscript. The emendation is based on Aeschylus φυλακτέον, which Thoreau has translated incompletely.

87.11 it: Followed in the manuscript by a pencilled question mark, apparently for Thoreau's own reference; it does not appear in Aeschylus.

87.14 attributed: "(attributed" in the manuscript, interlined above the line it completes. The open parenthesis indicates the proper position of "attributed".

87.25 raised: Underlined and followed by a question mark in the manuscript, apparently for Thoreau's own reference. In Schaefer the word is neither emphasized nor followed by a question mark.

89.30 to thee: "to the" in the manuscript. The emendation is based on Aeschylus σοι, "to thee."

89.34 no: Thoreau interlined "not" above "no"; the editor emends to accept the alternative on the line on the basis that "not" was the beginning of a revision that Thoreau did not complete.

90.20 (Ate's . . . fruit.): In Schaefer this line is bracketed as textually dubious.

90.23 any craft: Aeschylus πανουργίᾳ can also be translated "however skillful."

91.1 pomp: Thoreau transliterates πομπήν, "a sending away" or "a solemn procession."

92.23 (she): Thoreau adds this word, which does not appear in Aeschylus.

93.8 (the fact): Thoreau adds this phrase, which does not appear in Aeschylus, to complete his translation of ἐπωνύμῳ, "eponymously."

93.26 (her attention): Thoreau adds this phrase, which does not appear in Aeschylus.

95.4 Saying gain: Aeschylus λέγουσα κέρδος can also be translated "Speaking of gain."

95.32-33 (would be said): Thoreau adds the parentheses, which do not appear in Aeschylus.

95.33-34 be long: "belong" in the manuscript. The emendation is based on Aeschylus οὐδε χρὴ μακράν, "Nor must [the speech] be a long one."

98.25 (them): Thoreau adds this word, which does not appear in Aeschylus.

98.33-34 (water into the hold): Thoreau adds the parentheses, which do not appear in Aeschylus.

99.5 The seven the chiefs: In the manuscript "7th leader" is interlined below "chiefs"; a curving line encloses both. The editor emends to accept the alternative on the line on the basis of Aeschylus τὰς δ᾽ ἑβδόμας ὁ σεμνὸς ἑβδομαγέτας / ἄναξ Ἀπόλλων εἵλετ᾽, "Noble lord Apollo, the Commander of the Seven, has taken the seven great chiefs." Thoreau's confusion here may stem from his indecision as to which of two cult epithets of Apollo Aeschylus is using: Ἑβδομαγέτας, "Patron of the seven warriors attacking Thebes" or Ἑβδομαγενής, "He born on the seventh day of the month."

99.9-10 (The . . . seed): In Schaefer this line is bracketed as textually dubious.

99.12  hands * * *:  Thoreau's asterisks replace four dashes in Schaefer; the dashes mark the Chorus' interruption of the Scout.

99.18  (that):  Thoreau adds the parentheses, which do not appear in Aeschylus.

100.8  (taken away):  Thoreau adds the parentheses and a question mark, which do not appear in Aeschylus. The question mark is apparently for his own reference.

101.14-16  But, friends, with . . . Row:  "But friends with . . . Row" in the manuscript. The emendation is based on Aeschylus ὦ φίλαι κατ' οὖρον / ἐρέσσετ' which makes it clear that the friends are being addressed directly, and are not the subject of the clause.

102.10  fathers house:  Aeschylus πατρῴους δόμους, is literally translated "forefathers' houses," but Thoreau's singular construction is acceptable because of the context and the general usage of πατρῴους.

102.20-21  (Not . . . determined;):  Thoreau adds the parentheses, though this line is not bracketed in either the 1817 or 1819 Schaefer editions. Later editions of the Schaefer text, however, either bracket the line (1829) or provide it in an endnote (1843) as a textually dubious gloss. Thoreau's parentheses in his translation may reflect either an acquaintance with later editions of the Schaefer text he was using, or his reference to editions in the Harvard College Library which also omit or otherwise question the status of this line (e.g., those of Schütz, Blomfield, and Dindorf).

102.24  by well named:  Thoreau mistranslates Aeschylus εὐωνύμων, "inauspiciously," on the basis of its root elements: εὖ, "well," in combination with a form of the verb ὀνομάζω, "to name." The alternatives Thoreau interlines, "As was foretold" and "Auspiciously," are also incorrect and suggest that he failed to understand the ironic twist in this idiom, which is that someone "well-named" could come to be seen as "ill-fated" or "doomed."

103.14  it was just:  "it just" in the manuscript. The emendation is based on Aeschylus ὥστ' ἴσον λαχεῖν, in which the verb is explicit.

103.21  lots (fates):  Alternative translations for Aeschylus λαχαί.

104.2  Of:  "Off" in the manuscript. The emendation is based on Aeschylus προπασῶν γυναικῶν, "of all women."

104.11  By . . . strife:  Following this line in the manuscript, which occurs at the bottom of a verso page, Thoreau fails to translate the next five lines in Aeschylus:

νείκεος ἐν τελευτᾷ.
πέπαυται δ' ἔχθος.
ἐν δὲ γαίᾳ ζωὰ

φονορρύτῳ μέμικται
κάρτα δ' εἶσ' ὅμαιμοι.

In the ending of their quarrel.
Their enmity has ceased. On the land
Drenched with gore, their life
Has been mingled;
Their blood is truly one.

In this edition extra vertical space marks the omission.

104.16-17   of . . . making:   The position of a vertical line in the manuscript suggests that Thoreau may have intended to move "Mars making" to precede "of property"; his intention remains unclear, however, and this edition follows the manuscript.

107.32-33   he shall obtain:   Following this line in the manuscript, where it occurs at the bottom of a verso page, Thoreau fails to translate Aeschylus ἄγος, "the curse," which Polynices "shall obtain [of] his country's gods".

108.30   alive him dead with kindred mind:   Thoreau deals poorly with Aeschylus θανόντι ζῶσα συγγόνῳ φρενί, in which the dative θανόντι is dependent on συγγόνῳ. The phrase means that Antigone, alive, is of kindred mind with her dead brother.

110.13   mourners:   Thoreau added several strokes to the "m" but his intention is unclear; he may have meant to alter it to "M".

110.13-14   mourners; . . . unmourned:   In the manuscript a vertical line connects "mourners" and "unmourned"; Thoreau's intention is unclear.

110.31   Not . . . wave:   This line is at the bottom of the manuscript page; "of foreign men / Inundated for the most part.   (END)" is written vertically in the right hand margin.

110.34   (END):   Thoreau adds this stage direction in pencil; it does not appear in Schaefer's edition.

## Emendations

All of the emendations are based on the editor's judgment and informed by an examination of Thoreau's source.

| * 63.4 | Scout.] Messenger  ?  Scout. |
|---|---|
| 63.9 | Citizens]  Ctizens |
| 63.14 | city's]  cty's |
| 64.15 | besieged]  beseiged |
| 64.27 | all.]  *possibly* ~∧ |
| 65.3 | have]  hav |
| 65.13 | For]  Fo |

| | | |
|---|---|---|
| * 66.11 | Host] | *cancelled* |
| 66.27 | thou] | thout |
| 68.17 | Excited] | Eexcited |
| 68.22 | The] | Th |
| 68.28 | host] | ~. |
| 69.16 | groans;] | ~.; |
| 69.17 | descended] | descnded |
| 70.1 | blessed] | bessed |
| 71.27 | tumult] | tumullt |
| 72.10 | their] | ther |
| * 72.14 | gods.] | ~, |
| 74.9 | Zeus,] | ~,, |
| 77.12 | filthy] | filthly |
| 77.30 | declare] | decare |
| 77.36 | fire] | fire fire |
| 78.28 | obtaining] | obtaing |
| 80.12 | sufficient] | suffiient |
| 80.19 | shield] | shild |
| 81.35 | Lightnings] | Lightenings |
| * 82.2 | a device] | an device |
| 82.14 | tongue] | tonge |
| 82.31 | Polyphontes'] | Polyphontus' |
| 82.36 | another] | anothe |
| 83.10 | Eteocles] | Eteoclus |
| * 83.16 | And] | An |
| 84.7 | loud] | *interlined without a caret above* sound |
| * 84.26 | them, angry] | ~∧ ~ |
| * 85.17-18 | to be guarded] | to guarded |
| 86.16 | is probable] | probable |
| * 87.11 | it] | ~? |
| * 87.14 | attributed] | (attributed |
| * 87.25 | raised] | *underlined and followed by a question mark* |
| 88.30 | curls] | curles |
| 89.10 | Council] | Coucil |
| 89.12 | worthy of death] | *interlined without a caret above* leagued with him |
| * 89.30 | to thee] | to the |
| * 89.34 | no] | not |
| 91.1 | Aiming] | *possibly* Striving |
| 92.21 | a] | an |
| 92.23 | And] | An |
| 94.18 | there] | *possibly* their |
| 95.2 | curse] | *possibly* ~— |

| * 95.33-34 | be long] belong |
| 96.1 | Nay] Say |
| 96.3 | off] of |
| 96.4 | your] yor |
| 97.14 | counsels] cousels |
| 98.16 | From] Frm |
| 99.5 | seven the] *possibly* seventh (*see Textual Note 99.5*) |
| 99.5 | chiefs] *uncancelled* 7th leaders *interlined below* (*see Textual Note 99.5*) |
| 99.18 | indeed] inded |
| 100.5 | And] An |
| 100.7 | unhappy] *interlined without a caret above* the prayers |
| 100.8 | away)] ~)? (*see Textual Note 100.8*) |
| 100.28 | Bacchus] Bachus |
| 101.14 | But, friends, with] ~∧ ~∧ ~ (*see Textual Note 101.14*) |
| 102.2 | twisted] *interlined without a caret above* girdle |
| 102.20 | friendship] frindship |
| 102.30 | piercing] peiercing |
| 103.11 | account] accont |
| *103.14 | it was just] it just |
| *104.2 | Of] Off |
| *104.11 | By . . . strife] *vertical space added below* |
| *104.16-17 | of . . . making] *preceded by vertical line in MS* |
| 104.19 | They] The |
| 105.5 | And] An |
| 106.14 | And] Am |
| *107.32-33 | he shall obtain] *vertical space added below* |
| 108.3 | foreign] foreing |
| 108.9 | And] An |
| 108.28 | shares] share |
| *110.13 | mourners] *possibly* Mourners |
| 110.13 | mourners] *preceded by vertical line in MS* (*see Textual Note 110.13-14*) |
| 110.14 | unmourned] *preceded by vertical line in MS* (*see Textual Note 110.13-14*) |
| 110.32-34 | of . . . END)] *written in right margin* (*see Textual Note 110.34*) |

## Alterations

Unless otherwise noted, Thoreau altered his text in ink.

| 63.1 | Seven] seven |
| 63.1 | Against] against |

63.10      that which]  *interlined above uncancelled* whate'er
           (e'er *added*)
63.13      managing]  *interlined above cancelled* holding
63.17      thanked for]  *interlined above uncancelled* (cause
           of)
63.20      blamed]  *interlined above cancelled* sounded
63.24      called]  *inserted preceding* the Defender
63.24      the]  *interlined above cancelled* the
63.24      Defender]  *cancelled* so called *interlined below*
63.25      indeed defend]  *interlined above cancelled* Indeed
           be a defender to *and preceded by cancelled* Called
63.29      exceeds]  exceedeth it
63.30-31   Increasing . . . his body]  *interlined above uncan-
           celled* Adding much vigorous strength of body,
63.32      of whatever age]  *interlined above uncancelled*
           (having whatever season)
63.33      aid]  *interlined above cancelled* help
64.1       so]  that
64.1       ne'er]  *interlined above cancelled* never
64.3       And His]  *interlined above cancelled* And
64.3       children]  *followed by cancelled* too
64.5       your]  *interlined above cancelled* his
64.7       your]  *interlined with a caret above* of
64.13      And]  *followed by cancelled* (now)
64.13      is Heaven]  Heaven is *marked for transposing*
64.13      Heaven]  heaven
64.15      now this long while besieged]  besieged now this
           long while *marked for transposing*
64.15      now]  *interlined above*
64.15      long]  *interlined above with a caret*
64.16      war]  *preceded by cancelled* The
64.16      succeeded]  *interlined above cancelled* proceeded
64.23      This one]  *interlined with a caret above uncan-
           celled* He
64.25      intends]  *interlined above uncancelled* designs
           *which is interlined above cancelled* plots
64.28      now]  *preceded by cancelled* But *and followed by
           cancelled* therefore *interlined above with a caret*
64.28      ramparts]  *interlined below cancelled* battlements
64.28      the bulwark]  the *interlined above* and
65.4       to]  *preceded by cancelled* of
65.5-6     who . . . I trust]  who I trust will not loiter by the
           way *marked for transposing*
65.9       Sc]  E

| | |
|---|---|
| 65.13 | myself] *interlined above with a caret* |
| 65.13 | observer] *interlined with a caret above uncancelled* spy |
| 65.13 | the] their |
| 65.14 | forsooth] *interlined above with a caret* |
| 65.20 | Ares] ares |
| 65.22 | the] this |
| 65.31 | But] but |
| 66.8 | arrange] *interlined above uncancelled* Place |
| 66.10-11 | completely Armed the Host of Argives] *interlined below cancelled* the the well armed host |
| 66.11 | Host] host |
| 66.22 | a faithful] *interlined below cancelled* will have |
| 66.26 | the things] these things |
| 67.4 | express] *interlined above uncancelled* speak |
| 67.14 | speech] *preceded by cancelled* word |
| 67.14 | a] *added* |
| 67.15 | my] *interlined above cancelled* our |
| 67.16 | by] *interlined above with a caret* |
| 67.27 | succour] ~— |
| 67.30 | divinities] gods |
| 68.2 | clash] *interlined above uncancelled* noise |
| 68.2 | clash;] ~— |
| 68.15 | For] Of |
| 69.9 | who] and |
| 70.1 | queen] *followed by cancelled* O |
| 70.4 | O ye] *cancelled* and *interlined below* |
| 70.5 | And] and |
| 70.9 | To] So |
| 70.13 | divinities] ~— |
| 70.20 | sacrifice] sacrificing |
| 70.21 | city] *followed by cancelled* to thes |
| 70.28 | sigh] *interlined above cancelled* cry |
| 70.33 | insolence] *interlined above uncancelled* courage |
| 71.8 | worsted] *interlined above uncancelled* ruined |
| 72.1 | with] *interlined above uncancelled* against |
| 72.4 | Hastening] hastening |
| 72.6 | the roaring] *interlined above cancelled* a noise |
| 72.8 | indeed] *followed by cancelled* I |
| 72.15 | then as] *interlined above with a caret* |
| 72.20 | Desert] desert |
| 72.27 | power] *preceded by cancelled* Sup |
| 73.14 | composed] *interlined above uncancelled* calm |

| | |
|---|---|
| 73.18 | I] *interlined above cancelled* we |
| 73.20 | burst] *followed by cancelled* into |
| 74.7 | both] *interlined above with a caret* |
| 74.12 | bestowed] *followed by cancelled* on us |
| 74.19 | wouldst] would |
| 74.20 | thing] *interlined above uncancelled* end |
| 75.11 | enemy] *interlined above cancelled* enemy |
| 75.16 | At] As |
| 75.19 | saved] safe |
| 75.31 | at] all |
| 75.31 | mayst] may |
| 75.31 | thou] you |
| 76.6 | [EXIT ETEOCLES] ] *interlined in pencil below* set on fire by |
| 76.15 | some] *interlined above cancelled* they |
| 76.32 | emits] *interlined above uncancelled* sends |
| 77.5 | the] *followed by cancelled* citizens |
| 77.15 | heaven] *preceded by cancelled* the |
| 78.5 | and] *written in margin preceding* Against |
| 78.10 | new-born] *preceded by cancelled* The |
| 78.31 | Hope] Hopes |
| 78.33 | Semich.] Ch. |
| 78.34 | us] *followed by cancelled* of |
| 79.20 | raging] *interlined above* dragon with |
| 80.1 | excels] *interlined below uncancelled* is distinguished |
| 80.11-12 | before them] *interlined above cancelled* against him |
| 80.16 | And] *preceded by cancelled* But |
| 80.19 | a] *interlined above cancelled* the |
| 80.22 | one.] ~, |
| 80.23 | fall] *interlined above uncancelled* come |
| 80.24 | dying—] *interlined below uncancelled* deaad |
| 81.7 | His] his |
| 81.10 | field] ~— |
| 81.17 | fates] *followed by cancelled* on ac |
| 81.17 | to behold] *followed by cancelled* on ac |
| 81.26 | is conceived] *interlined above uncancelled* resolves |
| 81.28 | perform] *interlined below cancelled* fulfil |
| 81.29 | Heaven] heaven |
| 81.32 | Zeus] *interlined below cancelled* Jove |
| 81.35 | Lightnings] s *interlined above* |

* 82.2        device] *interlined above uncancelled* emblem

82.5        furnished] *interlined below uncancelled* prepared
            *with uncancelled* provided *interlined above* pre-
            pared

82.20        being mortal] *interlined above with a caret*

82.26        justice] *interlined above uncancelled* vengeance

82.26        made] *interlined above with a caret*

82.29        very] *interlined above with a caret*

82.34        His protectress] *interlined in pencil above un-
            cancelled* Standing before him

82.34        and by] *interlined above uncancelled* with

83.6        virgin apartments] *interlined above uncancelled*
            Colts seats

83.14        strike] *interlined above uncancelled* advance

83.16-17        bridles raging against] *interlined above uncan-
            celled* headgear storming

83.21        snorting] *interlined above uncancelled* nostril
            boasting

83.22        fashioned] *interlined above uncancelled* devised

83.26        enemys] *written over* enemies

84.1        Such an] *interlined above uncancelled* This

84.7        at] all

84.7        loud] *interlined above* sound

84.8        greedy] *interlined above uncancelled* furious

84.14        deck] *interlined above uncancelled* ornament

84.17        words] *preceded by cancelled* your

84.31        great] *preceded by cancelled* a

85.3-4        not indeed] indeed not *marked for transposing*

85.9        whirling] *interlined above uncancelled* varying

85.16        Raves] raves

85.24        dragon] *interlined above uncancelled* serpent

85.25        offspring] *interlined above uncancelled* son

85.29        practice] *interlined below uncancelled* combat *with
            uncancelled* trial *on-line and uncancelled* need *in-
            terlined above* trial

85.31        of his arms] *followed by cancelled* to be blamed,

85.32        fitly] *interlined above uncancelled* rightly

86.27        lay] *interlined above uncancelled* cast

87.1-2        above his eyes] *interlined above uncancelled* su-
            perior in his eyes

87.11        producing it] *interlined above uncancelled* grow-
            ing

87.19        reproach] *interlined above uncancelled* disgrace

| | |
|---|---|
| 87.29 | hurled] *interlined below cancelled* hurled *which is written over* hurling |
| 87.30 | retail] *interlined above uncancelled* make |
| 87.32 | delay] *interlined above uncancelled* passage |
| 87.34 | of Arcadia] *interlined above uncancelled* Arcadian |
| 88.31 | impious] *followed by cancelled* men |
| 89.2 | Amphiareaus] Amphiareus |
| 89.9 | Erinnys] *preceded by cancelled* the |
| 89.12 | worthy of death] *interlined above uncancelled* leagued with him |
| 89.13 | Inspecting his name] *interlined below uncancelled* Blaming by name |
| 89.15 | two] too |
| 89.19 | agreeable] *interlined above cancelled* friendly |
| 89.21 | those] *followed by cancelled* to |
| 89.24 | lay waste] *interlined above uncancelled* destroy |
| 89.33 | under] *interlined above uncancelled* in |
| 89.33 | hostile] *interlined above cancelled* foreign |
| 90.3 | But] but |
| 90.7 | in his] in *interlined above uncancelled* of |
| 90.14 | omen] *interlined above uncancelled* bird |
| 90.15 | the] *interlined above* |
| 90.19 | derived] *interlined below uncancelled* gathered |
| 90.23 | craft] *interlined above uncancelled* cunning |
| 90.24 | perishes] *preceded by cancelled* He |
| 90.28 | snare] *interlined below uncancelled* net *with* catching *interlined above* net |
| 90.33 | reverent] *interlined above uncancelled* pious |
| 91.17 | oppose] *interlined below uncancelled* range *with uncancelled* station *interlined above* range |
| 91.18 | blooming] *interlined above uncancelled* vigorous |
| 91.23 | it] is |
| 91.23 | heaven] *interlined above cancelled* go |
| 91.24 | be fortunate] *interlined above uncancelled* succeed |
| 92.1 | thyself,] *followed by cancelled* what fates |
| 92.2 | prays] *interlined above uncancelled* vows |
| 92.3 | against the city] *interlined above cancelled* against |
| 92.12 | requite] *interlined above uncancelled* punish |
| 92.14 | says] *preceded by cancelled* he |
| 92.17 | Polynices] Polinices |
| 92.21 | soldier] *interlined above uncancelled* armed man |

\* 92.23        (she)]  *interlined above with a caret*

92.28        home]  *interlined above uncancelled* house

92.29        inventions]  *interlined below uncancelled* devices

92.34        steer]  *interlined above uncancelled* navigate

93.2         brought . . . end]  *interlined above uncancelled* ac-
             complished

93.17        perhaps]  *interlined above uncancelled* quickly

93.21        education]  *interlined above uncancelled* nursing

93.30        quite]  *interlined above uncancelled* (all justly)

94.4         stones]  *interlined above uncancelled* rocks

94.7         Not]  not

94.29        obtaining]  *preceded by cancelled* to t

95.2         curse]  ~,

95.14        respect]  *interlined above uncancelled* honor

95.19        divinity]  *interlined above uncancelled* demon

95.24        rages.]  *interlined below uncancelled* boils

96.1         Nay]  *interlined above uncancelled* That

96.3-4       take off the edge]  *interlined above uncancelled*
             blunt

96.5         heaven]  *interlined above uncancelled* god

96.16        Erinnys]  *preceded by cancelled* desire

96.21        colonist]  *interlined below uncancelled* settler

96.23        distributor]  *followed by cancelled* of po

96.25        shaking asunder]  *interlined above uncancelled*
             Dividing by lot

96.32        bloody]  *interlined above uncancelled* purple

96.33        extend]  *interlined above uncancelled* perform

97.4         forsooth]  *interlined above with a caret*

97.22        insane]  *interlined above reformed* Insane

97.27        but]  *added in margin*

97.27        between]  *interlined above uncancelled* (In the
             mean while)

97.29        kings]  *preceded by cancelled* the

97.34        omitted.]  *interlined below uncancelled* (are not
             transpiring.)

97.35        wealth]  *interlined above uncancelled* happiness

97.35        grown]  *interlined above with a caret*

98.4         him]  ~,

98.9         fate?]  ~,

98.13        heart]  ~,

98.14        He]  *written over* A

98.20        Alas! alas!]  *written in margin*

98.20        bitter]  Bitter

| | |
|---|---|
| 98.21 | iron-lawed] *followed by cancelled* hand |
| 98.22 | Hand] hand |
| 98.35 | protects] *interlined above uncancelled* covers |
| 98.35 | And we fortified] *marked to move up from next line in MS* |
| 98.35 | fortified] *preceded by cancelled* have *and followed by cancelled* the |
| 99.1 | The] *written in margin preceding* gates |
| 99.2 | champions] *interlined above uncancelled* opponents |
| 99.7 | matter] ~, |
| 99.24 | Fate] *interlined below uncancelled* Demon |
| 100.1 | 2] *interlined above uncancelled* Both |
| 100.1 | shared] *interlined below uncancelled* (obtained by lot) *with* divided *interlined above uncancelled* (obtained by lot) |
| 100.7 | unhappy] *interlined above with a caret* |
| 100.12 | murder] *interlined above cancelled* hands |
| 100.17 | To] to |
| 100.17 | unhurt] *interlined above uncancelled* uninjuring |
| 100.18 | &] *interlined above* |
| 100.26 | heart] hart |
| 100.35 | prevailed] *preceded by cancelled* were |
| 101.13 | the houses] the *interlined above cancelled* our |
| 101.18-19 | conveys through] *interlined above cancelled* goes to |
| 101.31 | before] *followed by cancelled* relating |
| 101.33 | Erinnys] Erynnys |
| 102.2 | twisted] *interlined above* girdle |
| 102.12 | Unfortunate] unfortunate |
| 102.14 | Found] found |
| 102.14 | your] thy |
| 102.18 | Looking] looking |
| *102.24 | by well named] *interlined below uncancelled* Auspiciously *with* As was foretold *interlined above* Auspiciously |
| 102.32 | reproach] *interlined above uncancelled* recount |
| 103.2 | &] *added* |
| 104.14 | Foreigner] foreigner |
| 104.15 | Severe] *preceded by cancelled* & |
| 104.18 | True] *preceded by cancelled* Making |
| 104.19 | their] thy |
| 105.4 | By] With |

| | |
|---|---|
| 105.12 | exposed] *interlined above uncancelled* abandoned |
| 105.23 | to] *interlined above* sisters their |
| 107.7 | is] *interlined below* it |
| 107.13 | This] *preceded by cancelled* That |
| 107.13 | This] this |
| 107.16 | burial] *interlined above uncancelled* grave of earth *which is interlined above uncancelled* digging down. |
| 107.16 | burial;] *semicolon added* |
| 107.32 | His] his |
| 107.32 | But] but |
| 108.5 | it] It |
| 108.22 | disobedient] *interlined above uncancelled* incredible |
| 109.5 | otherwise] *interlined above uncancelled* again |
| 109.16 | wilt] will |
| 110.3 | Erinnyes] Erynnyes |
| 110.10 | aside] *followed by cancelled* by |
| 110.14 | But] but |
| *110.34 | (END)] *added in pencil* |

# Pindar.

*Headnote*

Copy-text:  *Dial* 4 (January 1844):379-390, as corrected by Thoreau (ICarbS).

Pre-copy-text:  For lines noted in table below: CSmH (HM 13204). 15 pages, [5, 10-12, 14-19, 21-25], of white wove "Ames" paper, 24.7 x 19.7 cm. (part of a group of 13 leaves); probably drafted August-September 1843.

Post-copy-text:  For Pythian 4.—59. (119.22-120.8), and lines from Olympic 7.—100. (113.16-19 and 113.29-32): *A Week* 1849, p. 258; *A Week* 1868, p. 260 (*A Week* 1980, pp. 243-244).

Previous editions:  1893, 10:337-355; 1906, 5:375-390.

Source:  Pindar, *Werke,* ed. Friedrich Thiersch, 2 vols. (Leipzig: Gerhard Fleischer, 1820).

Sources and pre-copy-text versions of individual poems:

|  | Title, Line Numbers in Pindar | Volume, Page Numbers in Thiersch | Selection of the Ode in HM 13204 (Line Numbers) |
| --- | --- | --- | --- |
| 111.19-112.19 | Olympic 2.67-91 | 1, 24-28 | 67-72 |
| 112.21-25 | Olympic 5.15-16 | 1, 48-50 | |
| 112.27-31 | Olympic 6.9-11 | 1, 54 | |
| 113.1-33 | Olympic 7.54-71 | 1, 76-78 | 64-71 |
| 114.1-3 | Olympic 8.72-73 | 1, 92 | 72-73 |
| 114.5-13 | Olympic 10.51-57 | 1, 122 | 51-57 |
| 114.15-23 | Olympic 10.74-78 | 1, 124-126 | |
| 114.25-115.4 | Olympic 10.95-100 | 1, 128 | |
| 115.6-116.10 | Olympic 14.1-24 | 1, 150-152 | 3-8 |
| 116.12-18 | Pythian 1.5-7 | 1, 158 | 5-7 |
| 116.19-23 | Pythian 1.13-14 | 1, 158 | |
| 116.25-30 | Pythian 2.86-88 | 1, 188 | 86-88 |
| 117.1-30 | Pythian 3.47-62 | 1, 198-200 | 47-62 |
| 117.34-119.19 | Pythian 3.81-115 | 1, 202-206 | 81-90 |
| 119.21-120.8 | Pythian 4.34-43 | 1, 214-216 | 34-43 |
| 120.10-14 | Pythian 5.65-67 | 1, 260 | |
| 120.16-19 | Pythian 8.99-100 | 1, 292-294 | |
| 120.21-121.5 | Pythian 9.17-26 | 1, 298 | |
| 121.7-23 | Pythian 10.22-30 | 1, 318 | |
| 121.25-32 | Nemean 3.19-21 | 2, 22 | |
| 122.1-21 | Nemean 3.40-52 | 2, 26-28 | 47-52 |
| 122.23-27 | Nemean 4.41-43 | 2, 38 | 41-43 |
| 122.29-123.11 | Nemean 5.1-5 | 2, 48 | |

| 123.13-28 | Nemean 6.1-8 | 2, 58 | 1-8 |
| 123.30-124.3 | Nemean 8.26-30 | 2, 90 | 26-30 |
| 124.5-13 | Nemean 8.40-44 | 2, 92 | 40-44 |
| 124.15-125.5 | Nemean 9.18-27 | 2, 100-102 | 18-27 |
| 125.7-33 | Nemean 10.82-90 | 2, 120-122 | 82-90 |
| 126.1-9 | Isthmian 1.47-49 | 2, 140 | |
| 126.11-22 | Isthmian 2.6-11 | 2, 146 | |
| 126.24-127.8 | Isthmian 6.39-48 | 2, 182-184 | |

## Textual Notes

112.22-23  virtues ... strive:  Pindar αἰεὶ δ' ἀμφ' ἀρεταῖσι
πόνος δαπάνα τε μάρναται means "always labor and expense
strive after the virtues." Thoreau mistakes the idiom ἀμφί followed
by the dative, and so does not make it clear that "virtues" is the
object of "around", not a subject of "strive".

113.14  For him warned:  Thoreau mistranslates Pindar μνα-
σθέντι, which comes from μιμνήσκω, "to make mention of; to remind oneself, then mention [to someone else]": the phrase means
"for him [Helios] who had called it to his [Zeus's] attention."

114.7-8  for before nameless:  Thoreau follows Pindar πρόσθε
γάρ νώνυμνος which omits the verb "to be."

114.18  And ... afar,:  Followed on the next line in D by a rule,
which Thoreau cancelled in CD. The passage is not divided in
Thiersch.

116.4  go Echo:  An imperative, following Pindar ἴθι, 'Αχοῖ.

118.3  But the wise:  Thoreau follows Pindar ἀλλ' ἀγαθοὶ which
omits the verb "to be." ἀγαθοί means "the good," not "the wise."

119.28  seizing:  49; "snatching" in D. This change is accepted
as revising the translation itself rather than adapting it for incorporation into A Week.

119.32  on:  49; "upon" in D. This change is accepted as revising the translation itself rather than adapting it for incorporation
into A Week.

120.18  ἄνθρωποι:  ἄνθρωπος in Thiersch's text with ἄνθρωποι
given in a note as a variant.

125.20  Thou wilt:  Thoreau revised D in pencil, cancelling "You
wish to" and adding "Thou wilt" in the margin. He may have been
uncertain about making the change, however; a mark following
"Thou wilt" may be a question mark.

## Emendations

| 111.8-9 | untranslatable] ed.;  untranslateable |
| *119.28 | seizing] 49;  snatching |

| *119.32 | on] 49;  upon |
|---------|---------------|
| 122.1 | NEM. III] ed.;  NEM.III |
| *125.20 | Thou wilt] ed.;  *possibly* Thou wilt? |

## Thoreau's Corrections and Revisions

| 113.8 | But] CD;  And  D |
|-------|------------------|
| *114.18 | And . . . afar,] CD;  *followed below by printer's rule in* D |
| 121.14 | And, living still, sees] CD;  ~∧ ~~∧ ~  D |
| 125.7 | NEM.] CD;  MEM.  D |
| *125.20 | Thou wilt] CD;  You wish to  D |

## Variants

| 113.16 | springing] D;  Springing  49 |
|--------|------------------------------|
| 113.18 | men,] D;  ~∧  49  68 |
| 113.19 | flocks.] D;  ~;  49  68 |
| 113.29 | The] D;  —"~  49  68 |
| 113.31 | genial] D;  Genial  49 |
| 119.26 | home.] D;  ~.—  49  68 |
| 119.27 | He] D;  "He  49  68 |
| *119.28 | seizing] 49;  snatching  D  CD |
| *119.32 | on] 49;  upon  D  CD |
| 120.8 | hour.] D;  ~."  49  68 |

# Fragments of Pindar.

## Headnote

Copy-text:   *Dial* 4 (April 1844):513-514, as corrected by Thoreau (ICarbS).

Pre-copy-text:   For entire text: CSmH (HM 13204). 3 pages, [1-3], of white wove "Ames" paper, 24.7 x 19.7 cm. (part of a group of 13 leaves); probably drafted August-September 1843. For 129.25-26, see *Thoreau's Literary Notebook in the Library of Congress,* ed. Kenneth W. Cameron (Hartford, Conn.: Transcendental Books, 1964), p. 62.

Post-copy-text:   For lines from "From Plutarch." (129.25-26): *A Week* 1849, p. 18; *A Week* 1868, p. 22 (*A Week* 1980, p. 16).

Previous editions:   1893, 10:355-357; 1906, 5:390-392.

Source:   Pindar, *Werke,* ed. Friedrich Thiersch, 2 vols. (Leipzig: Gerhard Fleischer, 1820).

Sources of individual poems:

| Thoreau's Title | Title, Line Numbers in Thiersch (Volume, Page Numbers in Parentheses) |
| --- | --- |
| 129.5-11   The Freedom of Greece. | Epinicean, fr. 6.3-8 (2, 216) |
| 129.13-19   From Strabo. | Hymns, Paeans and Prosodies, fr. 6 (2, 242) |
| 129.21-26   From Plutarch. | Quotations in Plutarch, fr. 14 (2, 272) |
| 129.28-130.3   From Sextus Empiricus. | Quotations in Artemidorus, etc., fr. 12 (2, 288) |
| 130.5-11   From Stobaeus. | Quotations in Artemidorus, etc., fr. 12 (2, 288) |
| 130.13-17   From Clemens of Alexandria. | Quotations in Clement of Alexandria, fr. 5 (2, 292) |
| 130.19-27   From the Same. | Quotations in Clement of Alexandria, fr. 7 (2, 292) |
| 130.29-30   [untitled] | Quotations from Grammarians, Lexicographers, and Scholiasts, fr. 21 (2, 300) |
| 131.1-6   From Ælius Aristides. | Non-Metrical Quotations, fr. 2 (2, 308) |
| 131.8-10   From Stobaeus. | Non-Metrical Quotations, fr. 5 (2, 310) |
| 131.12-14   From the Same. | Non-Metrical Quotations, fr. 6 (2, 310) |

*Textual Notes*

129.14   *Apollo.*:   Thoreau adds this name, the referent for "he" at 129.15; it does not appear in Pindar's Greek. Thiersch's note, "Ben Strabo B. g. S. 632. C. als 'der Spruch des Pindarus über den Apollo'," is probably Thoreau's source.

129.24-26   Thus . . . plough.":   The "old translator" is John Philips; Thoreau's source is Philips' "Wherefore the Pythian Priestess Now Ceases to Deliver Her Oracles in Verse," in *Plutarch's Morals. Translated from the Greek by Several Hands.* 5 vols., 5th ed., rev. and cor. (London: W. Taylor, 1718), 3:123.

130.5   STOBAEUS:   Here and at 131.8, the *Dial* text prints "Æ"; the type size used for these titles in this edition does not include ligatured letters.

131.2   [in praise of poetry]:   Thoreau adds this phrase, which does not appear in the Greek. Thiersch's facing page German translation for this fragment includes a parenthetical phrase, "(benm Lobe der Bildung)" (2:309)—"in praise of education"; however, Thiersch's note to the fragment that precedes this one contains the phrase "Lob der Poesie" (2:308) and is probably Thoreau's source.

131.4-6   "asked . . . song.":   Thoreau adds the quotation marks, which do not appear in Pindar.

131.9-10   "plucked . . . wisdom.":   Thoreau adopts the quotation marks from Thiersch's German translation; they do not appear in the Greek.

131.13-14   "hopes . . . awake.":   Thoreau adds the quotation marks, which do not appear in Pindar.

*Variants*

| 129.25 | heaven] | D; | Heaven | 49 | 68 |
|---|---|---|---|---|---|
| 129.26 | plough] | D; | plow | 49 | 68 |

# Pindaric Odes From HM 13204

## Headnote

Copy-text:  CSmH (HM 13204). 2 pages, [21] and [23], of white
wove "Ames" paper, 24.7 x 19.7 cm. (part of a group of 13 leaves);
probably drafted August-September 1843.

Source:  Pindar, *Werke,* ed. Friedrich Thiersch, 2 vols. (Leipzig:
Gerhard Fleischer, 1820).

Sources of individual poems:

|  | Title, Line Numbers in Pindar | Volume, Page Number in Thiersch |
|---|---|---|
| 133.3-4 | Olympic 1.33-34 | 1, 6 |
| 133.5-14 | Olympic 9.107-116 | 1, 108-110 |
| 133.15-16 | Isthmian 7.18-19 | 2, 190 |
| 133.17-26 | Isthmian 8.12-17 | 2, 198 |

## Textual Notes

These odes are given in the order in which they appear in Thiersch.
In the manuscript they appear as follows: Isthmian 7, Isthmian 8,
Olympic 1 on p. [21]; Olympic 9 on p. [23].

In addition, Thoreau translated the following six lines of Nemean
7 in HM 13204, p. [15], and then cancelled them. Because they are
cancelled, the lines are not printed in the text of this edition, but
since neither they nor any part of Nemean 7 appears in the *Dial,*
they are included here. Thoreau's revisions are incorporated:

>     But I expect that there is
>     More fame of Ulysses, than he
>     Performed, through sweet-worded Homer.

>     ―――――――――-

>     ―――――――――-

>     Since there is something awful
>     In his fictions, by winged invention; and wisdom
>     Deceives, leading astray with fables.

133.14   Olymp. IX:   " " IX" in the manuscript. The ditto marks
refer to "Olymp.", which is written above them in the manuscript.

133.15-16   Of . . . words:   A paraphrase of the source, not an
exact translation. This line appears at the top of a page in the
manuscript and probably completed a passage begun on a leaf that
does not survive.

## Emendations

All of the emendations are based on the editor's judgment and informed by an examination of Thoreau's source.

|   |   |
|---|---|
| 133.12 | Ways]  *possibly*  ~— |
| *133.14 | Olymp. IX]  ″ IX |
| 133.18 | an]   and |
| 133.21 | time]   tme |

## Alterations

|   |   |
|---|---|
| 133.3 | But]  *followed by cancelled* the |
| 133.8 | talents]  *interlined above uncancelled* virtues |
| 133.10 | no]   not |
| 133.14 | Us]  *written in margin* |
| 133.14 | All]  *followed by cancelled* of us |
| 133.14 | steep]  *interlined above uncancelled* arduous |
| 133.19 | which]   is |
| 133.24 | But]   but |

# The Transmigrations of the Seven Brahmans.

## Headnote

Copy-text: MH (bMS Am 278.5.12 [1]). 4 folios (8 leaves) of white wove "H & E Goodwin," pp. [1-3] lined, p. [4] unlined in each folio, 25.2 x 20 cm.; probably fair-copied 1849-1850.
Previous edition: *The Transmigrations of the Seven Brahmans,* ed. Arthur Christy (New York: W. E. Rudge, 1936).
Source: Mahābhārata. *Harivansa,* trans. S. A. Langlois, 2 vols. (Paris and London: The Oriental Translation Fund, 1834), 1:100-110, Lectures 21-24, as follows:

|  | Lecture | Page and Line Number in Langlois |
|---|---|---|
| 135.1-2 | 21 | 100.14 |
| 135.3 | 21 | 100.17 |
| 135.4-138.22 | 21 | 100.25-103.27 |
| 138.23-139.16 | 22 | 104.5-26 |
| 139.17-32 | 23 | 105.5-14 |
| 139.33-142.6 | 23 | 106.1-107.27 |
| 142.7-144.28 | 24 | 108.5-110.5 |

## Textual Notes

Alterations described in the Textual Notes are in pencil unless otherwise noted.

135.3 The ... *sraddha*: Thoreau uses the first half-line of the French text as his epigraph; he then omits the next five lines of the French.

135.3 *sraddha*[1]: Here and throughout the essay, footnote numbers replace the "x" or "*" that Thoreau used in the manuscript.

135.24-25 missing or wandering: Thoreau adds these words, which do not appear in Langlois.

135.28-29 no ... us: In altering the manuscript from "men will have no reproach to make us" Thoreau parenthesized "men will have" and interlined "l'on" above "men". He interlined "can be made to" above "to make"; "make" is followed by a left parenthesis.

135.32 rites ... Ancestors: Thoreau has brought the information here and at 135.33, 137.35, and 143.36 from earlier sections of the *Harivansa* to clarify the passages he has translated.

136.3 (the regard and): Thoreau adds parentheses, which do not appear in Langlois.

136.8 reappeared: Above this word Thoreau wrote the now erased "came back again".

136.23 (down): Thoreau adds parentheses, which do not appear in Langlois.

136.34-36 An . . . ended.: Thoreau's condensation of a footnote in Langlois.

137.3 (their): Thoreau adds parentheses, which do not appear in Langlois.

137.10 by . . . bare: Thoreau adds this phrase to the text; it summarizes information Langlois gives in a footnote.

137.35 An exercise: Thoreau wrote "8" below these words.

138.5 science: Thoreau interlined a question mark above this word, apparently for his own reference.

138.15 glorious or illustrious: Both words translate Langlois "éclatant".

138.19 (he) . . . desire: After adding "he" in ink, Thoreau added parentheses in pencil; Langlois reads "il forma ce souhait".

138.28 consulting: Thoreau first wrote "only consulting", then marked the two words for transposing. Then he cancelled "only" and wrote it after "consulting".

139.12 (in): Thoreau adds parentheses, which do not appear in Langlois.

139.13-14 past, . . . which: "past." in the manuscript, though the next word begins with a lower case "t". Langlois reads "d'une manière concise, un passé dont la conscience".

139.15 (then): Thoreau adds parentheses, which do not appear in Langlois.

139.17 (that): Thoreau adds parentheses, which do not appear in Langlois.

139.23 seven: Thoreau adds this word, which does not appear in Langlois.

139.32 devotion. + + +: The crosses indicate the omission of six lines of Langlois.

139.36 the . . . Indra: Thoreau's condensation of a footnote in Langlois.

140.15 all together & in harmony: Both phrases translate Langlois "tous de concert".

140.17-18 meditation, (&) penitence, (and) instructed: Thoreau adds "&" in ink, then both sets of parentheses in pencil; Langlois reads "la méditation, la pénitence, instruites".

140.31   (or *Pantchica*):   Thoreau adds parentheses, which do not appear in Langlois.

140.36   A spiritual teacher:   Thoreau's condensation of a footnote in Langlois.

141.33   (about):   Thoreau adds the left parenthesis; the right parenthesis is added in this edition to complete the alteration; neither appears in Langlois.

142.6   (their):   Thoreau adds this word, which does not appear in Langlois.

142.35   Abstracted:   Followed in the manuscript by a question mark, apparently for Thoreau's own reference.

143.21   (to):   Thoreau interlined this word and added the parentheses and a question mark, which do not appear in Langlois.

143.35   A fly-flap . . . cow:   Thoreau's condensation of a footnote in Langlois.

144.1   also at the same time:   "also" and "at the same time" may be alternative translations for Langlois "aussi," although Thoreau has interlined "at the same time" with a caret without cancelling "also".

144.3   giving him:   In altering the manuscript from "to whom they gave" to "giving him" Thoreau parenthesized only "to whom they"; this edition completes the alteration by removing "gave" as well.

144.12   route:   Thoreau altered "root" to "rout"; this edition emends to "route" on the basis of Langlois "route".

144.28   glory.:   Thoreau omits the last two paragraphs of this lecture.

## Emendations

All of the emendations are based on the editor's judgment and informed by an examination of Thoreau's source.

| | | |
|---|---|---|
| *135.24-25 | missing or wandering] | *interlined without a caret* |
| *135.32 | rites . . . Ancestors] | *interlined below 135.3 sraddha* |
| 136.18 | plunging] plonging | |
| *137.35 | An exercise] An exercise / 8 | |
| *138.5 | science] ~? | |
| 138.18 | dazzled] dazeled | |
| 139.13 | past,] ~. (*see Textual Note 139.13*) | |
| 139.35 | himself] ~, | |

| | |
|---|---|
| 139.36 | Indra]  ~' (*see Alteration 139.36*) |
| 140.2 | friends]  ~. |
| 140.2 | there.]  ~, |
| 141.6 | of]  of of |
| 141.8 | luxury.]  ~∧ |
| 141.32 | this]  ~: |
| *141.33 | (about)]  (~∧ |
| *142.35 | Abstracted]  ~? |
| 143.10 | counsellors]  cousellors |
| *143.21 | (to)]  (~)? |
| 143.22-26 | "The seven . . . behind?"]  *pencilled ? in right margin beside these lines* |
| *144.3 | giving him]  giving him gave |
| *144.12 | route]  rout |

## Alterations

Unless otherwise noted, Thoreau altered his text in pencil.

| | |
|---|---|
| *135.3 | The . . . sraddha]  *added (ink)* |
| 135.6 | spoken]  *followed by cancelled* to me |
| 135.6 | but]  *interlined above uncancelled* and |
| 135.8 | answering]  *interlined above uncancelled* conformable |
| 135.11 | dying]  *interlined above uncancelled and parenthesized* happening to die, |
| 135.13 | took care of]  *interlined above uncancelled* guarded |
| 135.15 | herself]  *interlined above uncancelled* she |
| 135.24 | possessed]  *interlined below uncancelled* haunted *with uncancelled* beset *interlined above* haunted |
| *135.24-25 | missing or wandering]  *interlined above* his brothers |
| 135.26 | to the Pitris]  to *interlined above uncancelled and parenthesized* on account of |
| *135.28-29 | no . . . us]  men will have no reproach to make us |
| 135.29 | Well]  *interlined above uncancelled* Yes |
| *135.32 | rites . . . Ancestors]  *interlined below* 135.3 sraddha |
| 135.33 | Worship]  *interlined above cancelled* Devotion *(ink)* |
| 136.2 | took]  *interlined above uncancelled* received *and preceded by cancelled* too *(ink)* |
| 136.2 | delivered]  *interlined above uncancelled* restored |
| *136.3 | (the regard and)]  *parentheses added* |

| 136.9-10 | However] *interlined above cancelled* Neverthe-less |
| 136.13 | remembrance] *interlined above uncancelled* memory |
| 136.16 | holding in] *interlined above uncancelled* retaining |
| 136.23 | bent] *interlined above uncancelled* bowed |
| *136.23 | (down)] *parentheses added* |
| 136.28 | surrendered] *interlined above uncancelled* gave up |
| 136.29-30 | retained] *interlined above uncancelled and parenthesized* had |
| 136.34 | collects] *interlined above uncancelled* abstracts |
| 137.1 | fear] *interlined above uncancelled and parenthesized* terror |
| 137.3 | going over] *interlined above uncancelled* reviewing |
| *137.3 | (their)] *parentheses added* |
| 137.6 | submitting] ting *interlined above uncancelled* submitted |
| 137.10 | pious] *preceded by cancelled and parenthesized* their |
| *137.10 | by ... bare] *interlined above with a caret* |
| 137.17-18 | occupied only] only occupied *marked for transposing (ink)* |
| 137.18 | divine] divines *(ink)* |
| 137.31 | crime] *interlined below uncancelled* error *with uncancelled* straying *interlined above* error |
| 137.32 | adding to] *interlined above uncancelled* augmenting *which is interlined above uncancelled* increasing |
| 137.33 | knowledge] *preceded by cancelled* science *(ink)* |
| 137.33 | at each new birth] *interlined above uncancelled* each time they were born |
| 137.34 | with] *interlined with a caret above cancelled* and under *(ink)* |
| 137.35 | penance] *interlined below uncancelled and parenthesized* penitence |
| 137.35 | or extreme devotion] *added* |
| 138.4 | states] *interlined above cancelled* births |
| 138.8 | in] *interlined above uncancelled* by |
| *138.15 | glorious or illustrious] *interlined above uncancelled* dazzling |

138.16          stately]  *interlined above uncancelled* magnificent
138.19          (he)]  *added in ink; parentheses added in pencil*
                *(see Textual Note 138.19)*
138.21          unhappy]  *interlined above uncancelled* unfortu-
                nate *with uncancelled* unlucky *interlined preced-*
                *ing* unhappy
138.27          in]  *interlined above cancelled* for
*138.28         consulting]  *preceded by cancelled* only *(ink)*
138.30          desires]  *interlined above uncancelled* vows *with*
                *uncancelled* wishes *interlined preceding* desires
138.32          thither]  *interlined below uncancelled* there
139.10          are]  *interlined above uncancelled and parenthe-*
                *sized* ought
139.10-11       science]  *interlined above uncancelled* knowledge
*139.12         (in)]  *parentheses added*
*139.15         (then)]  *parentheses added*
139.15          shall]  *interlined above uncancelled* will
139.17          As]  *added in margin*
139.17          saying]  *followed by cancelled and parenthesized*
                then
*139.17         (that)]  *parentheses added*
139.19          waste away]  *interlined above uncancelled* wither
                *with uncancelled* dry up *interlined preceding* waste
                away
139.30          his]  her
139.34-35       made his adieus]  *interlined above uncancelled* bad
                adieu
139.35          Brahmans]  brahmans
139.35-140.2    himself . . . there.]  himself, in order to do penance
                there, to the borders of the lake where he had seen
                the seven friends. *marked for transposing*
139.36          the Elysium of Indra]  *originally* Indra's Elysium
                *with* the *and of added in pencil,* s *of* Indra's *can-*
                *celled (see Emendation 139.36) and phrase marked*
                *for transposing in ink*
140.1           borders]  *interlined above uncancelled* shores *(ink)*
140.8           soon gave]  gave soon *marked for transposing*
140.11          Vebhradja]  *Vobhradja (ink)*
140.13          who had]  *interlined above with a caret*
140.15          together & in harmony]  *interlined above uncan-*
                *celled and parenthesized* in harmony *(see Textual*
                *Note 140.15)*
140.17          &]  *added (ink) (see Textual Note 140.17-18)*

| | |
|---|---|
| 140.17-18 | (&) penitence, (and)] *parentheses added (see Textual Note 140.17-18)* |
| 140.30 | in] is *(ink)* |
| *140.31 | (or *Pantchica*)] *parentheses added* |
| 141.5-6 | on account of] *interlined above uncancelled and parenthesized* by reason |
| 141.8 | requirements] *interlined above uncancelled* exigences *with uncancelled* occasions *interlined preceding* requirements |
| 141.8 | luxury] *interlined above uncancelled* riches |
| 141.9 | crowned] *interlined above uncancelled and parenthesized* consecrated |
| 141.29 | can] *interlined above cancelled* could *(ink)* |
| 141.32 | disconsolate father] *interlined with a caret above uncancelled and parenthesized* desolate *with uncancelled* afflicted *interlined preceding* disconsolate |
| 141.32 | father] *interlined above* We *and marked for inserting with a caret and a line* |
| *141.33 | (about)] *interlined above cancelled* going |
| 142.2 | crown at last] *interlined above uncancelled* satisfy in short |
| *142.6 | (their)] ir *and parentheses added* |
| 142.14 | picking] *interlined above uncancelled* gathering *(ink)* |
| 142.22 | told her] *followed by cancelled* what it *(ink)* |
| 142.22 | truth] *interlined above uncancelled* fact |
| 142.23 | was unwilling to] *interlined above uncancelled and parenthesized* could not |
| 142.24 | wounded feelings] *interlined above uncancelled* temper |
| 143.1 | for] *interlined with a caret (ink)* |
| 143.4 | thou] thee *(ink)* |
| 143.9 | object] *interlined above uncancelled* end |
| 143.11 | moment] *interlined above uncancelled* instant |
| 143.14 | performed] *interlined above uncancelled* made |
| 143.15 | chariot] *interlined above uncancelled* car |
| *143.21 | (to)] *interlined above with a caret* |
| 143.27 | was struck dumb] *interlined above uncancelled* remained speechless *which is marked off by an initial parenthesis and a terminal caret* |
| 143.31 | In a moment] *interlined above uncancelled* An instant after *with uncancelled* A moment / *interlined preceding* In a moment |

| | |
|---|---|
| 143.34 | borders] *interlined above uncancelled* shores |
| *144.1 | at the same time] *interlined above with a caret* |
| *144.3 | giving him] *interlined above uncancelled and parenthesized* to whom they |
| 144.9 | were acquainted with] *interlined above uncancelled* knew |
| 144.12 | are going] *interlined above uncancelled* go |
| *144.12 | route] root *(ink)* |
| 144.14 | there] *interlined above with a caret (ink)* |
| 144.15 | drowsy] *interlined above uncancelled* slumbering |
| 144.17 | might] *interlined above uncancelled* forces |

## End-of-Line Hyphenation

| | |
|---|---|
| 136.1 | without |
| 136.26 | themselves |
| 140.21 | themselves |

# Appendix

## Headnote

Διαλογος

Copy-text:   MH-UA 6834.37, *Exhibition and Commencement Performances 1834-1835;* 1 folio (2 leaves) of white wove, 24.4 x 20 cm., bound; July 13, 1835.

The Cliffs—a Cenotaph

Copy-text:   CSmH (HM 945 ["Index Rerum"], p. "39"); white wove, lined, 20.1 x 16 cm., bound; before January 15, 1837.

## Textual Notes

145.3-4  Δεκιος ... H.:   The number of dashes in these two lines has been regularized to give the effect of the manuscript.

145.22  Ὠ:   Here and at 146.8, 146.14, and 146.32, Thoreau uses the old script form "ω". The Greek in the text of this edition is printed in the Porson Attic font.

146.29  Καισαρι:   Thoreau's incomplete alteration of this word is emended in this edition. He first wrote Καιραι then superimposed a σ over the ρ. The context requires the dative form, Καισαρι.

148.19-21  "Wehquetumah . . . onk.":   After copying this verse, Thoreau inserted dashes to separate the Indian words. He neglected to add one after "ohkeoog", probably because it occurs at the end of a line in the manuscript. The lineation of the manuscript is not preserved in the printed version, so a dash is added in this edition to represent Thoreau's apparent intention (see Emendation 148.21).

Thoreau's source for this verse is John Eliot's Massachuset translation of the Bible (*Mamusse Wunneetupanatamwe Up-Biblum God Naneeswe Nukkone Testament Kah Wonk Wusku Testament,* [Cambridge, Mass.: Printeuoop nashpe Samuel Green kah Marmaduke Johnson, 1663]; same title and publisher, 1685). The edition he used is uncertain; the Harvard College Library catalogue published in 1830 lists both the 1663 and the 1685 editions (*A Catalogue of the Library of Harvard University in Cambridge, Massachusetts,* 3 vols. [Cambridge, Mass.: E. W. Metcalf, 1830], 1:72). Neither edition has the dashes between words, and Thoreau's transcription varies from each of them in two minor elements.

The diphthong "∞" is based on a photograph made of this verse in the 1663 edition in the Scheide Library, Princeton, New Jersey.

148.23-30 "Sachimaupan . . . N. E.: Thoreau's source for this quotation was probably Roger Williams' *Key into the Language of the Indians of New England*, in *Collections of the Massachusetts Historical Society*, ser. 1 (1794; rpt. Boston: Munroe & Francis, 1810), 3:237-238. He modifies the original slightly to fit the context—Williams gives the meaning of several Indian words and then explains, "These expressions they use. . . ."—and he adds a comma.

## Emendations

All of the emendations are based on the editor's judgment. For a discussion of why accent and breathing marks are not emended in Διαλογος, see p. 226.

| | |
|---|---|
| 145.9 | Δεκιος] Δεκος |
| 145.19 | νικων των] νικωντων |
| 145.26 | τον] τον |
| 145.30 | προσηκει] προϛηκει |
| 146.8 | Κατων] Κατον |
| 146.16 | της] τησ |
| 146.28 | κοσμων] χοσμων |
| 146.28 | προσφερομενων] προϛφερομενων |
| *146.29 | Καισαρι] Καιραι |
| 146.32 | ματαια] μεταια |
| 147.2 | δυναστεια] δυναστεια |
| 147.2 | ειλημενη] ειλημενη |
| 148.21 | ohke∞g—] ~∧ (*see Textual Note 148.19-21*) |

## Alterations

| | |
|---|---|
| 145.22 | κελευομαι] ν *interlined above with a caret* |
| 146.3 | εκτιθετι] *first* ι *interlined above with a caret* |
| 146.4 | τους] ν *interlined above with a caret* |
| 146.28 | κοσμων] *interlined above with a caret* (*see Emendation 146.28*) |
| 147.6 | πασα] *interlined above with a caret* |
| 148.5 | Sachimaupan,*] *added later* |
| 148.17 | esto.] ~! |
| *148.19-21 | "Wehquetumah . . . onk."] *dashes between words added later* |
| *148.23-30 | *"Sachimaupan . . . N. E.] *added later* |

*Translations of the Texts*

The editor made the following translations from Greek and Latin; the English version of Psalm 2:8 is quoted from Robert Aitken's 1782 edition of the Bible (facsimile reprint, New York: Arno Press, 1968).

A Dialogue.

Decius————————Manlius S. Clarke
Cato————————David H. Thoreau

Decius   Caesar bids you well.

Cato   If it were possible to bid my slain friends well, this would be agreeable. Is it not necessary for you to address the Senate?

Decius   I come to speak with you. Caesar perceives that your affairs go badly, and because he sets great store by you he is concerned for your safety.

Cato   The same fate is allotted to me and to Rome. If Caesar wishes to save me bid him not destroy his country. Tell this to the dictator, and that I set little by the life he has to give.

Decius   Rome and the Senate have given themselves up to Caesar completely. The consuls and the tribunes, who have impeded his victories and his triumphs, have come to an end. Why do you avoid laying up merit with Caesar?

Cato   Your very words prevent this.

Decius   O Cato, I bid you kindly turn from your schemes. Consider the danger hanging over you, and the destruction now threatening you. You will receive many honors from the citizens if only you are willing to accede to Caesar and earn his gratitude. Rome will rejoice and look up to you as the highest of mortals.

Cato   Enough of such stuff. It does not become me to look for life on such terms.

Decius   Caesar knows your virtues; that is why he values your safety highly. Inform him for how much he may receive [you] and set forth your terms.

Cato        Bid him disperse his marauders and give freedom back
            to the Republic, and refer what he has done to the Senate;
            which having been done, I will make friends with him.

Decius      O Cato, all praise your wisdom too highly.

Cato        Bid him, since my voice does not love those who have
            strayed into evil, abandon and wash away his sins. I will
            mount the rostrum on his behalf and persuade the people
            to pardon his sins.

Decius      Such words befit the conqueror.

Cato        O Decius, these words befit a Roman.

Decius      Why is any Roman an enemy to Caesar.

Cato        For greater than Caesar, he is a friend of virtue.

Decius      Remember where you are. You are [now] an alien; you
            head only a small party. You do not now give harangues
            in the Forum, playing the strings of all the Romans.

Cato        He who drove us to this must remember this: Caesar's
            sword has decimated the Roman Senate. Alas! His victory
            and fortune have wildly deceived your eyes; if you see
            him rightly, he is stained with murder, treason, impiety,
            and pollution; of which terrors he will seem the only mem-
            ory. I am aware that I am myself unfortunate and seem
            plagued by evils, but I swear by the gods that if a million
            such honors were offered me, I would not be such a Cae-
            sar.

Decius      Is this the answer Cato sends to Caesar, after all his kind
            considerations, when his friendship is freely offered?

Cato        His consideration is impious and vain. Oh overweening
            man! The gods have consideration for me; if Caesar wishes
            to show his greatness of soul, then he must have consid-
            eration for these my friends, and use well the power so
            evilly seized.

Decius      Due to your hard heart you forget that you are mortal.
            You are rushing headlong to your destruction. Enough of
            such stuff! When I report how this embassy went, all
            Rome will shed tears.

The Cliffs—a Cenotaph.

Stay, you who have climbed [thus far]!
Here
A Son of Nature,
TAHATTAWAN, Sachimaupan,
The Last of the Indians,
Has hunted, in this stream has fished.
Over fields, meadows, and hills he reigned,
But if tradition is to be believed,
He had no distant bands [of warriors].
Man, Chief, Christian,
Though unlearned, he is not unmourned.
In character clearly austere and without levity;
Great of speech, handsome, truly modest at heart!!!
In integrity and tested fortitude preeminent.

---

This crag shall be his cenotaph
Oh, Indian! Where have your people gone?
"Ask of me, and I shall give *thee* the heathen *for* thine inheritance,
and the uttermost parts of the earth *for* thy possession." Psalm, 2.8.
Carved A.D. 1836.

*Library of Congress Cataloging-in-Publication Data*

Translations.

  (The Writings of Henry D. Thoreau)
  "Textual Center, University of California, Santa Barbara"–Ser. t.p.
  "This volume collects Thoreau's literary translations for the first
time"–CIP galley.
  Includes bibliographical references.
  Contents: The Prometheus bound–Anacreon–The seven against
Thebes–[etc.]
  1. Greek literature–Translations into English. 2. English literature–
Translations from Greek. I. Thoreau, Henry David, 1817-1862. II. Van
Anglen, Kevin P. III. University of California, Santa Barbara. Textual
Center. IV. Series: Thoreau, Henry David, 1817-1862. Works. 1986.
PA3621.T7  1986      880'.8'001      83-42589
ISBN 0-691-06531-4